Had she died sometime during the night and this was Gabriel escorting her to heaven? If so, she'd go.

Slipping her arms around his neck, she pulled herself a mite closer to his warmth. With her head on his shoulder, she tried to focus on how good he felt as opposed to how much she hurt.

"Evie? You still with me?" He had a great voice. Kind of raspy and soft, very masculine. She let herself melt against him.

"I'm okay," she replied, not really certain she was. She opened her eyes to see him looking intently at her. He was gorgeous and he'd saved her life, and she was being carried in his arms and he hadn't rolled his eyes and made some joke about the strain on his back or anything. She felt her heart rate speed up a little more, and suddenly realized she didn't know who he was.

"I'm Evie Randall," she said softly.

"I know."

"And you are?"

He gave her a quick smile. Oh yes. He had a beautiful mouth. And then he opened it and said, "Galloway. Max Galloway."

While it was too dark to see the color of her eyes, the sudden scowl on her face was plain as day. She slipped her arms from around his neck in a ridiculous effort to pull away from him.

"I see my reputation has preceded me," he smirked.

Avon Contemporary Romances by
Marianne Stillings

MIDNIGHT IN THE GARDEN OF GOOD AND EVIE
THE DAMSEL IN THIS DRESS

MARIANNE STILLINGS

Midnight in the Garden of Good and Evie

AVON BOOKS
An Imprint of HarperCollinsPublishers

This is a work of fiction. Names, characters, places, and incidents are products of the author's imagination or are used fictitiously and are not to be construed as real. Any resemblance to actual events, locales, organizations, or persons, living or dead, is entirely coincidental.

AVON BOOKS
An Imprint of HarperCollins*Publishers*
10 East 53rd Street
New York, New York 10022-5299

First Avon Books paperback printing: May 2005

Avon Trademark Reg. U.S. Pat. Off. and in Other Countries, Marca Registrada, Hecho en U.S.A.
HarperCollins® is a registered trademark of HarperCollins Publishers Inc.

Printed in the U.S.A.

10 9 8 7 6 5 4 3 2 1

For my mother,
who gave me my love of reading,
and for the staff
of AllAboutRomance.com—
especially Laurie Gold, Blythe Barnhill,
Nora Armstrong, Robin Uncapher,
and Ellen Micheletti—
who were there at the beginning,
and who rooted for me
every step of the way.

Acknowledgments

I'd like to thank Bina Vachhani, a fan who became a friend, for the many hours she spent reading the manuscript and pointing out where improvements might be made. I hope I did right by you, Bina.

To Katie Stillings, who, at thirteen, isn't old enough to read *Midnight,* but who gave me a few pointers on being nine, ten, and eleven again, and helped me accurately craft Evie's youthful diary entries.

Additional thanks to Sharon Jones Spaulding, attorney at law, DNA expert, and dearest friend, who helped me get the details right, and who journeyed with me to Port Townsend, Washington, so she could see what the real "Port Henry" looked like—and whose mantra has become, "Shouldn't you be *writing*?!?"

Any goofs or gaffes are my own.

Chapter 1

Port Henry, Washington
July

I'm dead. Damn. I was hoping to see how the Mariners wind up this season. If they just had a better goddamned bullpen. . . .

Oh, hell. Since I'm dead, we might as well get on with it.

As I, Thomas Evanston Heyworth, write this codicil to my will, I am a month shy of turning seventy-one. This day and age, that's not so old, but the doc just informed me of a kink that may speed the end game up a bit. Therefore, I think I'd like to depart this world the same way I lived in it—by confusing and frustrating the hell out of everybody. You still with me?

I don't leave any heirs, but I do leave one helluva lot of moolah. Besides a big chunk of change in the bank and some sound investments, there's Hey-

worth Island, Mayhem Manor, its antique furnish-ings, the boats . . . Oh, how I have loved being rich!

I suppose I could divvy it all up and make be-queaths and bequests and all that crap, but that's no fun. Hell, I'm a famous mystery writer! If I have to die, why not go out with a little pizzazz?

So without further ado, here's the deal. I've set up a treasure hunt. Yes, you read it right . . . a trea-sure hunt.

The winner will be awarded my entire estate (au-dible gasp!). Some fun, huh? I checked it out. It's legal—unusual, but legal—so shut your trap.

Felix Barlow, the peckerhead shyster who calls himself my lawyer, will administer the treasure hunt, but once it begins, you'll be on your own.

Yesiree, a treasure hunt with a fortune at stake. Damn, I wish I could be there! Have fun, kiddies. . . .

Evie Randall blinked at the *peckerhead shyster* in question as he continued reading from Thomas's will, apparently unfazed by his late client's assess-ment regarding the phallic nature of his skull.

She blinked again. And again, trying to get her mental arms around the concept. A treasure hunt for all the marbles. Wow. Taking a deep breath, she forced herself to focus on the attorney, uncertain whether she should laugh or cry.

If she laughed, it would be because this whole treasure hunt idea was ludicrous . . . and *so* like the Thomas Heyworth she had known and loved. Knowing Thomas, he'd like it if she laughed.

But if she cried, it would be because she missed

him . . . much as a daughter would miss a doting father. It had been the notoriously "heartless" Thomas Heyworth, after all, who rescued her from the chaos of her childhood. He'd given her a safe home, gentle guidance, purpose. He'd changed the course of her life, and she felt she owed it to him to hound the police until his murderer was found. But the police had no leads, no clues, nothing.

Catching the attorney between subordinate clauses, Evie said, "Excuse me, Mr. Barlow?" She presented him with her most gracious smile, and waited.

Felix Barlow, surviving partner in the law firm of Barlow and Steele, looked up, obviously vexed at the interruption. Only his bespectacled black eyes were visible above the top of the page. When he didn't say anything, Evie widened her smile and forged ahead.

"Would now be a good time to ask a question? Because I have one." She cleared her throat. "A question. For clarification. Please."

The attorney adjusted his reading glasses, lowered the page, and gifted her with a courteous smile. "All questions will be answered in due time, Ms. Randall. If you'll be patient."

Evie nodded politely. "Of course."

He narrowed his gaze on the papers, mumbling words until he found his place, then began reading aloud where he'd left off. Evie tried to quell her mounting frustration by letting her gaze wander around the lawyer's office. Converted Victorian, Oriental carpets, carved stone fireplace. In front of the bay window overlooking Port Henry, Barlow's mahogany desk stretched before him, its surface area rivaling the square footage of several small nations.

She arched a brow. Compensating, she figured. Big ego, tiny dictum.

Felix Barlow appeared mid-sixties, tall, lean, and owned a face which could best be described as pinched. His nose was the exception. It was flat, giving him the look of a little boy who had been beaten up by schoolyard bullies one too many times. In his younger days he must have had thick blond hair, but now the scant strands that topped his dome had been combed over like the remaining strings of a broken harp.

She'd never cared much for Barlow, not that there was anything overtly bothersome about him. It was simply that the firm's senior partner, Charles Steele, had been an affable, avuncular type, and Thomas's friend and attorney for decades. At Steele's untimely death four years ago, Barlow had assumed the Heyworth account, and though he was always friendly and professional, she had never warmed to him the way she had to his partner.

Barlow finished reading and placed the papers in a neat stack in front of him. "You had a question, Ms. Randall."

"Yes," Evie said, leaning forward a bit in her chair. "I'm just curious about something. I guess I figured that, being Thomas's ward, he'd leave me something. Money, maybe, or some property. It's not that I want or need anything, you see. But he was so rich, and I was with him for so long. I—I guess I just naturally figured that . . ."

She let her voice trail off, unsure what to say, how

to put words to her disappointment. She didn't want to come off as some money-grubbing mercenary, and she knew if she continued to ask Barlow questions along these lines, he'd think she cared less for Thomas and more for his bank account. But, oh, how untrue that was.

She had loved Thomas Heyworth with all her heart, and would do anything, give anything, to see those flinty brown eyes once more. Hear that rough voice ranting about some trivial thing. Hug that wiry body until he chuckled and patted her head as if she were some fragile pet. Thomas was the second person in Evie's life to die suddenly, and neither time had she had the chance to say good-bye. It weighed heavily.

"Well," she said finally, since there really was nothing else *to* say. "I supposed Thomas had his reasons. I, uh, I guess I can assume, then, that I am to be included in the treasure hunt, or else I wouldn't be here now, right?"

"Correct."

"How many people will be participating?"

"Six." Barlow proceeded to shuffle through a different sheaf of papers and finally found the page he was looking for. Giving it the once-over, he said, "Ah, yes, here we are. Besides yourself, there is the butler, Edmunds, and Mr. Heyworth's secretary, Lorna Whitney. As for the remaining three, per the decedent's wishes, I've already taken the liberty of issuing each of them invitations. Two have accepted. Madame Ernestina Grovda, the renowned Russian psychic, and Dabney James, the famed, yet reclusive, poet."

"I see." She didn't, but life was like that sometimes. Thomas wanted a *psychic* and a *poet* to take a crack at his money? She shook her head as though that would suddenly make everything fall into place. It didn't.

"I'm a little confused. I don't recall him ever mentioning either of those people."

Barlow gave a disinterested shrug. "Though he did not confide his motives to me, I assume he invited individuals he believed would have fun participating in such a game. As to the relationship he had with each of them, I believe he was romantically involved with Madame Grovda some years ago. I do know that Mr. James is the grandson of a newspaperman with whom Mr. Heyworth shared a longtime friendship. Perhaps it was out of deference to his late friend that he included the grandson."

With a little laugh, she said, "So, we have me, a schoolteacher, as well as a butler, a secretary, a psychic, and a poet. What's left, a taxidermist? An interpretive dancer? The plumber?"

"Maxfield Galloway."

Evie nearly choked. "Max Galloway? Thomas's *step*son? I don't believe it."

"Be that as it may, Ms. Randall," Barlow said, not unkindly.

"Thomas *despised* Max Galloway, and my understanding is, the feeling was more than mutual. This makes no sense at all, Mr. Barlow."

"Have you ever met Detective Galloway?"

"Detect—He's a *cop*?" Shock waves jolted her system. "Look, I know for a fact Thomas loathed the man, and he *abhorred* cops on general principles. He believed they were all doughnut-munching nincompoops. I can't imagine he would—"

"Your lack of imagination aside," Barlow drawled in a dismissive tone, "Detective Galloway has been invited, but has yet to accept or decline."

Evie made a conscious decision to remain calm, to think this through if she could.

"Well, okay," she said softly, more to herself than Barlow. "For whatever reason, Thomas left none of his estate to me, and I guess I'll just have to accept that. Fine. This is me accepting that." She took a big breath, let it out, nodded, then forged ahead.

"If Thomas has chosen to have a treasure hunt to dispense of his fortune, then I guess he can invite whomever he wants. Besides, there's nothing that says I have to interact with this Galloway person." Satisfied, she smiled over at the lawyer.

"Ah, but you do, Ms. Randall."

Her brows snapped together. "Why?"

"The late Mr. Heyworth not only detailed *who* would participate in his hunt, but *how*."

"What on earth do you mean?"

"Simply put, Ms. Randall," he said, "For the sake of expediency, the treasure hunters have been paired. The Grovda woman with Edmunds, Mr. James with Mr. Heyworth's secretary, and you with Detective Galloway."

"W-What!"

"It's quite practical," he explained. "Three of the invitees are not local, and you, Ms. Whitney, and Edmunds are familiar with the island and its environs. As you were out of town and unavailable until today, I have already detailed this information to the others, who were all quite agreeable."

She nodded absently, trying to absorb this new turn of events. Why would Thomas leave nothing to her, yet ask her to participate in a treasure hunt for that which he might have bequeathed her, and then paired her with a man he detested?

"Do you have any coffee, Mr. Barlow? Maybe a shot of bourbon would be better. Got any bourbon?"

"Fresh out." He leaned back in his chair, tenting his fingers in front of him.

Wow. You go to L.A. for a couple of weeks to help with your best friend's new baby, and you come back to Bizzaro World. How long had Thomas been planning this?

"What's the date on the codicil?" she asked.

Barlow flipped to the back page. "Mr. Heyworth dictated and signed this document just slightly above six months ago."

"Were you aware he was ill?"

"I'm sorry to say, I was not. Mr. Heyworth's will and this codicil were handled by a firm in Seattle. I became aware of the decedent's medical history only when these documents were delivered to me several weeks after his death, and via the autopsy findings, of course. Apparently, he wished to keep his cancer, and the plans for his estate, a complete secret from everyone who knew him."

As Evie sat trying to absorb all this strange information, Barlow handed her some papers. "It's all there. Your copy of the will and codicil, information on the treasure hunt, roles and responsibilities, time frame—"

"Time frame?" she interrupted. "What kind of time frame?"

"The treasure hunt must be completed within two weeks, which begins when the guests are all assembled. There are seven clues of some kind. It's my understanding that each one leads to the next."

"You don't know what or where they are?"

"I do not. As I said, the deceased set this whole thing up in secret." His voice remained bland, but there was a glint in his eye that told her he was none too pleased with how his client had chosen to dispense of his fortune.

She furrowed her brow. "This is very vague, Mr. Barlow. What if we can't find all the clues within the time frame?"

"In the event there is no winner, Barlow and Steele has instructions to liquidate the estate and distribute the funds to the various charities outlined in the codicil."

"So, whichever team finds the last clue first wins Thomas's estate and splits fifty-fifty. Money, Mayhem Manor, the livestock, Heyworth Island, the works. Or else it all gets sold." Her heart suddenly felt as though it would crack in two.

"Yes," Barlow confirmed. "There are some special dispensations to staff, but that money has already been set aside and does not figure into the terms of the hunt."

Evie thought of Heyworth Island. It was a world all its own, a dollop of earth floating on the sea, ar-

rayed with wild blackberry vines and sweet grass
and isolation, and thick with majestic evergreens,
carpets of wildflowers in summer, a wandering
stream, a duck pond. She had meandered through
the woods as salty breezes played with her pigtails.
The sun warmed her back while she'd plucked bou-
quets of white daisies to clutch in her small fist. The
island had been her sanctuary since her mother's
death. It would be difficult to see it put into some
stranger's hands to become a place she could no
longer even visit.

If she wanted to keep that from happening, she'd
better well win the damned treasure hunt.

"Have you heard anything from the police?" she
said. "It's been six weeks since Thomas was killed,
and they *still* don't have any leads?"

"Not to my knowledge. I am sorry, Ms. Randall."

She huffed in frustration. "That's just plain
ridiculous. I've called that Detective McKennitt guy
at least a dozen times, and he insists they're doing
everything—"

"As I believe they are, Ms. Randall," Barlow interrupted. "Forgive me, but do you have any questions pertinent to Mr. Heyworth's will or the
treasure hunt as I have described it?"

Mayhem. Murder. Max Galloway. Yes. She had
questions, about a kajillion of them.

But instead of badgering the poor man, she caved
in to the inevitable and said, "When do we start?"

"This Saturday, the ninth," he said. "Four days
hence. The competitors—guests, I should say—will
be assembled on the island by then, including Detective Galloway, should he decide to participate."

"Why do you think Thomas invited him?"

"I have no idea."

"Do you think he'll come?"

"Couldn't say."

"He could get millions of dollars from a man who had hated him," she reasoned as she rose to her feet. "Why wouldn't he come?"

Barlow eyed her, his mouth set in a perfect smile. "Why not, indeed?"

A few blocks down from the Port Henry ferry, Evie pulled into the private lot reserved for guests and employees of Mayhem Manor. Locking the silver BMW roadster convertible Thomas had given her for her last birthday, she slung her purse over her shoulder, picked up her suitcase, and headed for the boat that would take her out to Heyworth Island.

The hot July sun bleached the sky as she waved to the security guy who tended the small parking facility. Boarding the twenty-foot runabout docked in one of the slips, she tossed her things onto the bench behind her and started up the engine.

Twenty-five minutes ticked by as she guided the boat out of the harbor and across the bay toward the privately owned island.

For the first ten minutes she thought about how much she missed Thomas and how she wished she had him back again—just so she could read him the riot act about this dumb treasure hunt of his.

For another five she tried to move past how stunned and, yes, admittedly intrigued she was by the whole idea. What kind of clues had he left, and where?

A tingle of excitement slipped up her spine, and she had to concede a treasure hunt might be fun—if only Thomas were around to participate.

Another five minutes she devoted to the fact that he hadn't said anything about their relationship. For fifteen years she'd suspected they had blood ties, yet he'd said nothing. Had she been fooling herself all that time? Had it all been a lonely child's wishful thinking? Or had Thomas simply not wanted to acknowledge her publicly? Perhaps she would never know.

The remainder of the trip was spent considering the illustrious Detective Max Galloway. According to Thomas, his despised stepson was no prize. Galloway had apparently been so against Thomas's marriage to his mother that he never set foot on Heyworth Island, not even when she lay dying.

What a creep. Well, maybe His Arrogance would decline to attend and she wouldn't have to deal with the jerk.

She *putt-putted* the runabout past the twin beacons at the entrance to Heyworth Island's dock, and slipped the runabout into its moorings, tossing a line around a dock cleat. Leaving her dour thoughts behind, she grabbed her things and hurried up to the house to change.

Mayhem Manor. It was a grand place. Three stories of white clapboard, a deep, wraparound porch, and five red brick chimneys. Emerald and cream variegated ivy climbed up the many pillars of the porch, and pink roses bloomed along the rails. It looked like one of those old East Coast places where the Vanderbilts and Rockefellers summered by the sea, the ladies in pastel silk shifts and wide-brimmed white hats playing croquet in the afternoon.

Mayhem Manor had once known such a time. But all the Heyworths were gone now . . .

Scurrying up the grand staircase to the third floor, Evie chose a bedroom she'd never stayed in before. Her own room, the one she lived in for most of the fifteen years since she'd come to the island, was being spruced up; new wallpaper, new curtains, the hardwood floor being refinished. Of course, if the house were sold, it wouldn't be her room anymore.

She put that out of her head for now as she chose the last room at the end of the wide hallway. Hopefully, with twenty bedrooms in the place, this one was as removed as possible from where Max Galloway would be sleeping.

Opening the massive mahogany armoire, she hung up her blue business suit and changed into jeans and a long-sleeve white top, then left the house and headed off toward the north end of the island, practically running in her haste to get to the barn.

Though she owned a small house in town where she lived during the school year, holidays and summers had been spent at Mayhem with her "family," doing what she loved best.

A smile on her lips, she topped the rise to gaze down at the old barn and the ancient, hand-hewn corrals that had stood for nearly a century.

The minute the gate creaked open, Fernando lifted his beautiful head and strolled over to greet her. Lorenzo appeared from behind the barn and sauntered up, followed closely by pregnant Lily. Soon all three llamas had gathered around her, humming and smiling, filling her troubled heart with serenity and joy.

Fernando stared into her eyes and blinked slowly, his lashes long and silky, his lids perpetually drowsy. She tickled his nose.

"Hello, handsome."

The llama responded by humming a bit louder and nudging her cheek with his forehead. Evie laughed and gently shoved him away.

"Okay you few, you happy few," she said on a laugh. "It's feeding time at the zoo, and this means you and you and *you*." Fernando nudged her again. "Did you miss me?"

The llama continued to stare placidly at her.

"Not talking, huh," she joked, then headed for the barn, stroking Fernando's soft neck as he plodded along quietly beside her.

Inside the barn door, she opened the feed bin and lifted out a layer of alfalfa, setting it into the trough by the window. Glancing about, she looked for the oat bucket she usually left hanging on a nail next to the bins, and spotted it on a hook in front of one of the empty stalls on the other side of the barn.

"What in the world was on my mind when I hung it clear over there?" Fernando nudged her ear. Leaning into him, she stroked his shaggy wool. "So impatient, my dear."

She started for the bucket, when a board beneath her foot shifted. Startled, she paused. What on earth? Straw covered the planking, but as far as she could tell, the floor appeared as solid as ever.

Deciding the shift must have been her imagination, she stepped forward. Behind her, Fernando let loose with a rapid, pulsing squeal—a llama warning.

Evie spun toward the animal just as the floor beneath her feet gave way. It was as though the earth opened up to swallow her whole. She screamed and made a frantic grab with her hands for solid wood, but there was none.

She plunged downward, into darkness. Her body slammed into something hard, knocking the air from her lungs. Pain ricocheted through her shoulders and hips, and her head fell back, hitting solid rock.

Dazed, Evie lifted one hand to the back of her head and felt a thick stickiness. Groaning, she shifted position, but the incline was steep, the rocks slimy, and she began to slide. She flipped onto her stomach as she skidded several feet, slamming her jaw against the rock. The salty metal taste of blood filled her mouth. Clawing at the precipice, her nails bent and broke as she tried to get a handhold.

Panic swelled her throat nearly closed. She tried to take a deep breath, but the air seemed to have disappeared. Beneath her body the rocks were slick, her grip weak. She lost her grasp, her footing. Her body tumbled out of control until she finally hit bottom, crashing hard into the uneven floor of the cavern.

Cold water seeped into her clothes. She was panting, crying, her head ached, her muscles felt bruised and cramped. She caught the scent of muck and mold and blood. In the darkness, something skittered close by her head, and she forced herself to bite down on a scream.

Around her loomed vague shapes, suggestions of things. *Rocks, a wall maybe? What was this? A well? A cavern? An old basement of some kind?*

Her teeth began to chatter. Her fingers, numb with cold, trembled as she tried to find a hold on the rock so she could sit up, maybe even stand.

A noise high above brought her head up. There, in the hole through which she'd fallen, was the muted outline of a shaggy head, fuzzy banana ears, and two luminous eyes blinking serenely down into the darkness.

"*No!*" she choked, her voice thin and reedy. "Get away, Fernando. Go. *Go!*" Tears stung as she envisioned the llama plunging to his death right before her very eyes.

"*Fernando.*" Fear and worry tightened her throat, forcing her voice to a whisper. "Go, sweetie," she begged. "Get away from there, *please.*"

She closed her eyes, praying the llamas would stay far away from the hole in the barn floor. When she looked up again, Fernando was gone, and she was alone in the dark.

Chapter 2

Dear Diary:

mommy forgot my birthday. Mrs. Burke brought cup-
caks to school for the whole class! She's my teacher.
And she gave me this really really cool diary. She says
that somtimes it helps for people to rite things down
when they are sad or lonely or just want to rebember
stuff. She says when i become a grown up, i can look
back and see how i was when i was little, and maybe
undorstand things better. i think she means my mom.
i love Mrs. Burke. i think when i grow up that i'm
gonna be a teacher just like her.

Evangeline—age 9

"I can . . . *do* this," Evie panted to the rocks, as
though she expected them to put up a fight.
"Won't . . . quit."

She'd emerged from the depths of unconsciousness to realize time had passed. How much, she couldn't tell. She'd never fainted in her life, and the thought of lying in the muck, unaware of things going on around her, made her queasy. As it was, her head throbbed and her muscles ached like they'd been ripped from her bones. Her fingers were sticky from her own blood.

High above, the vaguely visible break in the floor remained thankfully empty. No shaggy head filled the space, no large eyes peered into the darkness. Intelligent creatures that they were, the llamas had probably moved away to safety and were clustered together, wondering when she was going to climb out of that stupid cavern and finish feeding them.

She attempted turning onto her knees, but her head pounded, forcing her to take things slowly.

"Stay awake," she cautioned herself through labored breaths. "Stay awake. Don't pass out. Stay awake . . ."

It took all her concentration, but at last she was able to turn onto her stomach. She felt like a mackerel, soggy and smelly and flopping about.

With a bit more effort, she forced herself onto her knees and moved forward. Her hands shook. Her fingers were icicles, brittle, numb. Her whole body trembled from the exertion.

Forcing herself to concentrate, she moved up the rocky incline a few inches. Around her hovered ghostly shapes, suggestions of solid matter, but it was so dark, there could be ten people standing behind her and she wouldn't be able to see them.

The air smelled of rotten driftwood and stagnant

water. She raised her chin and tried to see the gray opening high overhead. It was distant and dim, but it gave her something to aim for.

Well, she thought, clamping her jaw tightly closed. Nowhere to go . . . but up.

Shoving her foot against the rock, she pushed herself along, edging her way back up the harsh incline. The dark was like a predator, intimidating, smothering, terrorizing. It was as though she'd been enclosed in a tomb. Thank heaven for that jagged bit of gray above her head; without it, she might have gone insane.

Evie gave herself a mental shake. *Not going to think of that now. Just one hand in front of the other. One foot in front of the other. I . . . can . . . do . . . this.*

She blinked and looked up again. Was it her imagination or had the ragged edges of the gap become more defined? Dear God, was it *daybreak?* Had she been down here all night?

A flash of light crossed the chasm.

"Here!" she shouted, or tried to, but it came out more like a dry croak. Swallowing, she tried again. "Be careful!"

"Miss Randall? Evie?" A deep voice. Young. Unfamiliar.

"I'm here!"

A beam of light slammed straight into her eyes. She blinked, closing her lids against the brightness.

"Are you hurt?" he shouted.

She didn't recognize his voice, but she didn't care. As long as he wasn't the Grim Reaper coming to take her away, she was thrilled to see him.

A second man called out. "Evangeline?" An older man, his voice blessedly familiar. She nearly burst with joy.

Edmunds? Thank God. "I'm okay!"

"Stay where you are," the first man shouted. "I'll come down and get you."

I am so for that, she thought, feeling vaguely weary, as though she were a helium balloon that had sprung a leak and begun to crumple.

She closed her eyes. Whoever he was, he sounded *strong*. Certainly stronger than she felt at the moment.

Light filled the opening once again, and she watched as a tall man with a flashlight in one hand edged his way through the broken boards to drop onto the rocks about fifteen feet above her head. He flattened his body on the incline and descended, hand over hand, until he was even with her.

Without prelude he said, "Anything broken?" She felt his breath on her cheek, warm, reassuring. Her rescuer. God, she was so cold.

"I d-don't know," she stumbled. "I don't think tho."

"You don't think though?"

"Tho," she repeated. "Eth, O. Tho."

"Oh," he drawled, suddenly comprehending. "*So*. You don't think *so*."

"Yeth."

"You must have hit your mouth or bitten your tongue. Can't say your S's, right?"

"Yeth." Ouch. She *had* bitten her tongue, and hard. She didn't realize it had swollen until she'd begun to speak.

"Did you lose consciousness at any time?"

She nodded, which hurt like hell to do. "What time ith it?"

"Ten-thirty."

"Then I've been down here for about four hourth."

"Four hours. You going to stay with me now?"

"I—I think tho. How did you know I wath in trouble?"

"The llama came to the houth, er, house. The butler said that was unusual, so we started looking for you."

Fernando had gone to the house? Like Lassie? *Evie's fallen in a big hole underneath the barn and she can't climb out!* Her throat closed against tears of joy and gratitude.

The man ran his flashlight up and down her body. "Are you bleeding anywhere or is that just from scratches?"

"No bleeding."

The beam from Edmunds's flashlight above them shone down on her rescuer, giving him a pale aura. She still couldn't make out his features, but he had dark hair and a firm jaw.

"You're a cool one under pressure," he said, and she was sure she heard a smile in his voice.

"Would you prefer I become hythterical?" she challenged. "I gueth I could manage a little hytheria after being trapped in the bowelth of the earth for hourth in total darkneth with only thlimy, crawly thingth to keep me company."

"Jerry Springer and Geraldo are here?"

She waited a heartbeat. "You know, I'd laugh at

that, but it might kill me and then you'd have to drag my poor, dead carcath up these rockth."

"I feel like I'm rescuing Daffy Duck. Maybe you shouldn't talk. Give that tongue a retht."

High overhead, Edmunds moved, shifting the beam of his flashlight, and for an instant her rescuer was illuminated.

Early thirties, clean features, impressive shoulders. Had she died sometime during the night and this was Gabriel escorting her to heaven? If so, she'd go.

"I'm going to touch you," he advised her. "Just checking for broken bones. Okay?"

Touch her? He'd spoken with such authority, how could she deny him? " 'Kay."

She licked her lips, which hurt a whole hell of a lot. Was her mouth swelling up, too? She had a vague memory of her face slamming against a passing rock, and her stomach squeezed painfully.

Fighting nausea, she focused on her rescuer's warm breath wafting against her cheek. She was certain she could hear the steady thudding of his stalwart heart. He'd climbed down here to help her. He wasn't like her mother's boyfriends, and she wasn't a scared little girl anymore. She was a scared adult woman, but that was beside the point.

She lay still and let his hands rove over her body, ready to shove him away if he took advantage. But he kept the contact light and didn't touch her anyplace or in any manner he shouldn't. His hands were large and warm, and she was so cold. For an instant she wished he would wrap his strong arms around her, whoever he was.

"Nothing seems to be broken," he said finally, "so here's what we'll do. I'm going to get behind you and help you up ahead of me. Can you do that?"

"I got thith far on my own. I can crawl a few more feet."

There was silence for a moment. "You fell all the way to the bottom?"

"Yeth."

He paused, sent the beam of his flashlight down into the darkness far below. "You weren't by any chance a Girl Scout?"

"You want to thee me tie a theepthank?"

"A sheepshank?" He laughed. "A bowline would have been just as impressive, and doesn't have any S's in it."

Then he was moving over her, careful not to press down on her body. Settling against her backside, he wrapped his arm around her waist and pulled her close.

Oh my, he was so big and warm, and she was so terribly numb with cold. If he could just curl around her like that, she could go to sleep. That would feel like heaven.

But no sooner had she thought it than she felt him lift his other arm. Shining the flashlight ahead of them, he said, "Scoot, Scout."

She reached out, pulling herself along as he pushed, keeping himself between her and the slide of rock that would take her back down to the floor of the cavern. Every muscle she owned screamed in protest, but she moved steadily upward until they were just below the floor.

When they reached the top of the rocks, he stood and brought her slowly to her feet. Her head began to spin, and she fell against him, grasping the sleeves of his shirt for support while she worked at not being sick.

"You doing okay, Scout?"

Her knees hurt as she carefully straightened them. She was weak, but she stayed upright. *And his arms. Oh, God, his arms* . . .

"Well," she panted, "I'm not going back down there again."

"Then let's do it."

As he put his hands on her waist and raised her toward the opening, she extended her arms, reaching up as Edmunds reached down. The old man clasped her under her arms, and with a strength she would not have believed he possessed, lifted her while her rescuer put his hands on her butt and pushed her up and through.

Edmunds quickly moved her to safety far away from the gaping chasm. A mere few seconds later the other man was beside them.

"Evangeline?" Edmunds choked as he took her hand in his. He was trembling more than she was. "Are you all right, my dear?"

She looked up at the butler's face, all shadows and soft lines in the darkness of the barn. He was pale, his lips thin and bloodless. She had never seen him so frightened in the entire time she'd know him.

"I'm all right," she whispered, barely able to get a breath. Suddenly, she felt as though she'd just scaled Everest. Her muscles turned to jelly, her bones dissolved, her teeth chattered so hard she sounded like a maraca.

"I have a little h-headache," she stuttered, "b-but, I. . . . oh!"

She closed her eyes as strong arms lifted her. Him again. Warm and solid.

"Don't l-let the llamath fall in," she pleaded.

In the distance Edmunds spoke, but she couldn't make out what he was saying. She thought she heard the barn doors slam shut, and she relaxed, letting her lids drift down.

"Evie?" It was *his* voice, her rescuer, commanding, harsh. "Stay awake," he ordered. "Stay with me now."

" 'Kay." She nodded sleepily and made a valiant attempt to open her eyes. Slipping her arms around his neck, she pulled herself closer to his warmth. With her head on his shoulder, she tried to focus on how good he felt as opposed to how much she hurt.

"Evie? You still with me?" He had a great voice. Kind of raspy and soft, very masculine. She let herself melt against him and barely thought about her usual aversion to being touched.

"I'm okay," she replied, not really certain she was, but she was alive and that was ninety-nine percent of the battle right there. "Thank you for rethcuing me."

He must have lowered his head, because when he replied, she felt his breath against her brow and the bridge of her nose.

"It was my pleathure, ma'am."

"You're making fun of me."

"Would I do that?"

She opened her eyes to see him looking intently at her. The line of his nose, limned by the amber light of the moon, was straight, his jaw square. She could see his mouth, firm lips, sort of curvy, like a Renaissance sculpture. The words *sensuous* and *succulent* slid into her head, and she did nothing to slide them out again.

He was gorgeous, and he'd saved her life, and she was being carried in his arms and he hadn't rolled his eyes and made some joke about the strain on his back or anything. She felt her heart rate speed up a little more, and suddenly realized she didn't know who he was.

A man like this would certainly have a good name, something as solid and heroic as he was. Eric or Alexander or Christopher or Nicholas. He would not have a name like Orville or Albert or Maurice or Uriah.

"I'm Evie Randall," she said softly.

"I know."

When he didn't say anything else, she said, "And you are?"

Her rescuer locked gazes with her again and gave her a quick smile. Oh yes. He had a beautiful mouth.

And then he opened it and said, "Galloway. Max Galloway."

Max gazed down on the face of the woman he'd just rescued.

It was an odd thing, holding a woman he barely knew in his arms. He felt heroic, like he'd saved the fair damsel from the dragon, except this damsel was sopping wet and smelled like three-day-old bait.

Her long hair was a muddy tangle and lay sort of flopped over one eye. She was sporting bruises on her cheek, a scratch on her brow, and her lip was swollen. While it was too dark to see the color of her eyes, the sudden scowl on her face was plain as day.

She slipped her arms from around his neck in a ridiculous effort to pull away from him. He was holding her, for Christ's sake. Just how far did she think she could get?

"I see my reputation has preceded me," he smirked.

"I can walk," she said. "Put me down."

The herniated frog impression was not particularly commanding. Her voice was toast, she looked like she'd been dragged though a kelp bed behind a speedboat, she smelled like a swamp rat, and was bleeding all over him. Any man in his right mind would be *desperate* to put her down.

"No," he said.

"I feel thick," she lisped.

"Sick?"

"Yeth."

"I thought I told you not to talk," he said. "It's hard to take an injured woman seriously who looks like Guttersnipe Raggedy Ann and sounds like a puddy tat."

She glared up at him.

"Sorry," he growled. "I'm having a bad day."

"*You're* having . . ." She waited a beat, then said thickly, "Let me tell you about a bad day, mithter."

Why was he so damned aggravated with her? She

hadn't done a thing wrong, except nearly get herself killed. But she was safe now, thanks to him. So why did he feel like somebody'd just shoved a burr under his attitude?

He began walking back up the path, Evie Randall's body tight to his chest. His strides ate up the ground as he headed toward the massive porch encircling the north side of the mansion. Edmunds moved to the front, illuminating the way with the beams of both flashlights.

Evie slowly slipped her arms around his neck again, and smiled. As they neared the house, the porch lights winked on, flooding her face with amber light.

He looked down into her eyes, and his brain stopped functioning. Her eyes were blue. Blue like a hot summer sky or a cold mountain lake. Blue so pure, it seemed he could see every thought whirling around inside her brain. She lowered sooty lashes. Her pale cheeks flushed.

"Thank you for your help," she lisped softly. "I wath thcared thtiff until you came along."

"*Scared stiff.*"

She nodded, then laid her head on his shoulder and closed her eyes.

"Yeah," he growled. "Well, like I said, don't talk."

Inwardly, he cringed. He was no knight in shining armor, and just because he'd climbed down into that damn pit didn't mean a thing.

He shifted her weight in his arms. Her muscles were firm, her bones delicate but sturdy. Okay, she was no Victoria's Secret model, but she sure had curves in all the right places.

Damn Girl Scout.

Jesus, she'd fallen all the way to the bottom of that cavern and had clawed herself halfway back to the top before he and the butler found her. She was lucky the fall hadn't killed her outright. It took guts and determination to do what she'd done.

He gave himself a mental smack. She was just a woman bent on survival. That was all. The comfortable heft of her in his arms didn't mean she was anybody special. The feel of her breasts smooshed against his chest, the curve of her butt against his belly, were very nice, but it didn't mean a wedding band, a mortgage, and a couple of kids. Sexual attraction could be had any day of the week. His body would get over it. Eventually.

Besides, any friend of Heyworth's was no friend of Max Galloway's. End of story. After what Heyworth had done to his family, anybody who sided with the bastard was on his personal Enemies List, and that included the slightly sumptuous, gutsy as hell Evie Randall.

As Max climbed the porch steps, Edmunds swung open the French doors, their ancient hinges squealing against the effort. Carrying Evie into the parlor, he carefully set her on a tan brocade sofa.

Edmunds made a hasty exit, then reappeared with a first aid kit and a blanket. Behind him, a young woman carried a water pitcher, glasses, and a clean washcloth.

"This is Lorna Whitney," Edmunds said quickly

as the woman set the tray on the end table. "Lorna, this is Detective Max Galloway of the Olympia Police Department."

Lorna seemed a bit confused, then nodded a greeting and stepped back. Her brown eyes filled with concern when she got a good look at Evie. "What on earth . . ."

Evie blinked up at Max, her summer blue eyes clouded with pain. Turning to Edmunds, he said, "When I arrived today, I saw a big Hatteras in the boathouse. How many knots does that son of a bitch make?"

They made the trip across the bay to the hospital in Port Henry on the sixty-five-foot luxury yacht Heyworth had kept to ferry guests to and from the island. By the time Max got Evie back to Mayhem, the sun had just begun creeping up behind the mansion, casting the elegant lines of the house in dark silhouette.

The news had been good—no concussion, nothing broken, just cuts and bruises that should heal quickly, and a headache, a little rest, and some painkillers would alleviate.

Despite her protests, Max carried Evie to her bedroom, then asked Edmunds to have his things moved to the room adjacent to hers. If she hadn't been woozy from painkillers, he was certain she would have put up a helluva fight—which he may even have enjoyed under different circumstances.

He left Evie with Lorna, who would help her bathe, wash her hair, and settle her in for some much needed sleep. Heading swiftly down the hallway, his footfalls absorbed by the thick rust-colored carpet, he shoved his hands in his pockets, ignoring the fine landscapes and pieces of art lining the walls of the long corridor. His mind was on that barn floor, the rotted wood, and how it had nearly cost a young woman her life.

As he approached the barn, the llamas in the pen raised their heads and blinked at him, then moved forward to investigate. He walked past them, opened the barn door, and shut it quickly so they wouldn't follow him inside.

Approaching the gaping chasm, he bent on one knee and felt around the jutting boards that had remained in place. He reached out and picked up a bent nail.

In the back of his mind a red flag began to wave wildly. The hairs on the back of his neck prickled. He'd been a cop long enough to know when his instincts were trying to tell him something, and right now they were rocking and rolling too loudly to ignore.

The nail made a dull *ping* as he tossed it onto the floor. He rubbed his chin. No rotten wood, no inferior planking. This wasn't an accident he was looking at.

It was a trap.

Chapter 3

Dear Diary:

Last night i dreamed that i was a beautiful princess
and lived in a really big and pretty castle and rode on
a wite horse with red and gold ribbons tied in her
long flowing hair. And the prince from the next kingdom saw me and fell madly in love with me and
asked me to marry him and i said Yes! Because he
was so handsome and nice. It was a very good
dream but i don't think it will happen though. Well,
maybe.

Evangeline—age 9

There was a term for people who became giddy after facing death and surviving. PTS? Post-traumatic
silliness? No, that wasn't it. Evie gazed at her reflection in the steamy bathroom mirror and beamed,
thrilled to be alive, whatever the term for it was.

She turned her head to the right. Slight bruise on the jaw, little cut on the forehead, swollen lip. Not bad. But her tongue was sore as hell where she'd bitten it.

Six silver swans, she thought. *Say it*.

"Thix thilver thwanz," she said. *Forget it*. Sylvester the cat on pain medication. Her vocabulary would have to be confined to non-S words until that tongue healed up a bit.

She brushed her hair and twisted it into a loose braid, idly wondering if Max Galloway liked redheads, then gave herself a mental shake.

Why should she care what Max Galloway thought? He was the avowed enemy of a man she had loved. They were, therefore, adversaries by default.

But Max *had* risked life and limb to rescue her. There was no getting around that, and she didn't want to appear ungrateful. It was only fitting she find some way to thank him.

Slipping on a pair of gold minihoops, she wondered if there was a Hallmark card that fit the occasion. The front would read *For My Hero* in swirly, twirly gold-embossed script. Inside, there'd be some generic, one-size-fits-all sentiment:

> *What you did, it was great.*
> *You really are first rate.*
> *I was scared, you were strong.*
> *As to Thomas, you're dead wrong*
> *You jerk.*

Okay, so pop poetry wasn't her strong suit. She donned a summery print blouse and buttoned it, then tucked it into her jeans. Since she was going down to the barn after breakfast, she tugged on her old brown muck boots.

With one last glance in the mirror, she decided this was as good as it was going to get under the circumstances, and headed downstairs.

As she entered the grand dining room, she was greeted by the heady scent of coffee, and the even headier sight of Max Galloway.

Oh, damn. She'd hoped to be down tending the llamas before he got up.

He stood as she approached the table, a coffee mug in one hand and a linen napkin in the other. He was dressed in jeans and an indigo T-shirt, which showed off his athletic build to perfection. Reluctantly, she had to admit that finding a sexy hunk like Detective Max Galloway across the breakfast table in the morning would not be much of a hardship.

Flicking a glance at her mouth, his hazel eyes glimmered with mischief. "It looks like you stubbed your face."

At least I didn't stub my brain, she thought, but didn't say because it would have come out "thtubbed," which would have thounded thtupid.

"Actually," he continued, giving her what he probably considered a charming grin, "I think it's very sexy. The Angelina Jolie look is hot right now."

Did he think comparing her to a superthin movie star was going to make her feel *better?* When she didn't respond, he tapped his jaw with a finger and said, "Tough to talk?"

Yeth, you thtupid ath.

She nodded.

"How are your bruises?" he asked gently, almost as though he cared. He poured coffee into her cup. "Do they bother you much?"

Yeth, you thtupid ath.

She shook her head. The fact was, her left shoulder and hip were badly bruised, deeply purple, and tender as hell. Her muscles were stiff and sore, and she fought the need to limp when she walked.

Max pursed his lips and tilted his head as though assessing whether she was telling the truth. When his gaze grazed the bruise on her jaw, she thought she saw genuine concern in his eyes. That assumption, however, was shot to hell when he grinned and said, "So what are you going to give me for saving your life?"

Thomas had been right. Max Galloway didn't have one compassionate bone in his body. Not in his whole disturbingly perfect body.

"According to ancient Celtic cultures and the customs of my ancestors," he said, "I own you now." Again with the cute grin.

"The Clan MacOaf, no doubt," she muttered as she took the seat across from his. Adding cream and sugar to her coffee, she stirred it, then wrapped her hands around the porcelain's warmth.

Ignoring her sarcasm, Max sat down and said, "It's true. My mother was an amateur archaeologist. She did a lot of work in Britain."

Is that where she dug you up? she said with a look, then nearly flinched when their gazes locked.

His eyes were a light hazel green, flecked with gold, brown, and gray. And they were piercing.

When Max Galloway looked at you, you knew you were being looked at, that he was focused wholly on you and nothing else. It was an intoxicating feeling, and she imagined he'd gotten a lot of women into bed just by flashing those babies, and turning that beautiful mouth into a "come hither and you won't be sorry" smile.

She was not impervious to such sexuality, but she wasn't *thtupid*, either, which meant she was going to have to work hard at keeping him at an arm's length. Not because he might want her, but because she was very much afraid she might want him.

He bit off half a slice of bacon. "I've already done a prelim investigation of the barn where you fell, but I'd like you to come with me and answer some questions. Can you walk that far?"

I can walk anywhere you can, buster. Like a slug, but speed isn't everything. Okay, so slugs don't exactly walk, but that's beside the point.

She took a sip of coffee and nodded.

"You sure?" he said. "I'm more than willing to carry you again, if it would help." He popped the rest of the bacon in his mouth, which quirked up on one end.

He was trying to *charm* her? What was *that* all about? Did he think they had some special bond because he'd rescued her?

Shaking her head, she tucked into her eggs and bacon, spooning strawberry preserves on a toasted English muffin. She ate carefully to avoid hurting her tongue, and relished every bite, letting the warm food energize her. A day and a half of sleep had worked wonders in helping her body mend, but the food would help even more.

She polished off her orange juice, set her napkin down, then rose to leave. Before she could get far, however, Max was around the table, beside her, his palm under her elbow.

"You doing okay?" His eyes narrowed as he assessed her. "Honest. You look a little pale. Maybe I should go get one of the llamas and you can ride it."

She scowled at him. "Can't *ride*," she said, talking out of the side of her mouth that didn't hurt.

"Why not? They look big and fat and strong to me."

Shaking her head, she said, "All wool. Too thin. No riding. Blockhead." Then she clamped her mouth shut.

"What was that last part there?" he challenged. "It sounded like you called me a blockhead."

She widened her eyes innocently and blinked, giving him a *Who me?* look.

It took only a few minutes to reach the barn. Cool morning air wafting up from the water kept the temperature down and felt good against Evie's skin. As they approached, the llamas turned in their direction, each fuzzy snout curved into a placid smile.

"That black one," Max said. "That's Fernando, right? Lily is the white one and Lorenzo is the spotted one?"

"Fernando, dark brown," Evie corrected. "Truly black llama . . . rare."

The llamas. Her babies, her family, her closest confidants. They had been her saving grace since the day she'd come to Mayhem Manor and Thomas had told her the llamas would be her responsibility. There had been different llamas on the island back then, but Fernando and his son Lorenzo were descendants of the original herd. Lily had been purchased a few years ago and was Lorenzo's dam.

Gesturing toward Fernando, Max said, "He's kind of cute, in a giant, alien, dust-mop sort of way."

He opened the gate and walked through ahead of Evie, but the llamas only blinked at him with quiet curiosity. As a group, they moved forward to inspect him, and he let them. He reached out and stroked Fernando's coat. "He's soft. Do you clip them like sheep?"

"Yeth."

"That so? Tell me more." He gave her the cock-eyed grin that had probably gotten him everything he'd ever wanted all his life.

She looked into his eyes and it occurred to her that if Max Galloway were a product on a grocery store shelf, he'd be labeled "SEX APPEAL!" in big red letters, under which would read: *Surgeon General's Warning: Proximity to this product hazardous to your virtue. Women have been known to ignore logic and rip off their clothes when coming into contact with this product. Can cause rash, nervous stomach, thundering palpitations. Has been known to break hearts into itty-bitty pieces.*

"I see those wheels turning," he chided. "What are you thinking right now?"

Evie lifted her chin. "None of your beethwaxth."

Max's gaze dropped to her mouth. "That's adorable. *Thay* it again."

She set her jaw and gave him her haughtiest glare.

And he gave her back a smile that would melt the polar caps.

"Okay, then," he challenged. "Try 'suffering succotash.'"

What do you think I am, a performing theal?

When she didn't respond, he said, "Better yet, skip the succotash. Say something worthwhile. Say . . . 'sex.'"

Her eyes widened, then narrowed.

"Ah, c'mon," he coaxed, moving forward a step. "That's got to be a tough one. Give it a try."

His gaze locked on hers. Sparks, nearly visible to the naked eye, flared between them. He was seducing her, plain and simple. Or trying to. She knew it. He knew it. He'd issued a challenge. The succotash was in her court.

She pursed her lips. Okay, hot shot, she thought. Two can play at this game.

Starting at his boots, she slowly lifted her gaze. She lingered when she reached his crotch, trying desperately not to blink and blush. Button fly. A bit on the bulging side, she thought. Boxers or briefs? Mmm. Briefs. Definitely. And tight.

She felt her cheeks warm, but she wouldn't stop now.

His hips were encircled by a brown belt with a dull brass buckle. A little frisson of heat made its way to her stomach and then on down a little farther. She resisted the urge to clamp her legs tightly together.

Her gaze reached his chest. The chest she'd lain her weary head against. She knew he was solid, his muscles firm and strong. Her eyes assessed the breadth of his shoulders. His neck was strong, too, and not bulging in the least. It led up to a firm chin and jawline, hollow cheeks with a hint of dimple on each side of his sensual mouth.

Cute ears, not too big, not too stuck out. Finally, she let her gaze meander to his eyes, and stop. Uh-oh.

Her heart ceased beating. She'd come this far . . . couldn't chicken out now.

His eyes glittered, his jaw seemed locked in place. Oh, yes. She'd gotten his attention.

She tilted her head to the side and licked her lips until she was pretty sure they glistened.

"Thexth." It was as low and slow and deliberate as she could make it without running out of air.

He went still. His eyes darkened as his lids went sleepy. He seemed to stop breathing for a moment, then appeared to breathe too fast.

Silence, thick and tense, stretched taut between them. He lowered his gaze to her mouth, then returned it to her eyes. A moment earlier he had just been some hot-looking guy teasing her. But now he was a predatory male on the scent of a female he wanted, and Evie thought that perhaps she had played the game a little too well. She'd simply thought to give him a taste of his own medicine, but instead had given him a taste of something else, something he now seemed interested in devouring.

He took a step toward her.

She turned away—away from his expectant stare, away from his body heat, his masculinity, the attraction for him she would deny to the death.

"You don't like me, do you, Evie?"

Lowering her head, she kept her back to him, unsure how to answer. Why would he care one way or the other about her feelings for him? She didn't even *know* him.

He moved closer. She felt his presence, the weight and substance of him, and it disturbed and excited her at the same time.

"Look," he said, his voice edged with frustration, "I . . . you're . . . you caught me off guard, that's all. I've been behaving stupidly. Sorry."

Yeah, well, if I could only say "thtupidly," I'd give you a piece of my mind.

She turned to face him. For a moment he said nothing, just looked into her eyes. Then, "Ready to check out the barn? There's something I need to show you, and I don't think you're going to like it."

Chapter 4

Dear Diary:

We moved again. this place is ok. It doesn't smell as bad as the last one. mommy said the new job she got pays more and that we can go shopping at Value Village for some school clothes in a couple of weeks. Then she took off the moon neklice she always wears and put it on me. she told me to hang on to it and to not let her sell it no matter what, because it was the only thing of any value she had, axcept for me, of course. She smiled when she said it, so it must be true.

Evangeline—age 9

Inside the barn, Max got down on his knees and ran the beam of his pocket flashlight around the perimeter of the gaping hole in the floor. Without taking his eyes from it, he said, "Does anybody else come out here besides you?"

Evie paused before answering, looking down at the yawning chasm like it was going to expand and engulf her once and for all. Licking her lips, she said slowly, "When I'm in town, teaching, vacation, whatever, Edmund feed them, take care of them. Me and him, only."

"Did you know there was a cavern underneath the barn floor?"

She shook her head. "No."

Tapping the flashlight rhythmically against his thigh, he said, "The frame under the boards is made of two-by-fours, probably pine. The one-by-five planks have been nailed over it to form the floor."

He swept some of the straw away. "See here? The nails have been removed and the planks set back in place across the foundation struts."

Evie frowned at the wood, then at him, confusion and shock plain to see in the depths of her blue eyes. She swallowed.

"The wood is healthy, Evie," he continued. "No sign of rot. There are marks from a claw hammer where the nails have been pried up and removed. Before Tuesday afternoon when you fell, when was the last time you walked across this floor?"

"Don't remember." She paused a moment, licking her lips, pressing her fingertips to her jaw.

He hated to do this now, knowing she was in pain, but he had to find out what had happened.

"Hardly ever go to the back," she said. "No need."

"Why did you do it on Tuesday?"

"Oat bucket." She gestured to the tin bucket hanging on a peg a few feet away. Shaking her head, she said, "Didn't put it there."

It wasn't rocket science. "So someone placed it way over there to get you to walk across the floor, and fall through." Shining the light down into the chasm, he said, "Yesterday, while you were sleeping, I went down there. It's just a big rock cavern. The bottom is sandy in places and was covered with a few inches of seawater, so it must seep in from somewhere, maybe only during really high tides or storm surges."

In silence, she frowned, studied the bucket, the floor, and the ragged planking surrounding the hole through which she'd fallen. Without a word, she turned and walked out of the barn and into the sunshine.

He let her go. Snapping the flashlight off, he sat on the floor, resting his elbow on his knee, and watched her. Against his better judgment, he allowed himself to appreciate her quiet strength and intelligence. It was attractive. She was attractive.

She stood in the sun, her back to him, her arms crossed, thinking. She had an alluring, feminine shape, soft lines, cambered hips. With her dark red hair, gentle blue eyes, a dash of freckles across her nose, she probably captured the heart of every little boy in her class on the first day of school.

But at the moment, his eyes were focused on the way her blue jeans cupped her butt. Her perfect butt. Crass, disgusting, lusty male that he was, he'd have been dead not to notice how sexy the woman looked from behind.

He picked up a piece of straw and twirled it in his fingers. She had no criminal record, not so much as a parking ticket. No complaints on file from parents or students or the school board, and no history of substance abuse. She had a small circle of friends, most of whom were teachers and most of whom were out of town for the summer, but she had no boyfriends.

The field, as the saying went, was clear. And he had the ball. Play or pass? She turned a little and he caught her profile, the line of her nose, the fullness of her upper lip.

Play.

He twirled the straw in his fingers again, then let it fall to the floor. If she'd had a motive for killing Thomas Heyworth, neither the Port Henry PD nor the Seattle PD had been able to find it. While she couldn't be ruled out as a suspect, she wasn't exactly high on the list. In fact, in the weeks since Heyworth's death, she'd apparently been hounding Detective McKennitt to hurry up and find the old guy's killer.

All in all, Evangeline Randall *seemed* to be exactly what she *appeared* to be: a nice young schoolteacher who had loved her mentor, had a thing for llamas, and seemed to scramble his brain whenever she was near.

He gave himself a mental jab. As nice as she seemed, she absolutely wasn't his type, so why did his skin feel too tight for his body, his throat constrict, and his palms itch whenever she was around? When he'd pulled her out of that cavern, she looked like a broken toy that had been tossed in the recycle bin, but today, well, she sure cleaned up good. Better than good.

Crossing her arms over her stomach, she turned back to him.

"That hole," she said, giving a slight nod in the direction of the floor. "To hurt me?"

Without taking his eyes from hers, he nodded. "It's possible."

Her frown deepened and she turned away from him again, leaving Max to consider exactly what the point was of laying a trap for Evie.

Thomas Heyworth, the rich and famous mystery writer, had been shot to death in his own library, most likely with his own gun. And now an attempt had been made to harm his ward.

Was there a connection? And if so, what in the hell was it?

Evie closed her bedroom door and leaned against it, trying to slow her hammering heart. Thomas was dead, and now somebody had set a trap for her. To hurt her? To . . .

No, not kill her. Surely not to kill her.

She closed her eyes and held her breath for a moment, then let it out slowly. The thought of somebody wanting to kill her was ludicrous. That couldn't be it. There had to be some rational explanation. Maybe some kids had sneaked onto the island and thought it would be funny to put a hole in the barn floor. Or maybe they were just vandals. Or maybe . . . Or maybe what? What possible explanation could there be?

Resting her forehead in her palm, she worked to control her fragile emotions.

Between the heartbreak of Thomas's death, the stress of his funeral, the frustration of a police investigation going nowhere, then the awkward visit to Barlow's office, which culminated in the surprise of an impending contest for Thomas's estate, the trauma of falling through a hole in the floor to near death and then coping with the injuries to her body . . . And then there was the confusion and asperity she felt over Max Galloway . . .

Damn, was she going insane, or did it just feel that way? Insanity might not be such a bad idea. At least they'd lock her away in a safe place where she didn't have to worry about anything except what color socks she preferred, and whether to use straw or bamboo strips in basket-weaving class.

Letting her tired mind drift, she remembered back to when she'd first come to Heyworth Island.

She'd been barely eleven, a little girl. Alone in the world with no family or friends, she'd needed a home and an outlet for her love. Thomas had provided both.

Over time, she'd discovered what a complex man he was. Kind and generous, selfish and cruel. How he treated a person depended on his mood at the time, what he wanted, and how he felt about them.

Her heart felt bruised inside her chest as she remembered the first time she'd seen him. She'd looked up from her chair next to her mother's coffin to see him standing in the doorway of the dingy funeral home, gazing at her.

Fifteen years ago Thomas Heyworth had been lanky and a bit worn around the edges, but he hadn't seemed frightening, not like Maggie's boyfriends. He'd seemed fatherly, right from the very first moment. Approaching her, he'd hunkered down to her level.

"You Maggie O'Dell's girl?"

She'd nodded.

"What do they call you?"

"Evie," she replied. "Evangeline May Randall, sir."

He blinked, hard, the way people do when they're caught off guard, and even at eleven she'd known that to be true. "Randall, eh?" He seemed to search her face for a moment, then gave an absent sort of nod.

His brown eyes were kindly as he'd smiled at her. "My name's Thomas Heyworth. I'm a famous writer. Not a very good one, if you want the truth, but a famous one. You ever heard of me?"

She'd shaken her head.

"You got any family anywhere, Evangeline May Randall?"

"They're looking," she whispered.

He nodded again. "Do you know what a ward is, Evie?"

"It's a place in a hospital where they keep sick people."

"Yes, that's one definition. But a ward the way I

mean it is when a grown-up takes care of a kid, like me taking care of you. I've arranged for that to happen. Would you like that?"

Her little body had stiffened, and she eyed him with suspicion. "I don't know you. Why do you want to ward me?"

He'd chuckled, then grown serious. "I knew your mother, Evie. Not very well, apparently, but I assume she'll rest easier knowing you are being well cared for. Uh, you see, last year, I lost my wife."

"I'm sorry." She leaned forward. "Did you need me to help you look for her?"

For a moment he'd gone silent, licking his lips and swallowing. Finally, he said gently, "Not that kind of lost. Lost, like you've lost your mother."

She'd felt her cheeks flush. "Oh. I see. I knew what that meant, but I forgot. You probably think I'm dumb, and now you won't want to ward me."

He'd lowered his head for a moment, and when he looked at her again, his eyes were rimmed with red. "I don't think you're dumb at all. And I think offering to help me find my lost wife tells me everything I need to know about you, Evangeline May Randall. And more." Tapping her on the knee with the back of his finger, he said, "I haven't got anyone now, and neither do you. So, what do you think, kiddo? Shall we be alone together?"

Since Maggie O'Dell's child care system had been somewhat haphazard, Evie wasn't sure if her mother would care one way or the other about her future, but she didn't want to tell this nice stranger that. Instead, she'd looked at him, trying in her child's mind to make some sense of his remarks.

"Sort of like, would you be my father?"

He'd blinked that hard blink again and said, "No. But I can make sure you have a roof over your head, food, clothing, and safety. Above all, a little girl needs to feel safe. Am I right?"

Since Evie had never felt particularly safe, she wondered just what that might feel like.

He'd reached his hand out to her, and she hesitated only a second before taking it. Many times over the years, she'd replayed that first meeting in her head, looking for clues, coming up with nothing.

While he may not have admitted to being her father, she had certainly thought of him as one. Her innocent heart had opened to him, accepted him, and made him her own.

He'd brought her to the island, to Mayhem Manor, where she met Edmunds. Wonderful, gentle-hearted Edmunds. Between the two middle-aged men, she'd never felt safer in her life. While they were each emotionally distant in their own way, they'd done their best. She'd never gone hungry, always had decent clothing, excellent health care, and a good education.

If she didn't get as many hugs and kisses as most little girls needed, well, that was okay. She couldn't complain. She loved Thomas with the love a daughter feels for a beloved father, even though, as she grew older, she came to realize he was not a very kind man to most other people, and in fact could be an obnoxious son of a bitch.

But not to her. Not ever to her.

She walked over to the window, brushed the curtain aside and placed her open hand on the glass. It

felt cold, brittle, just like her insides. Past her fingertips, she could see the west end of the island, and beyond the treetops, the sea, sparkling like a meadow
of hand-hewn jade.

Typical of the Northwest, the morning's sun had
disappeared behind a thick layer of clouds, and now
rain splattered against the pane. Droplets formed,
slid down and away, out of sight. Her world became
a blur, the hard edges softened, gentled by the
cleansing rain.

She let her forehead rest against the back of her
hand on the glass. Somebody had killed Thomas, on
his own island, at his own house, in his own library.
She had been the one to find his lifeless body.
Thomas, I miss you. . . .

Trying to shake off her melancholy, she checked
the time on the clock on her bedside table. The
guests would all be gathered tonight, and Thomas's
ridiculous treasure hunt would begin. Worse, to win
the game and keep her island, her world, intact, she
would have to work closely with Max Galloway—a
man who both fascinated and terrified her.

How would it go for them? Could they possibly
win? What kinds of surprises did Thomas have in
store?

As she went to the armoire to slip into her dress,
she thought of what a tricky guy Thomas could be.
If he'd devised this little treasure hunt, there was
probably more to it than met the eye—probably a
lot more.

Chapter 5

Dear Diary:

sometimes i wonder what it would be like to be somebody else. somebody who has both a mommy and a
daddy. If i had a dad, he'd probbaly be tall and handsome and very, very brave. And he would make
mommy stay at home. But even if she did go out, he
would be here with me. i know there are lots of people
who don't have both a mom and a dad, and i love
mommy and everything, it's just i think having two
parents instead of one would be nice. You can never
get too much love, you know!

Evangeline—age 9

At a few minutes before six Evie took one last
glance in the mirror. She had wiggled into her knitted rose silk dress, then slipped on a pair of dangly

earrings and her mother's necklace. A little blusher and touch of lipstick . . . yep, good to go and not half bad.

She'd almost convinced herself she simply wanted to look nice for dinner, that her primping had nothing to do with impressing a man she didn't like and with whom she would become involved when they sold raspberry iced tea in hell. Sure, the look in Max's eyes had the power to send her blood pressure skyrocketing, but she'd always held sway over her hormones before, and didn't see any reason to worry about them tonight. Too much.

As she walked toward her door she reminded herself that her response to him was just one more reason to stay away from the man. He disturbed her equilibrium, the status quo, her carefully planned life. Being near him made her *feel* things, intense things, desirable things. She became like a little kid fascinated by a candle's flame. Her fingertips had been burned, yet the potent allure of the fire was so powerful, she wanted to touch it anyway.

When she entered the dining room a few minutes later, Max was seated at the table looking like a million bucks and change. But, thank God, he was not alone, for seated to his right was an older woman, and to his left, a handsome, bespectacled blond man.

The treasure hunters had arrived.

She approached the table, and Max rose from his seat. He was a gentleman, she'd give him that. He was freshly shaved, and wore a dark blue suit and dark tie. He looked like he'd just stepped off the pages of the *Totally Hot Guys Way Out Of Your League Gazette*, and he knew it, the bastard.

He winked at her, and his mouth kicked up at one end in a flirty smile. Wowee-zowee, what a hunk.

Her heart fluttered. She ignored it. All this fluttering heart nonsense was probably taking years off her life.

"Evie Randall," he said, "this is Madame Grovda, the world-renowned Russian psychic, and Dabney James, the poet."

James stood and extended his hand, but before she could take it, Madame Grovda bolted from her seat. Practically trotting around the end of the table, she flung her arms about Evie and gave her a breath-stealing hug.

"*Privet*, dahlink! I, Madame Ernestina Grovda, have arrived. I am saving the day!" Her voice was husky, her accent pronounced. Holding Evie at an arm's length, she gave her the once-over and said, "You are pretty one, yes?"

"*Spasiba*, madame," Evie managed without too much trouble. She'd noticed that, over the course of the afternoon, the swelling on her tongue had reduced considerably, allowing her to speak normally again. The bruises on her backside, however, were still weeks away from healing.

"What is this? *Govorite li vy po Russki*?"

Evie blushed and shook her head. "*Nyet*. Not really. I learned a few words, in your honor. I am a schoolteacher, and I thought it would be nice—"

"*Da!* The teacher of children. This is good!" Madame Grovda seemed thrilled enough by that to pull Evie to her bosom again and practically hug the life out of her. Pain shot through her body.

Evie realized she must have reacted, because she suddenly felt Max's presence beside her, felt his hands gently prying her out of the psychic's abundant arms.

"Madame," he said, wedging himself between Evie and the woman. "Ms. Randall is suffering injuries from a fall two days ago. She's still healing."

Evie felt her eyes mist. Doing her best to smile at the psychic, she said, "It's okay, madame. I'm fine, really."

Madame Grovda was a woman well past her middle years, stout of build, strong of limb, who appeared not so much clothed as upholstered. Everything about her was large—from her shock of white hair, to the dinner-plate earrings swinging heavily from her lobes, to her necklace of ping-pong-ball-sized red beads.

Her round, friendly face was flushed, her broad forehead dotted with perspiration. Whiskey-brown eyes glittering with enthusiasm were small and deeply set, and her generous mouth had been painted a shade of orange Evie was sure didn't exist in nature.

"I regret, my dear," she crooned, cupping Evie's cheek in her palm.

Abruptly, she spread her arms wide, like a 747 preparing for takeoff. Her eyes drifted closed and she set her fingertips to her temples. Humming and rocking back and forth on her heels, she moaned, "Your hand, child. Give to me your hand."

Evie glanced at Max, then hesitantly extended her

right hand. Madame grasped it as though it were the lifeline that would save her from going down for the third time. Her eyes pinched tightly closed, her head nodding, she resembled a malfunctioning bobble-head toy.

"Yes, yes. Clearly, I see," she announced dramatically, her voice pitched high and breathy, like the shriek of a terrified chipmunk. "Soon, you will undertake trip of heart. Ah, and with such beautiful man."

She paused a moment to smile knowingly. Then her lips curved down and her voice deepened. "But trip holds many dangers. This man will protect you, but you should give him a key to secret which you hold buried deeply in your heart, *milaya moya.*"

Evie's aforementioned heart skidded and hopped for several beats and nearly went into arrest. Everybody had secrets. That was a pretty safe *prediction.* The woman could not possibly know anything.

Madame Grovda's eyes were still closed, her forehead furrowed in distress. "This man," she rasped. "He does not wish for me to see him clearly, but he is handsome devil. You will marry him when the trees turn to red and gold, and the cool wind, it kisses your brow. You will have three children. Two sons. One daughter. *Dover'sya mne.* It is so."

Right. "*This* fall, madame?" Evie laughed, not quite sure what to make of her own personal psychic reading. "Well, that doesn't give me much time. So much to do. The dress, the church, the guest list, the china pattern. Did you happen to notice if my future husband prefers floral designs or tone-on-tone?"

Madame Grovda opened her eyes and smiled at Evie as though she knew all her most intimate dreams.

"You doubt me, child?" she said softly, arching a thinly painted brow. "But is truth."

Max took a sip of wine and slid a glance around the table. They had become five for dinner when Lorna joined them a few minutes ago and was seated next to her treasure hunt partner, Dabney James. Edmunds, who would be Madame Grovda's companion for the hunt, hovered in the background, ready to provide whatever the guests needed.

"So tell me, Mr. James," Lorna said. "What are you working on now?"

James appeared to be in his early thirties and had the kind of blond good looks that seemed to appeal to most women. Max wasn't sure what famed, yet reclusive, poets were supposed to look like, but if they resembled a quarterback for the Seahawks, then Dabney James was your man.

The poet smiled shyly at Lorna and said, "Have you read any of my work, Ms. Whitney?"

"Since we're going to be partners," she said, "perhaps you should call me Lorna." She lowered her lashes as her cheeks flushed a girlish pink.

Smitten. The poor woman hadn't been in James's presence for more than ten minutes and she was smitten with the bastard. Well, he'd better not try that frigging charm on *his* partner.

Max took a sip of wine, then set his glass well into Evie's personal space on the table. She didn't seem to notice, but James shot a quick glance at the overt territorial male gesture, and came that close to smirking.

"Hey, James," Max said, feeling peeved enough to act on it. All eyes turned to him. "Why don't you recite one of your poems for us? One of the short ones. You *do* have a *short* one?"

From across the table James's light brown eyes assessed Max. With a single finger, the middle one, he pushed his glasses back up on his nose, then smiled. Long dimples formed in his cheeks and Max could have sworn he heard Evie's breath catch.

Son of a bitch.

"Um, Detective Lollygag, was it?" the famed, yet reclusive, poet answered, arching his brows. Both of them.

"Galloway."

"Sorry. Well, in your honor, I could recite my shortest poem. It's called 'Poor Little Inchworm.' I don't bring it out much, sort of keep it tucked away since it's such an embarrassment. Limp, no rhythm, no staying power. Always leaves the reader frustrated, wanting more. You understand, I'm sure."

Lorna smiled, transforming her somewhat plain features into a delicate prettiness. "Oh, please do recite something, Mr. James. I'm a huge fan."

He turned to her and said, "Please call me Dabney."

Dabney, Max thought. What kind of a puke-assed name was that?

Next to him, Evie spoke up. "My favorite poem of yours is 'Lamentation of the Lilac.' I have parts of it memorized, but I'd love to hear you recite it the way you, the poet, intended." She beamed at the guy, and Max felt like he'd been sucker-punched right in the gut. What would it take to get her to smile at him like that? He was no good at poetry, but if she appreciated an ardent and somewhat lyrical homicide report, he had it covered.

James picked up his wineglass and held it to his lips. "Actually," he said over the rim, "I think it would be wonderful if *you* recited it. I never tire of hearing my own work." He laughed as though he were poking fun at himself. Yeah, right.

All eyes turned to Evie. She put her hands in her lap and closed her eyes. Her lashes were dark and thick, her cheeks flushed from the warmth of the room. With her lips slightly parted, she looked like a woman about to be kissed, and it was all he could do to refrain from swooping in. Damn, she was pretty.

" 'O to be a lilac fair, amethyst petals, dew like fairy sequins sewn one by one with gentle hands, gliding, stroking the silken flesh of the flower, ever opening, yawning, gaping, beckoning the sword that knights my love in passion and in pain.' " Her lashes fluttered open, and she smiled . . . at James. "Did I do it justice?"

Max stared at her, then at the lovestruck Lorna, and at the Russian psychic, grown silent and wistful. Dabney James wrote pornographic crap, and they loved it?

In response to her recitation, James lifted his glass in a toast to Evie. "Very nicely done."

Edmunds approached and placed another bottle of wine on the table. The man's blue eyes rested for a moment on Evie, and when she looked up at him, he gave her a quick smile and continued on about his duties.

Refilling his own glass with the excellent cabernet, Max said, "That was great, but it was written a while ago. Why don't you give us a couple of lines of what you're working on now? I'm sure the ladies would love something hot off the presses."

The poet glared at him over the rim of his wineglass as the women begged and pleaded for more.

Finally, James said, "Well, let's see. Uh, okay. There is a little something I've been working on, but it's still in the rough draft stages so you'll have to forgive me if it seems unpolished."

"Oh, you're just being modest," Max scolded. "I'm sure it's of the same quality as your published work."

Tossing back a huge gulp of wine, the poet resettled himself in his chair. "Right. Uh, okay. It's called, uh, yeah, it's called 'Ode to Wine.'"

The women smiled and nodded their approval, leaning forward in their chairs in eager anticipation, while Max stared innocently into James's face.

The poet cleared his throat. "'Wine is good and red and tasty, and when drunk slowly, it won't make you hasty, to depart . . . in passion and in pain.'"

There was silence for a moment at the table, then the women burst into enthusiastic applause. James blushed and polished off the rest of his *good and red and tasty* wine.

"As I s-said," he stammered. "Very rough." He

sent another meaningful glare Max's way, and the two men locked gazes for a moment.

While James had babbled on, Edmunds placed chilled plates in front of each guest, and Max realized he was starving. As he took a healthy bite of his cracked crab appetizer, Madame Grovda broke off a section of French bread the size of a Volkswagen and applied butter to it with the enthusiasm of Van Gogh smearing yellow ochre on a fresh canvas.

He refocused his attention on the woman seated next to him—the prickly woman apparently determined to avoid him. She seemed to be picking away at her food, absently pushing it around but not really eating anything.

"Evie?" he said, and she lifted her gaze to him. Man, she had gorgeous eyes. Clear blue. Stunning blue. Wary and suspicious blue.

She slowly blinked those big blue eyes and tilted her head as if asking him what he wanted.

"Allergic to shellfish?" he asked, gesturing to her plate.

"Oh, no," she said, lowering her lashes. "I, uh, I have an emotional aversion to crab."

"An *emotional* aversion? Like what? An edible complex?"

Across the table, James snorted.

With a little shake of the head she said, "Detective Galloway, you are far too immature to understand. Forget I said anything."

He sat back in his chair and narrowed his eyes on her. Twirling the stem of his wineglass in his fingers, he said, "No, really. I want to know."

Evie carefully readjusted the napkin on her lap. She was wearing a soft pink dress that complimented the richness of her auburn hair and brought out the scatter of freckles across her nose. It also accentuated the tantalizing swell of her bosom as the scooped neckline displayed creamy skin and a hint of deep cleavage. Encircling her throat, a gold chain held a sparkling crescent moon. She pursed her lips and looked at him steady on, and he felt himself tighten all over.

"It's a silly thing," she said finally. "You wouldn't understand—"

"Not true," he interrupted, feigning insult. "I'm a very understanding guy." Giving her an encouraging grin, he urged, "I'm sure Madame Grovda and Ms. Whitney, not to mention old James over there, would be interested in the story."

Across from Evie, Max could see that Madame Grovda's mouth was full, but she encouraged Evie with a poof-cheeked smile, while Lorna and that dickhead James both nodded their approval.

Evie stared at Max for a moment, then relaxed. "All right. Okay, last year, I showed my sixth grade class a marine documentary—"

"Hoo-ha!"

She halted and looked over at James, who was grinning.

"No, Mr. James," she said patiently. "Not 'Marine,' as in 'a few good men,' but marine as in sea creatures. Besides, 'Hoo-ha' is the Army. I believe 'ooo-rah' is the Marines."

Max considered this. "What's the Air Force?"

Her brows dipped together as she glanced at him in obvious irritation. "I'm guessing 'up-up-and-away.'"

"Negative. That's Superman." Max crossed his arms over his chest. "What about the Navy?"

"'Glub-glub,' for all I know," she snapped. "Do you want to hear the story or not?"

"I do."

Madame Grovda swallowed and said, "*Pozhalujsta, milaya moya.* Please speak to us of seeing the craps."

"The *sea crabs*," Evie corrected. "Fine. Anyway, the documentary was about the reproductive habits of crabs."

"Oh," Max said dryly. "Did I miss that one? And I had so wanted to tape it."

"You're ruining the moment," she said icily.

"What *moment*? You're talking about the sex life of *crustaceans*, for Christ's sake."

She condemned him with the arch of a brow. "I knew you'd have some juvenile response. Which reminds me. You hated Thomas, so why did you agree to join the treasure hunt?"

"None of your beethwaxth," he growled.

"Are you making fun of me again?"

"Would I do that?"

"*Yeth,*" she said, mimicking herself. "I'm participating so I can keep the island and the llamas, because I grew up here and I can't imagine living anywhere else, and if I had millions of dollars, I wouldn't have to teach anymore and could live here all the time. Why are *you* here?"

He shrugged. "Curiosity, mostly. Then there's all

that money. I figure Heyworth owes me, and I mean to collect."

"Owes you? For what?"

Glaring at Evie, he said, "Let us return to your fascinating crab story, shall we?"

She sent him a stern, teacherly look, and said, "Are you going to behave?"

Max stifled a laugh and put up his hands in mock surrender. "I'll be good," he said smoothly, like when he was seventeen and he'd tried to get Merilee Vandermore into the backseat of his car. "So, what about the mating habits of marine crabs? Do they have little bumper stickers that say, 'Crabs Do It in a Pinch?'"

"You are *such* a jerk."

Okay, so she was no Merilee Vandermore. And maybe that was a good thing.

Evie ignored his apologetic smile, sent him a glare, and continued.

"It seems that when two crabs mate, the female must first completely shed her shell."

"Works that way for humans, too." Max waggled his brows.

"When a female and a male crab get together, she sheds the shell, and he, uh, crawls on top of her, sort of like nesting tables, you know?" She demonstrated this by cupping one hand over the other. "Then, very gently, he uses all his legs to turn her onto her back, underneath him. He has to be extremely gentle, because she doesn't have her shell anymore to protect her. Then he lowers himself onto her until their bodies are touching, um, intimately."

Max willed Evie to look up at him, but she wouldn't.

"As they m-mate," she stumbled softly, "he curls his legs around her body, sort of like an embrace. Then he, you know, um, deposits his sperm."

Max took another slug of wine, but said nothing. Was it getting hot in here, or was it just him? Who would have thought the sex life of some ugly-assed crabs could be so erotic?

"When he's done," she continued, "very, very gently, he uses all his legs to turn her right side up again, then he stands over her, guarding her, with his legs acting as a sort of bulwark against predators. They stay like that until her new shell hardens. It's the most vulnerable time of her life. She has completely let her guard down, and must rely totally on him for protection, and somehow they both know it."

Lorna reached out and patted Evie's hand, sympathy plain to see in her eyes. "And then?"

Evie lifted her chin to stare at Max. "He leaves her, of course, pregnant, to fend for herself. Just goes on his merry way, feetloose and fancy free."

Madame Grovda shook her head then knocked back the rest of her wine. "So typical. Men. *Phooey*." She made a rude noise with her lips.

Lorna's mouth flattened. "How true."

"Wait just a minute," Max said. "He probably thought she used protection. Besides, just how many baby crabs does she have?"

"Two million."

His brows shot up. "Well there you go. What guy crab in his right mind would stay? Two *million*? What if the little crablettes needed braces or glasses?" He grinned at her. "Why, the cost of back-to-school shoes alone would be staggering."

Shifting her gaze to the rose-and-cream flocked wallpaper, Evie murmured, "That's beside the point. A *decent* crab would have stayed. They were half his responsibility, after all, whether he loved her or not."

Max studied Evie's profile as she continued to ignore him. He'd been mistaken when he first saw her and thought she was passably pretty. She was absolutely stunning, in a fresh and unassuming way. The dock out front should be crammed with motorboats from her hoards of suitors, but there were none. Just why was that? he wondered.

With a wistful smile, she said, "Well, you'd have to have seen it, I suppose. It was a beautiful thing, really. I mean, he *knows* to protect her, and she *knows* she needs to let him because at that very moment she's completely vulnerable. I . . . I sort of thought it was romantic."

Romantic? Horny crustaceans, romantic?

"It's ridiculous, I guess," she continued, "but ever since I saw that documentary, I can't eat crab."

As she took a sip of water, Max studied her. Sure, her story was silly, but it was also very tender, and enormously revealing.

He wondered if she had any idea just how revealing.

Chapter 6

Dear Diary:

Adam Blane is like, a total snot. he thinks he's sooooo great just because his daddy's a cop. Adam said that his daddy told him that he knows my mommy really well. he said she has a reputashan. The way he said that made me so mad, I punched him in the nose. He squealed and even cried just like a big baby. I know you're not supposed to hit, but I just couldn't help it!

Evangeline—age 9

The atrium garden at Mayhem Manor was exquisite. As Max meandered down flagstone pathways, through thick stands of leafy palms, around tropical ferns and flowers, he was amazed at the visual beauty of the place, the mix of heady scents. The warm, damp air made him want to strip off his clothes and dive into the deep pool at the base of the waterfall, submerge himself in the cool water. . . .

He glanced at Evie, walking next to him, pointing out various flora and fauna. Naked, under the waterfall, Evie and him. The mental picture was enough to make his fingers tremble.

Dinner had ended an hour ago. It was nearly eight, and even though chairs had been set up in the garden in anticipation of Felix Barlow's arrival—and the start of the treasure hunt—the attorney hadn't yet arrived.

"It's not a greenhouse," Evie was explaining, flashing those big blue eyes at him. "It's a fully enclosed atrium, three stories tall, and takes up the entire south side of the mansion. This time of year, the glass panels on top are open, but in the winter they're closed so the more exotic species can be kept at an even temperature."

And so you could swim naked under the waterfall, he added silently, envisioning her pale skin under the splash of water, her rich mahogany hair flowing down her bare back, a fairy nymph in some secret woodland grotto.

Disconcerted by his own thoughts, he flipped back the edges of his jacket and slid his hands into his pockets. As he did, his right hand met the uneven edges of the coin, and he automatically curled his fingers around it.

He didn't have to take it out and look at it; over the years, its every detail had been etched into his brain. Since his mother had given it to him, he'd carried it with him and invariably found himself clutching it whenever he needed to clear his thoughts, focus his mind on something important—something emotional.

Remove his thoughts from something emotional was closer to the truth.

He ran the tip of his finger over the face of the coin, over the smooth swell of the image struck there ages ago in a land far removed in time and place from the world he knew. He skimmed the metal with his thumb, wishing, in a way, it was Evie he was touching, glad, in a way, it was not.

He'd come to perceive the crudely struck gold disk much as he did his own heart. Like his heart, the coin was warm or cold, depending on whether someone touched it . . . or not. It was a thing separate from his body, away. He sensed its presence and could touch it when he needed to, but it did not touch him.

Sitting now in his palm, the coin reminded him he could look all he wanted, but his heart would remain his own. It had been a hard lesson for him to learn, but between his father and Melissa, he had learned it well.

He'd tried it once, giving away his heart, but she'd given it back. A little battered, a bit bruised, still, it was his own again, and it was going to stay that way.

Inside his head, his father's words jabbed at his brain.

Women make you soft. You start screwing up. Everything goes to hell. You can't let them get to you. Do that, and you're only half a man.

Was Evie getting to him? He couldn't help but

wonder. When he decided to join the treasure hunt, he hadn't counted on running into somebody like Evie Randall. As a cop, he wasn't fond of surprises. As a man, however, he seemed to come alive with her in a way he hadn't for years.

His arms remembered the weight of her body as he carried her to the house that first night. At dinner tonight he'd wondered what it would be like to have sex with her, but he knew enough about women to know Evie Randall probably wouldn't have sex . . . she would make love.

As they passed a trio of exotic palms, she caressed a shiny leaf, and he focused on her fingertips, imagining them gliding down his chest, followed by that moist, plump mouth—

". . . capable of sucking the whole thing down, no matter how big it is, until it dissolves into a gelatinous ooze."

He shot her a confused look, then looked at the plant she was pointing to.

"Oh, uh, sorry," he said, feeling his cheeks heat. "My mind seems to have wandered."

"A rare occurrence, I'm sure," she said dryly. "I was referring to the Venus flytrap over there. When a fly wanders in—"

"Never mind. I know what happens next. Tell me about the flowers."

"Sure. In the past hundred years," she explained, "flowers and trees have been collected from all over the world. The waterfall is made up of island rock—"

"And here I took it for granite."

She stopped and stared at him, fighting a grin, if the dimples in her cheeks were any sign.

"There are children in my class," she said, "who have an infinitely more sophisticated sense of humor than you, Detective."

He shrugged and smiled down into her eyes. "Damn kids these days. I'll bet they don't even know any good elephant jokes. Why, when I was a kid—"

"And when was that, last week sometime?"

"Don't let these boyish good looks fool you."

Pursing her lips, she gave him the once-over. "Not a problem." She turned to the rocks in question and said, "The waterfall is three stories high and takes up the entire west side of the atrium. It was designed to look like a cataract Thomas sketched years ago while on safari."

"It's like a jungle in here," Max said, lifting his gaze to a coconut palm that nearly touched the skylights. "Very 'Me Tarzan, you Jane' kind of thing."

She slid him a glance. "Sorry. No Tarzan, no Jane, no Cheetah."

He shrugged. "And cheetah's nevah prospah?"

"Just because you're funny doesn't mean I will ever like you," she said evenly. "Thomas had some pretty disparaging things to say about you, Detective."

"Likewise, I'm sure." He stopped and tried to catch her gaze, but she avoided him. "So why'd he invite me to join the treasure hunt?"

"Believe me," she said, "I've been wondering *that* myself. After the things he said concerning your mother and how—"

"Leave my mother out of this."

She looked shocked. "I'm sorry," she said softly. "I only meant, well, he adored her. She died just before I came here, but Thomas has kept her portrait hanging above the fireplace in his room all these years. She was very beautiful, Max. You . . . you look like her."

Max tightened his jaw. There was no way in hell he would be drawn into a conversation about his mother, Thomas Heyworth's one and only wife. He'd been against the marriage and had told his mother so. He'd even gone so far as to boycott the ceremony, but she married the son of a bitch anyway, and within months was dead. He had never even had a chance to say good-bye. In the sixteen years since, his hatred of Heyworth had only increased.

Turning away from Max, Evie continued on up the path. "The atrium's my favorite place at Mayhem Manor," she said lightly, obviously changing the subject. "When I first arrived, I felt very unsettled, especially at night. I'd bring the quilt from my bed, and sneak down and sleep in here on the deep grass by the waterfall. The rhythm of the falling water seemed to soothe me. I didn't feel so lonely then."

"How old were you when you came here, Evie?" He knew the answer, knew her whole history, but he wanted to keep her talking. He liked her voice, the slight huskiness of it. It was the kind of voice a man liked to hear whispering his name in the dark. His name, and other things.

"Eleven," she said, and walked away from him to face the waterfall.

Light from the dying sun bounced and glimmered off the ribbons of water slithering and splashing down the rough edges of the rocks. He could see why she had slept here when she'd been afraid. The sound of the water was calming, musical, maybe even healing. He imagined her as a little girl, alone and frightened, and he wished suddenly he'd known her then. He would have stood by her, protected her, been her stalwart defender. There was something about Evie that brought out the knight gallant in him, and even knowing how destructive those feelings were, he hesitated shoving them away.

Just then the glass doors at the far end of the atrium swung wide, allowing in a distinguished-looking man in a black suit. Mid-sixties, balding, elegant, he held a briefcase in his left hand as though it were a natural extension of his arm.

"Felix Barlow," Evie said under her breath. She crossed her arms under her breasts and stared across the garden. While she focused on the lawyer, Max stole a quick look at her alluring breasts, then flicked his glance away. Dumbasses stared and drooled, which pissed women off. Smart men knew how to get a quick eyeful without offending. He considered himself a very smart man.

Edmunds stepped through the door next, holding it open as Madame Grovda swooped in, chattering away in a blur of Russian. She wore a black velvet dress and a thousand scarves in various shades of red, yellow, and orange, all of which fluttered about her as she walked, giving the impression she was on fire.

The cook and gardener—Ada Stanley and her

husband Earl—shuffled in, neither one apparently enthused about a treasure hunt in which they would not take part.

The little parade culminated with Lorna, looking pretty in the yellow sundress she'd worn to dinner, and Dabney James, who had slipped his arm through hers and was apparently spouting more "poetry." His slacks and white shirt made him appear as if he'd just jetted in from Palm Beach. He caught sight of Max and scowled, then returned his attention to the enraptured secretary.

After the guests had entered, Edmunds released the door and followed a wide flagstone path to the waterfall, where everyone was busy seating themselves.

Conversation trickled off as Barlow rose from his chair and prepared to address the group, the twenty foot red banana tree at his back making him look like an overdressed castaway.

A hush fell over the guests. Even the loquacious Madame Grovda had zipped her lips and seemed to be holding her breath. Next to Max, Evie sat on the edge of her chair, her hands folded neatly on her knees, her attention fully on the lawyer. Inhaling, Max let her soft floral scent wrap around his senses like a silk ribbon—a ribbon that tied him into more knots each time he looked at her.

Barlow cleared his throat, clasped his hands behind him, and began to pace in lawyerlike fashion. Max half expected him to begin with, "If it please the court."

A smile on his lips, Barlow said, "Welcome to the treasure hunt. Except for the Stanleys and myself, of course, all of you in this room are participants in my late client's plan to dispose of his sizable fortune through an elaborate game of hide and seek."

He paused for a moment, then shifted direction and paced back the way he'd come. "Be that as it may, the game will officially begin as soon as this meeting has concluded and any questions have been answered. You already know who your partners are, and that you have two weeks from midnight tonight to find the final clue and claim the Heyworth estate, which, as of this morning, is worth somewhere in the neighborhood of thirty million dollars."

"Nice neighborhood," Dabney mumbled.

As Barlow cleared his throat to continue, Edmunds rose from his seat, clutching a thin packet.

"Beg pardon, Mr. Barlow."

All eyes turned toward Edmunds, who stood looking so regal as to be a long-lost member of the royal family.

Barlow raised his brows. "What is it, Edmunds?"

"A package was delivered via certified mail a few hours ago." He raised the packet for all to see. "It contained this sealed envelope addressed to Miss Evangeline. An accompanying letter to me instructed she open it at the commencement of the treasure hunt when everyone had assembled."

Next to Max, Evie made a small sound of surprise. Rising from his chair, he stretched out his hand. "May I see that, Edmunds?"

The butler sketched a brief bow and handed the packet to Max, then returned to his seat. The address on the envelope was a prominent law firm in Seattle.

"Do you know what's in it, Edmunds?"

"No sir. I do not."

Max looked down at Evie. "Do you?"

She shook her head. "No. I can't imagine. . . ."

"Barlow? You know anything about this?"

The lawyer stared at the envelope in dismay, as though it had just plopped to earth from the outer reaches of space. "I couldn't begin to guess. However, if its contents involves the game, it should come to me."

"I couldn't begin to second-guess Heyworth," Max said, handing the envelope to Evie. "But if he addressed it to her, I'd say he wanted it to go to her."

Everybody looked at everybody else, and a small hum of anticipatory conversation bubbled through the group.

Standing, Evie moved to the front and turned to face the others. She broke the seal on the packet and opened it, pulling out a single sheet of paper.

Barlow reached over to snatch it from her hand, but she quickly turned away, smashing it against her chest. "Excuse me, Mr. Barlow."

"But it may be a legal document that I need to evaluate before you—"

"Take a seat, Barlow," Max said.

The attorney's mouth turned town and he looked like a cat who had just been denied a bowl of cream. Then he smiled at Evie and returned to his seat.

"It's dated seven days before Thomas died," she said. "He must have written it while he was on tour."

Max considered the timing. "He was on a book

tour all during May, right? And was shot the day he got back?"

"Yes, h-he was." She looked at the paper, her brows knitted in a frown. Licking her lips, she began to read aloud.

" 'Don't you just love surprises? What kind of host would I be if there weren't a few twists and turns thrown in to keep you on your toes? You didn't really think I was going to make this easy, did you?

" 'True, you were all invited to take part in my treasure hunt, and I wanted you to have a good time. But something has happened to change my original plans, turning my treasure hunt into the hunt for a killer.

" 'You see, a few days ago, somebody tried to kill me. Shocking, isn't it? Since this codicil only kicks in if I was murdered, they must have tried it again, and succeeded! I'm sure the cops are running around with their heads up their assumptions, as usual, so it's up to you to make sure justice is done.' "

Evie raised her eyes and locked gazes with Edmunds, who had risen from his chair to stare at her. Returning her attention to the paper, she read, " 'Let me cut right to the chase, folks. It was one of you who k-killed me, and I know which one.' "

A collective gasp rose from the room. Barlow choked, Lorna cried out, and Madame Grovda gave a sharp laugh. James stayed where he was and glanced quickly around the room, while Mrs. Stanley began muttering under her breath and her husband slapped his knee and muttered, "No, shit."

Edmunds stood stock still and neither said nor did anything, the look on his face unreadable.

Max considered each person in the room. They'd all had alibis for the time of the murder—save for Madame Grovda and Dabney James, who hadn't been investigated because they hadn't been suspects, until now.

Heyworth had lived on an island. Anybody with an axe to grind, and a boat, could have motored up, gained entry to the house, shot Heyworth, then gone fishing, and nobody would have been the wiser.

Clearing her throat, Evie cut a glance at Edmunds, who gave her an encouraging smile. She resumed reading.

" 'There are seven clues. Each one leads to the next. Originally, they simply led to my treasure. Now, they lead to my murderer.

" 'The only clue I need to change is the last one, Lucky Number Seven, which I'll do as soon as I return home.

" 'So you don't all trip over each other, there are three separate sets of clues. Each set is unique except for Number Seven. That's the kicker. Find it, and you inherit my estate, *and* get the goods on my killer. Some fun, huh? Damn, I wish I could be there!

" 'You're thinking, why don't I just name him or her right now and have done with it? I could, but why? I'm a mystery writer, for Christ's sake! This is the best mystery I've ever come across—better than Clue or a Mystery Train or spooky tales around a campfire! Besides, the whole time my Treasure–

cum–Murder Hunt is in progress, my killer gets to sweat. That alone's worth the price of admission, kiddies. Hell, I had little enough time left on this planet, and now this interloper has stolen it! It's only right I should make him, or her, suffer.

" 'Oh, and one more thing. It probably wouldn't be wise for any of you to skip town right now since I have no doubt the cops would be mighty interested in anybody who did, if you get my drift.

" 'Okay! Are we ready? Clue Number One for each team is in a sealed envelope inside this packet. Damn, I love a good mystery! Let the Murder Hunt begin!' "

"That's all there is," Evie said. "It's been signed and notarized."

Outside, a crow screeched and scolded, and a brisk wind rustled the branches of a nearby alder tree. Inside, only the burble of water as it tumbled down the rocks broke the thick silence. Max viewed each guest in turn.

Lorna looked like she'd just been slapped. Next to her, James locked gazes with Max, then looked away. Barlow's face was the picture of amused calm. Mrs. Stanley glanced questioningly at Barlow, then refocused her attention on Evie, while Earl sat shaking his head as he cleaned his fingernails with a penknife. Madame Grovda smiled wistfully; there were tears in her eyes. Edmunds moved forward to stand next to Evie, his blue eyes clouded with confusion and concern.

"Oh, Edmunds," Evie whispered, placing her open hand on his chest. He immediately covered it with his own. "How awful. Thomas was dying of cancer and never said a word. I wish I'd been able to comfort him. And then someone tried to kill him, and he carried that burden by himself, too? After all he did for me, I feel like I should have known some-how, like I let him down in the end. . . ."

Edmunds's eyes darted around the room as though he were searching for words he'd never used before. "Please don't blame yourself, Evangeline. He said nothing to me, either, nor gave any indica-tion. I—I am at a loss as well, my dear."

Max watched the interaction between Evie and the butler with growing displeasure. Okay, sure, she'd known the guy for half her life and didn't know Max at all, and what she did know, she didn't like. So why did it bother him so much she'd turned to Edmunds and not to him for solace?

Dammit. He needed to get a girlfriend. A woman whose only interest was getting into his bed, screw-ing him blind, and then moving on down the high-way. *That* was his kind of woman. He didn't need to stand here and wish a woman like Evie Randall with her soft eyes and tender heart would turn to him for comfort. Didn't need it, didn't want it.

Reaching into the packet, Evie pulled out three identical envelopes and read the labels. She handed one to Edmunds, another to Lorna, and kept the third.

Barlow rose from his chair and began gathering up his things. "As the treasure hunt has now begun, I'll be heading on back to the mainland."

"Not planning on leaving town, are you, Bar-low?" Max said.

"And wouldn't that be a stupid move," he answered with a congenial grin. "Guilty or innocent, a mad dash for the Canadian border to buy imported Irish lace in a Victoria shop would be ill advised, I should imagine. Call my office if you need anything, Detective. And remember, if the seventh clue is not found by midnight in two weeks' time, there will be no winner. Neither the will nor the codicil provides for the dilatory nature of a police investigation, inclement weather, acts of God, or simple bad luck. Good night."

When the lawyer had gone, Evie turned to Max and said, "Thomas accused one of us of killing him. If we don't find the seventh clue, we may not get the evidence the police needs to nail his murderer. I don't care if I get a penny of the estate," she said, her eyes narrowed, her jaw clenched. "I want his killer found and brought to justice."

"As do I," urged Edmunds. "If Mr. Heyworth believed one of us to be his murderer, he must have had enough evidence to convict. Even despising the police as he did, he was aware of how the system works."

"It isn't simply about pointing the police in the right direction," Max growled, still pissed at his response to seeing Evie and Edmunds having their moment. "Unless hard evidence is found, the D.A. can't prosecute. Hell, Heyworth could name the killer outright, but without evidence, it's virtually meaningless. Can you see the D.A. going to court based on a dead man's Murder Hunt game and Clue Number Seven?"

Evie shrugged. "What if Clue Number Seven is a signed affidavit stating that—"

"And what if it is? Heyworth would have written and signed it based on *conjecture*. The murder hadn't taken place yet. Whoever he thought might want him dead, might not *actually* have killed him. What if it was someone else? The D.A. could never convince a jury with that kind of evidence unless it was written in blood on a photograph of the killer pulling the trigger. And even then. Remember the Rodney King tapes? Remember O.J.? A slick lawyer can spin a jury right into an acquittal."

Max looked at the envelope Evie held in her hand, then let his gaze drift to her face. Her eyes were incredibly blue, her lips were parted, her cheeks flushed. Again, he was struck by how attracted he was to her, and again, he shoved his feelings around the corner of his heart and out of sight.

Around him the others had assembled, expectant, nervous, staring at their envelopes. Hell, the last clue might very well name Heyworth's killer, and if it did, it was more than McKennitt had at the moment.

"Okay," he said to Evie. "Open it. Let's see just what the son of a bitch had in mind."

Chapter 7

Dear Diary:

Today Kevin Ingers and Tommy Jenkins got really
mad at each other and got into a big fight! Kevin hit
Tommy in the eye and Tommy slugged Kevin in the
stomach. The playground moniter pulled them apart
and then sent them to the office to see the princa-
pal. I couldn't believe how mad they were at each
other, but when I saw them after school, they were
smiling and telling jokes and poking each other like
nothing had happened, and like they were best
friends or something. Boys are sooooooo weird.

Evangeline—age 10

Evie glanced at the envelope marked EVIE AND DE-
TECTIVE SMARTASS, then raised a brow and sent
Max a wry look.

The corners of his eyes creased in a very attractive way as he grinned and gave her a mock bow. "I am many things to many people."

I'll just bet you are, she thought as her gaze lingered a little too long on his incredible eyes. She felt her cheeks flush. Sometimes it was as though she were hooked up to faulty wiring that zinged her nervous system whenever he looked at her in that intense way he had. He was an enormously masculine man, and even a quick glance from him was enough to make her brain stutter.

Turning her attention to the envelope in her hand, she carefully opened it and slid out the folded sheet of paper.

I seen him come in, swaggering, the way cops do when they think they're impressing the hell out of some poor sap. But how else could he walk since his brains was in his pants? I watched as he leaned against the bar and let his beady eyes run over every dame in the joint. Cops. They was all alike.

T. E. Heyworth, 1952
The Case of the Cocky Dick

Evie's fingertips flew to her mouth just in time to stop a laugh. "Oh, my God," she said. "It's a passage from one of his books." She searched Max's eyes. "I wonder if all the clues are lines from his books."

Max turned to Dabney James, standing with

Lorna a few feet away, concentrating on their clue. "Does he name anybody?" he asked.

The poet pushed his glasses up on his nose. "No. Seems to be a couple of lines from one of his books."

"Same here, sir," said Edmunds, huddled with Madame Grovda under a mammoth fern. The psychic seemed more concerned with adjusting her scarves than deciphering their clue.

As Max took their own clue from Evie's hand, their fingers touched, and sparked. She jerked her hand away as though he'd smacked her, but he seemed not to notice.

He read it, then read it again, then frowned. "I wish the goddamned son of a bitch hadn't—"

"Stop that," Evie snapped, feeling her anger rise. She didn't care how hot Max Galloway was or what kind of relationship he'd had or not had with Thomas. She wasn't going to allow him to continue making snide remarks any longer. "You've called poor Thomas bad names ever since you got here. I loved him, and I miss him, and I'm not going to stand by while you curse him."

Max squared his shoulders and frowned. "Well, I didn't love him, and I don't miss him," he growled, "but I'll keep my comments to myself, if that will make you happy." By the tone of his voice, her happiness wasn't something he particularly cared about, but at least he had agreed.

"Thank you," she said. Thomas hadn't been gone that long—two months. She thought she had begun to come to terms with her grief, yet now, suddenly, her anguish felt fresh and new and sharp. Her heart seemed hollow, and she sought out Edmunds with her gaze.

Perhaps he sensed she was in stress, because he looked up, narrowed his eyes in concern, then smiled at her.

Much relieved, she smiled back, thanking the powers that be that dear Edmunds at least was still in her life.

She took a moment to compose herself, then returned her attention to Max, who suddenly seemed furious about something, if the hard glint in his eye was any sign.

"Look, I know you and Thomas had problems," she said, "but he was good to me. I don't know what would have happened to me if not for him. If you feel you must hate Thomas, at least do it in silence."

"Yes, ma'am," he snapped. "Anything else?"

She scowled at him. "What's gotten into you? I don't think I'm being unreasonable."

"No, ma'am," he growled, glaring at her.

Well, this pretty much proved it, didn't it? Thomas had been right. Max Galloway was showing his true colors. He could be an arrogant unreasonable jerk when he didn't get his way, and she'd be wise to keep that in mind.

Max fought down his envy. He was a complete idiot. The look Evie had given Edmunds spoke volumes about the kind of relationship they had, and it had been hard for him to watch. He'd never had that kind of connection with another person, not even with his sister, Frankie.

Midnight in the Garden of Good and Evie 89

Christ. His mother had been right—he'd turned out just like his old man. The thought scalded his brain.

Taking a body-cleansing breath, he pushed past his emotions. Time to concentrate on the clue. There was work to be done, and to hell with his frigging jealousy.

Rubbing his jaw with his knuckles, he said, "I'm going to apprise Detective McKennitt of what's happened. See what he wants to do, if anything. As a member of the treasure hunt, and apparently a *suspect* in Heyworth's murder . . ." He sent Evie a sardonic leer because he didn't call the son of a bitch a son of a bitch. ". . . I can act in no official capacity."

"Hey, you get my vote," James said as he and Lorna wandered up. "I say you did it. You have that sort of evil, hidden agenda look about you." He shoved his hands in his pockets; looking pretty damn smug, Max thought.

"I'm sorry," Max drawled. "Did you say something, James? It wasn't in the form of some sucky poem, so I must have missed it."

The man huffed. "Jealousy," he said. "I've seen it before. You're just one of thousands of brain-dead public servants, while I'm a touted, albeit reclusive, modern-day Homer who touches people's hearts with my words."

"If you're not careful, I'll tout your Homer with my knee, pal."

James straightened. "Is that a threat, Detective?"

"Nope. Simply poetic justice."

James scowled and started to say something, but Max cut him off with, "What does your clue say?"

The man smirked, patted his shirt pocket and said, "I'm not telling *you*."

"Police business," Max growled. "What does your clue say?"

James cleared his throat. Not a good sign. "This clue is mine," he announced, "though I'm not a hoarder. If you want to see it, *pal*, get a court order."

Until then, Evie had been quiet, but with James's last comment, she snorted a laugh and lowered her head, ruthlessly studying the toes of her shoes.

Lorna, on the other hand, widened her eyes in obvious appreciation. "Did you just now make that up?" she all but gushed.

James's cheeks pinked a bit as he looked down at her. "Why, yes. I did. Did you like it?"

"You forgot the part about passion and pain," Max accused. "Or hasty red wine."

James flattened his mouth and looked over at Max. "That's *tasty* red wine, and just what in the hell do *you* know about poetry?"

"I know *good* poetry when I hear it."

"Well, this may come as a shock to you, Detective Lollygag, but good poetry does not begin with 'There once was a man from Nantucket—' "

"Madame and I will keep our clue private," Edmunds interrupted, "until such time as the law requires we reveal it."

Glancing between the butler and the so-called poet, Max said, "Aren't you two a pair? Fine. Here's the deal. It's getting late. I'll call McKennitt first thing in the morning. I have no authority to confiscate your clues, or I would. So tonight we all just hang tight until we know how the clues might affect the murder investigation."

"But the treasure," Madame Grovda protested. "Are we not in the mad race to find it? What if *you* are sneaking out and finding the money while we are all sleeping? It is not fair!"

"Madame," Evie said, "do you know what your clue means?"

She shook her head so hard one of her gigantic earrings nearly smacked her nose. "*Nyet*. I am not understanding at all."

"Does anyone else understand their clue?"

James looked loath to admit it, but he said, "No," while Lorna shrugged and Edmunds pursed his lips.

"Well, until you understand what your clue means," Evie said, "you can't go anywhere anyway. This will give all of us a chance to rest up and analyze the situation, then, when we get the go-ahead, we can make a mad race of it in the morning."

Max watched Evie as she spoke to the group. It was obvious she was used to dealing with many different personality types in her students. With her air of gentle command, she captured everyone's attention and helped them see reason.

As the guests agreed to wait until morning, she smiled up at him, a satisfied gleam in her eyes. As much as he knew he should look away, he kept his gaze locked with hers until he saw her cheeks flush.

To the group, she said, "There's no way off the island except by yacht, or the runabout. Edmunds can lock the keys in the safe until morning. Then, if the police let us continue, we can pick up where we left off. Agreed?"

"I guess I thought all the clues would be in the house somewhere," Lorna said. "What makes you think we'll have to leave the island?"

Evie shrugged. "Just a hunch. Knowing Thomas, I think he'd want to give us a run for his money."

"So to speak," Max added.

"So to speak," she said, sending him a flirty smile.

There was a general mumbling and milling around, but since this was just the first clue and nobody was certain what theirs meant, there was no use fighting the inevitable. They were all stuck at Mayhem Manor for the night.

Edmunds cleared his throat. "If anyone would care for coffee or tea, please assemble in the dining room in ten minutes."

"You got anything stronger than tea?" James growled. "I could use something with a little more personality right now."

"As you wish, sir," Edmunds replied, turning toward the atrium's exit. Madame Grovda joined him, and the two of them meandered away. James offered his arm to Lorna, and as she took it, she smiled shyly up at him.

When everyone had gone, Max turned his full attention to Evie.

"About this clue," he said, gesturing to the paper in her hand. "Heyworth wrote forty books, but I've only read a couple, and that was years ago. Do you know what the quote means?"

She cocked her head and purred, "Fortunately, Detective Smartass, *I* have read every one of Thomas's books. Twice. Some, three times."

"Who was holding the gun to your head?"

"Now, now," she warned. "When you live on an island, and it rains a lot so you're indoors a lot, you find you tend to read . . . a lot."

Her blue eyes became wary as he stepped closer to her. She lifted her chin. It was as though they were lovers saying good night at her door. All he had to do was bend his head and their lips would touch. He felt his heart start to pound in his chest like exotic jungle drums.

"So," he whispered, "*do* you know what it means?"

Evie raised her hand, straightened her index finger, and poked him squarely in the chest.

"As a matter of fact, *partner*," she said. "I know *exactly* what it means."

Max checked his watch. Nearly twelve. The July night was unusually warm, making the wind blowing off the sea damp and salty. Behind him the llamas in the pen were quiet and attentive to his presence, but apparently not alarmed.

He heard a noise. Footfalls, coming quickly down the path that led from the mansion to the barn. The same path over which he'd carried Evie that first night.

That first night. Ever since then he'd tried countless times to eradicate the memory of her softness against his body, her warmth in his arms, her breath against his neck, and he'd failed. He was disturbingly attracted to her, a fact that would have thoroughly disgusted his father.

The footsteps slowed, stopped. A man stood a few feet away in the clearing. His blond hair was disheveled from the wind and he needed a shave. Tall and broad-shouldered, he was dressed in jeans and a suede jacket. Max knew, under the jacket, the man held a .38 strapped close to his body.

Silently, Max stepped out from his hiding place. "What kept you, Darling?"

Detective Nathan Darling rested his hands on his hips, turned toward Max, pushed his glasses up on his nose and swore.

Hell, it wasn't Max's fault the guy had such a ridiculous last name. At six-two and two hundred pounds, the former Marine had undoubtedly used his fists all his life defending himself and his family name, yet whenever Max addressed him, the guy nearly went ballistic.

"Give it a rest," Max said. "I've tried every intonation I can think of in saying your name. What in the hell am I doing wrong . . . Darling?"

"There you go," Nate accused. "It's not *what* you say, it's the *way* you say it. Don't think I can't hear the sarcasm buried in your voice, Galloway. Cut it out."

"Oh, come on. Must be great for your sex life. You can be a total loser in bed and the women will still call you darling."

"Sounds like you know a lot about being a loser in bed, Galloway."

"You want notarized testimonials?"

"Look," Nate snapped, "I don't like this any more than you do. This should have been *my* case, with *me* calling the shots."

"Really? Based on the quality of the poetry you were spewing tonight, *Dabney*, and how the women were lapping it up, I would have thought you were right in your element. 'In passion and in pain' my ass."

"I only volunteered to go undercover because I wanted to stay with the case, but because you're part of this frigging murder hunt thing, *you're* getting the visibility *I* should have."

"You'll get your turn, newbie. Just think, undercover on your first case. Something to tell your kids." Max shoved his hands in his back pockets. "Can we get down to business now, *Nate*?"

"Yeah, yeah." Nate Darling had the reputation of being a good cop, sharp, thorough. And he obviously didn't like coming in second. Max understood completely, which didn't mean he was going to cut the smug bastard any slack.

"Okay," Max admitted. "I've got a problem here."

"There's always Viagra."

"Oh, you have some left over?" Max jibed. "Look, you've read all the files on the Heyworth murder, right?"

"Yeah," Nate groused. "So T. E. Heyworth was your stepfather. His books are crap."

Max smirked. "Well, if you think that's going to hurt my feelings, guess again. Heyworth wrote mysteries because he already had money. Writing was a hobby, not a driving force in his life. His family made their millions during Prohibition bringing bootleg liquor into the States from Canada." Taking a breath, he said, "Did Edmunds tell you anything about his clue?"

"Just that it was a passage from one of Heyworth's books."

Max looked up at the moon as an owl screeched and circled high overhead. "I need you to help me keep an eye on Evie in case there are any other attempts on her life. I've already talked with the staff. Nobody claims to know anything about how that hole got in the barn floor."

Nate ran his fingers through his hair. "What about the accusations Heyworth made, about one of the treasure hunters being his killer? Do you really think he knew who killed him?"

"Beats the hell out of me," Max said. "All we can do is follow it up and hope for some viable evidence."

Max shifted his position and stretched his back. Behind him, he heard Fernando snort.

"You know anything about llamas?" Max asked.

"Yeah. My sister-in-law did that with both her kids."

"Not Lamaze, you bonehead. *Llamas*." He pointed back over his shoulder with his thumb.

"Oh. Uh, yeah. I think they spit."

"Well that helps. Tell me about Lorna Whitney."

Max wasn't sure, but he thought Nate blushed at the sound of the secretary's name, yet when he spoke, his tone was professional and detached.

"Lorna Anne Whitney. Age thirty. Moved to Washington from California to work for Heyworth two weeks before he left on his book tour, but because she was new on the job and settling in, she didn't go with him." He cleared his throat. "She has an alibi for the day of the murder, and absolutely no motive. As for the rest of the staff, we have Mrs. Stanley, the cook, and her husband Earl. He's the gardener. Nothing on either of them."

"Then there's the butler," Max said. "Let's see. Alexander Edmunds. Born in London, came to the U.S. thirty-five years ago and went to work for Thomas Heyworth. Eventually became a citizen. No arrests, no convictions, nada."

"And no reason to kill his boss?"

"Nothing obvious."

"That leaves us with Evie and the psychic. Is the Randall woman a viable suspect?" Nate asked.

"They're all viable suspects," Max said.

"You know what I mean."

"No I don't."

"Yes, you do. I may be new at this, but I'm not blind and stupid. You're attracted to her."

"Nate, old man," Max said, glaring into the other detective's eyes. "I'm not new at this, and I'm not blind, and I'm not stupid, either."

"What in the hell's that supposed to mean?"

"Lorna Whitney is a suspect, and I've seen the way you—"

"Max?" A woman's voice, coming from up the path somewhere behind the trees. "Max! Are you out here?"

Evie. She sounded panicked. If somebody had tried to hurt her again . . .

"Max?" As she quickly approached, Nate stepped into the shadows and disappeared.

"Here, I'm here," Max said as he grabbed her by the arms to keep her from running smack into him, not that he would have minded.

"Oh! Max," she panted, her chest heaving. "They've . . . I can't believe . . . don't understand—"

"Hang on. Whatever it is, it's okay." His arms had automatically wrapped around her as she clung to him trying to catch her breath.

He slid his knuckles under her chin and lifted her face to his. Oh, man. The look in her eyes by moonlight went straight to his soul.

"Tell me," he said.

"They're g-gone," she panted.

"Who's gone?"

"I never would have believed it, but they've taken the yacht and gone ashore."

"*Who?*"

"E-Edmunds," she stammered. "And Madame Grovda. They've gone after the next clue."

Chapter 8

Dear Diary:

Last night the police came to our house again. My mother's new boyfriend was yelling at her really loud and he shoved her. I sneaked into the kitchen and called 911, but I didn't know what to say, so I hung up. But the policemen came anyway. I didn't want my mother to get into trouble, but I was afraid he would hurt her like the last one did. I just wanted the yelling to stop so I could go to sleep. When I grow up, I am going to be very careful about getting boyfriends.

Evangeline—age 10

Max stared down into Evie's eyes, not sure how to react. While he was furious that Edmunds and the Grovda woman had bolted, the image of the austere butler and the flamboyant Russian psychic hot on the trail of Clue Number Two seemed too ludicrous to be real.

"How long ago did they leave?" he asked as Evie caught her breath and pushed herself out of his arms.

Bathed by the light of the moon, she looked like some kind of ethereal maiden, her red hair down and flowing around her shoulders. She wore a white nightgown and robe, and looked as though she should be haunting a man's dreams rather than running about the woods at midnight. He hadn't missed the soft fullness of her breasts pressed against his chest as he held her close. He hadn't missed a damned thing.

"I was asleep," she said. "A noise woke me and I realized it was the yacht's engines. I can't *believe* Edmunds did this, Max. It's so unlike him to be so . . . well, rash."

"Why would he take such a risk, Evie?" Max said. "Does he have some special incentive? Something to hide, maybe?"

She scowled at him and put her hands on her hips, which opened the front of her robe, revealing the thrust of her breasts under the thin fabric.

"If you mean, did Edmunds kill Thomas," she snapped, "no way, José."

"Oh, so Heyworth is off limits, and now so is Edmunds? Your loyalty is admirable, even if a little misplaced."

"Says you," she huffed.

Her loyalty *was* admirable, and for a split second he wondered what it would be like to have her on his side, doubling her fists on her hips, challenging all comers in his defense.

Reaching for her robe, he grasped the lapels and yanked them together, covering her bosom. Unfortunately, the action caused his knuckles to brush her nipples, sending hot blood surging through his body to the point where his brain damn near emptied. "Keep that thing shut, will you?"

She looked down and curled her fingers around the robe, clasping it tightly to her throat. "Oh. Sorry. I just threw it on and came looking for you. When you weren't in your room, I checked the house, then figured maybe you'd gone for a walk or something."

"Couldn't sleep," he lied. "Let's go."

Taking Evie by the arm, he ushered her back up the path. As they walked he said, "We can compare our clues with Dabney and Lorna's. If we're lucky, maybe we can figure out where Edmunds and Madame Grovda have gone."

As they hurried up the path, Max pulled out his cell phone and called the PHPD. The Port Henry Police Department was small, but so was the town, so he hoped there was one available officer this time of night who could get down to the dock and meet the Hatteras. Unless, of course, Edmunds had put ashore elsewhere.

By the time they reached the mansion, he'd put in a second call, to the Harbor Patrol. Unfortunately, since Edmunds hadn't done anything illegal, neither agency could be expected to drop everything to look for a butler and a psychic motoring around Puget Sound in an expensive yacht.

Edmunds had seemed stable, reasonable. What in hell was he doing racing off in the middle of the night? Had he killed Heyworth and was desperate to find the last clue and destroy it? Or was he trying to get away, flee to Canada? Did he want to win the money so much he'd basically break the rules they'd agreed on? Or, maybe, he was trying to protect someone. . . .

By the time they'd awakened Lorna and both women had dressed and come downstairs, it was nearly one in the morning. Max and Nate Darling, aka Dabney James, sat at the dining room table, trying to make sense of their clues, while Evie and Lorna had gone to the kitchen to make coffee.

According to the Port Henry Police Department, the Hatteras had already anchored at Heyworth's private dock, but the Dippity Duo was nowhere to be found. Since none of the Mayhem Manor cars had been taken, it was assumed they'd used Madame Grovda's vehicle, which had apparently not been parked in the secured lot.

Max rubbed his eyes. "Why's the coffee taking so long?"

Nate shoved away from the table and stood, stretching his arms. "Maybe they've stolen the runabout and left us stranded here."

Max rose from his chair and approached the closed kitchen door, stopping just outside to listen.

Feminine voices, the *swoosh* of running tap water, the *tink* of metal against porcelain . . . the women were in there all right.

". . . blockheads . . ."

Max's mouth flattened. It was the second time he'd heard that term recently. Just who was Evie calling a blockhead now? Nate sidled up next to him and cocked an ear to the door.

". . . all jerks, if you ask me." Evie. Loud and clear.

Max stifled a laugh.

"That Max Galloway," she fumed. "He's . . . he's . . . he's arrogant and controlling and smug. I'll bet, when it comes to women, he's only after one thing."

"Aren't *we* after the same thing?" Lorna's softer voice challenged Evie.

"Sure we are," Evie said. "But women generally like to have their hearts engaged when they become physically involved with a man. But you know what they say: Men are like mascara; they run at the first sign of emotion."

Lorna snickered. The quiet secretary didn't seem to have a lot of experience with men, Max thought, so she probably wouldn't—

"I think men are like commercials," the quiet secretary who didn't seem to have a lot of experience with men said. "You can't believe a word they say."

Max flicked a glance at Nate, who pursed his lips.

Evie again: "I don't know. I think men are like blenders. You know you have to have one, you just don't know why."

"Men are like copiers," Lorna mused. "You need them for reproduction, but that's just about *it*."

The two women burst out laughing while Max and Nate scowled.

"Men," Evie said, elongating the *n*, "are like

coolers. You just load them up with beer and you can take them anywhere." Then she made a noise that sounded a lot like a snort.

Cooler, my ass, thought Max. The poor woman was obviously delirious from lack of sleep after all she'd been through.

Lorna sighed. "Well, I think men are like lava lamps. Interesting to look at, but not all that *bright*."

Next to him, Nate was glaring at the closed door.

"Men are like chocolate," Evie purred. "Tasty, smooth, and they head *right* for your hips."

Okay, he'd give her that one. He imagined Evie's hips, the nip of her waist, the firmness of her bottom. Then he imagined his hands on those hips, pulling her snuggly into his crotch.

His smile faded as the aforementioned crotch began to respond.

"Men are like spray paint," accused Lorna. "One little squeeze and they're all over you."

"You said it, sister," growled Evie. "And they're like plungers. They spend most of their lives in hardware stores or the bathroom."

Lorna laughed for a moment, and when she'd wound down, she said, "Men are like coffee. The best ones are rich, hot, full-bodied, and keep you up all night."

As the two women giggled and snorted themselves into a stupor, Max flicked another glance at Nate, who was pushing his glasses back up on his nose and shaking his head.

Evie gasped for air, then choked, "No, wait. Men are like vacations. Never long enough." Tittering like a giddy hyena, she stammered, "Or like surprise snowstorms. You never know how many inches you'll get, how long they'll last, or when they're coming!"

The two woman erupted into guffaws and giggles as Max and Nate met each other's eyes. Finally, Max said, "Enough of this crap."

Pushing the door open, he stepped into the kitchen, Nate right on his heels.

"Is that coffee ready yet?" he said, looking pointedly at the coffeemaker burbling and sputtering away on the counter. "Mmm. Smells great. Rich, hot, full-bodied, just the way I like it."

The women's laughter ceased abruptly and they eyed the men, then looked at each other.

"Sure you want a cup?" Nate said. "Liable to keep you up all night."

Evie scowled and passed a glance from one man to the other.

As Max pulled a coffee mug from the cupboard and handed it to Nate, he said, "Hell, I don't need caffeine to keep *me* up all night, buddy. I could outlast the Energizer Bunny."

Lorna blinked, raised her chin and slid a look to Evie.

"Hey, James," Max said, pouring coffee for the two of them. "Where are you going on vacation this year? I hear it snows like hell up on Snoqualmie Pass."

Evie crossed her arms under her breasts and stood with her weight shifted to one leg.

Nate took a sip of his coffee. "Yeah, well, you know what they say about winter vacations. They're too short, and all the women are like lava lamps, kind of pear-shaped with a cold glob of wax where their hearts should be."

"How true, how true," Max said, shaking his head. "Actually, I think it's more that the women are like cans of spray paint. Cylindrical, with little heads that you've got to keep your thumb on if you want to get anything out of them." He rolled his eyes, then took a sip of coffee.

"Yeah? Well, I heard that the women are all like chocolate bars."

"Ah, right. Stiff as boards and nutty as hell—"

"You were *eavesdropping* on us?" Evie blinked in wide-eyed astonishment while Lorna turned ten shades of pink.

Max sent Evie a sardonic grin. "You know what they say. Men are like broken toasters . . . always popping up at the wrong time."

Evie and Lorna glanced at each other, then back at the men, and scowled.

"You're disgusting," accused Evie. "Both of you."

Max took another sip of coffee, then said, "I love your rules, sweetheart. It's against the rules for me to bust Heyworth's chops. It's against the rules to say anything even remotely negative about Edmunds. However, you can dis the male of the species with impunity, huh?"

Evie shrugged. "Works for me."

"Fine," he groused. "Well, if you two have gotten all that man-hating vitriol out of your systems now, can we get down to business?"

She glared at him, but nodded. Lorna and Nate

exchanged glances, but neither said anything.

Reining in his temper, Max said, "Did you mean it when you said you knew what our clue meant?"

"Yes."

"Okay. I want you to take a look at Dabney and Lorna's clue and tell me if you think they lead to the same place."

Her haughty glare still in place, she reached for the coffeepot and said, "Happy to oblige, Detective."

Then, turning to face him, her fingers curled around a mug of steaming coffee, she said, "What, uh, what are you going to do to Edmunds when we catch up with him?"

"That depends."

Her blue eyes snapped with anger. "That's a pretty ambiguous answer."

"Yes," he said. "It is."

"These two clues are definitely from the same novel, but different passages have been quoted," Evie mused, her gaze still on the pieces of paper on the table in front of her. "I'd say they lead to the same physical location."

Max nodded. "I guess Heyworth didn't want whoever got there first to destroy the clue, so he planted three, one for each team. Seems fair."

Evie smiled to herself. "That sounds exactly like what Thomas would do. For my thirteenth birthday, he wanted to give me a party as a surprise, but he didn't know who my friends were and was afraid of leaving somebody out. So he invited the whole school. All the kids and all the teachers, even the custodian and the cafeteria staff." Her smile widened. "He turned the island into a play park for a whole weekend, with games and circus performers and incredible food. It was an absolute blast." He'd spent a fortune on that party, but the only gift he'd given her was a porcelain figurine of a llama. That, and a memory she could cherish forever.

"Th-That sounds wonderful," Lorna said, her lashes fluttering as though she had something in her eye. "What a thoughtful thing to do."

Max sat back in his chair and crossed his arms over his chest. "Thanks for that touching little walk down memory lane," he growled. "Heyworth had a heart. Go figure. Now tell me about the clues."

He was hopeless. Evie gave her head a shake, then returned to the pieces of paper on the table in front of her.

She'd examined both passages, and there was no mistaking where Thomas intended the search to begin. If the same held true for the third team, Edmunds and Madame Grovda were well on their way to finding their second clue.

"Thomas made this one easy for us," she said, gesturing to the paper. "*The Case of the Cocky Dick* took place in Seattle. The villain of the story was a cop who used his uniform off-hours to approach women and question them about some facetious crime, then kill them. I'm guessing the clue is at one of the Seattle precincts."

"Which one?"

At Max's words, Evie made the mistake of lifting her gaze and looking into his eyes. There went that brain stutter thing again, she realized, then swallowed and tried to gather her wits about her.

This sexual attraction problem was almost more than her system could support and still maintain primary functions. Her mind and heart were in constant turmoil over what to think of him. There was so much about Max she found appealing, yet Thomas had despised him, and he had hated Thomas. According to Thomas, Max had abandoned his own mother. And when things didn't go his way, he became sullen and snappish and downright surly.

Reminding herself that sexual attraction did not necessarily mean a man was right for you, she resolved to fortify her resistance to him. Sure, she could acknowledge that she desired him physically, but emotionally, unless she found out what drove him, what made him tick—what, if anything, he hid behind his churlish behavior—he was off limits.

She returned her attention to the clues. "I'd say it's at the North Precinct since that's where the villain in the story committed his crimes. Most of his victims were college girls, and that precinct is near the university. He'd target a girl while making his rounds, follow her and find out where she lived, then come back later."

Max seemed to mull this over for moment. "Heyworth hid one of the clues inside a police precinct? I find that really hard to accept."

Evie crossed her arms and quirked her lips. Such a know-it-all. Here he'd asked for her opinion, and when she gave it, he decided to ignore it.

"You got a better idea, Detective?"

With a bit of a shrug, he smiled and said, "Well,

you're the expert. Okay, Miss Smarty Pants. *Where* in the North Precinct?" The sparkle in his eye told her he didn't believe her, but it was the only lead they had.

She quirked her lips again. Boy, just when you thought you had somebody pegged, they went and surprised you.

"I'll tell you that, Detective Smartass," she said, "when we get there."

Chapter 9

Dear Diary:

Today was Saturday, and Pete, that's my mom's boyfriend, took us to the Woodland Park Zoo! It was awesome! And Pete bought us hot dogs and ice cream, and I got a balloon, and peanuts to feed the elephants. Pete's really nice and he has kind eyes and I asked my mom if she was going to marry him. If she did, then he could be my dad! I think Pete would make a great dad, so I hope he falls in love with my mom!

Evangeline—age 10

The first ferry out of Port Henry sailed at six o'clock in the morning, so by the time they reached Pier 52 in Seattle, it was nearly nine. As Max drove off the boat and into the heavy morning traffic on Alaskan

Way, he was feeling the effects of only three hours' sleep.

"Is there a drive-through Starbucks around here somewhere?" he said, making eye contact with Evie in the rearview mirror where she sat just behind him.

"I don't know," she said. "We can stop and ask."

"That's okay. It can wait. We're cutting it pretty close as it is. I alerted the precinct to be on the lookout for Edmunds and the woman, but if they caught the ferry last night, they've been in Seattle for hours. If *their* clue is not at the precinct, they may already have found it, and are well on their way to Number Three."

In the seat next to Max, Nate yawned. "I think you should turn left here."

"Why? Do you know where the precinct is?"

"No, but we're supposed to proceed north and—"

"We can stop and ask," Evie said from the backseat. In the mirror, he saw her nudge Lorna.

Max downshifted and moved in front of a Metro bus. "I'm sure it's up this way."

"Do you have a map?" she persisted.

"No, but I've been in this part of Seattle before. I'll find it." He put on his signal to turn.

"I don't think you can turn here. It's one-way."

He flicked her a glance in the mirror. "Then I'll turn on the *next* one."

Lorna blinked sleepy eyes and looked out the window. "Didn't we pass that sporting goods store once already?"

"Maybe we should stop and ask for directions,"

Evie said, an evil gleam in her eye. "You're not the kind of man who refuses to ask for directions, are you?"

"I am fully capable of asking for directions, Ms. Randall," he groused. "But it just so happens I know exactly where I'm going, so I don't *need* to stop and ask for directions."

Nate sighed. "Up one hill and down, driving through the town, ignoring suggestions that do vex, coming from the fairer sex—"

"Give it a rest, *Keats*. I liked you better when you were reclusive."

Lorna leaned forward and put her hands on the back of Nate's seat. "Oh, that was wonderful, Dabney. You can make up poems right on the spot, just like that. I'm so *impressed*."

Was this woman nuts, or thoroughly devoid of any kind of taste, or was she so smitten that her ears had clogged up?

Nate pushed his glasses up on his nose and turned to her. "Thanks. It's not so hard," he said gently, then looked over at Max and frowned. "Especially when you're highly motivated."

Due to the time of day and the amount of traffic they had to deal with, it took nearly an hour to reach the North Precinct. When they pulled up in front, Max caught Evie's gaze in the rearview mirror and sent her a look that said, *See? I got us here and I didn't have to ask for directions.*

She sent him a look in return that said, *Idiot.*

Max opened the car door for Evie, then reached in and took her hand, helping her from the backseat of his midnight-blue Lexus IS sedan. Her fingers curled around his in a reflexive action, which he in no way took for flirting but wished he could.

Her skin was warm, her hands soft, and as she stepped out of the car, he made certain to stand his ground, not move back, not give her enough room so she'd have to come into close contact. He had her trapped between the open car door and his body, and for a moment let himself enjoy her clean, soapy scent, the gleam of morning sunlight on her glorious red hair, the flash of irritation in her blue eyes.

She was on to him and didn't budge. Lifting her chin, she met his gaze with a challenge. "So, here we are. Amazing. Do you *ever* ask for directions, Detective?"

"I do," he said softly, locking gazes with her. "When I've never been . . . somewhere before with . . . someone. Unfamiliar territory, so to speak. I'll ask if there's anything I can do to make her journey better. If she directs me to shift my attention a bit more to the left, I will. Or perhaps I'm doing lickity-split through a narrow tunnel, and she asks me to slow down. I can go very, very slow. Exquisitely slow. You may not guess it to look at me, but I'm highly responsive to . . . directions."

Evie swallowed and pressed her plush lips together. She took a deep breath, which made her breasts rise and fall under the thin blue sweater she wore.

"I'm sorry," she said. "I've obviously underestimated you. And here I was prepared to give you a good tongue lashing."

His heart stopped, then jumped ahead. Without

thinking, he moved his hands to cup her shoulders. His gaze dropped to her soft mouth, then back up to her eyes, which were gleaming with satisfaction.

"I'll take a rain check on that," he murmured as Lorna and Nate came around to stand behind them.

Letting his hands fall away from Evie's shoulders, she moved away, and he closed the car door, took her arm, and started toward the precinct. "I still can't imagine how, with all these police officers and patrol cars around, Heyworth would have been able to hide three clues somewhere inside the station."

"He didn't."

At Evie's words, Max stopped and turned her to face him. "What did you say?"

She looked dynamite in her sweater and blue jeans, but he forced himself not to notice the sweet curves of her body as she put her hands on her hips and said, "The clues aren't in the precinct. At least, I don't think they are."

He bit down on his temper, which had more to do with acute sexual frustration than with actual anger. "Well then where the hell are they, Miss Marple?"

"My, my," she all but purred. "We really *do* need our coffee, don't we?" Lifting her arm, she pointed across the street. "Tavvy's Tavern is open. I'll bet they have coffee."

Nate murmured, "A tavern. Right across the street from the precinct. I'll bet a lot of cops hang out there."

"The passage in one of the clues," Lorna said, "referred to a bar. The villain walked into a bar. . . ."

"Since *The Case of the Cocky Dick* was fiction," Evie explained, "I wasn't sure there'd be a real tavern near the station or if Thomas had made it up. That's why I couldn't say much until we got here. I don't think the clue is in the precinct house. I think it's in the tavern."

They entered the old brick building and walked across the highly polished hardwood floor. An ancient man behind the bar stood peering into an open ledger.

" 'Morning," he said as the four of them approached. "You folks want coffee?"

"That'd be great," Max said.

"Suze!" the old man shouted over his shoulder. "Four on the floor! You can sit anywheres. Suze be out in a minute with your coffees."

"Thanks," Max said, showing his badge. "I'd like to ask you a few questions first."

The old man looked at the badge, then at Max. "You know, son," he said with a slight chuckle, "police station's right across the street. I seen more badges than Carter's got pills. You got a question, ask it."

Behind them a few of the round tables were occupied with uniformed officers sipping coffee, digging into a hot breakfast, bullshitting about a good or a bad bust they'd made last night.

The woman named Suze appeared with four steaming mugs of coffee on a tray. As Max gratefully took one, he nodded his thanks and took a long gulp, letting the scorching liquid warm his insides all the way down.

"We're looking for a man and a woman, may

have been in very late last night or early this morning." Max took another slug of coffee. Not bad. Not half bad. "Tall, thin man, short, round woman. She's Russian and—"

"They was here. I gave 'em their envelope and they left."

"Envelope?"

"Sure. Tommy Heyworth gave 'em to me, oh, must have been a good six months ago, with instructions to pass 'em along to the right folks when they showed up and asked."

"Them," Max repeated.

"Sure. Had three of 'em. Now, I only got two." The old man smiled, showing crooked yellow teeth. He had gray hair, what there was of it, and sharp black eyes. "The envelopes is marked with the names. I didn't know what it was all about, but Tommy was an old friend of mine, son of a bitch that he was. Told him I'd do as he asked when the time came."

"How long ago did the man and Russian woman leave?"

"Was waiting for me when I opened this morning, 'bout five-thirty."

Great. Edmunds and Madame Grovda had a nearly five-hour head start on them for Clue Number Three, wherever in the hell *it* was.

Evie stepped forward and put her hands on the smooth bar. "Is there one for Evie Randall and Max Galloway?"

He presented Evie with a charming smile, then slid his glance over to Max and frowned.

"There's one marked 'My Darling Evie and Detective Dickhead.' That'd be you, I figure."

Max scowled. "Yeah, that'd be me."

The old fellow opened a drawer, removed an envelope and slapped it down on the bar.

"The other one's for us," Lorna said softly. "Lorna and Dabney, or whatever he may have called us."

Another envelope smacked wood. Nate reached over and picked it up.

Max tossed some bills onto the bar to pay for the coffee. "You've been a great help. Thanks."

The man nodded as he collected the money, grinning like a cat that had just popped a canary. "By the way," he said, chuckling low in his throat, "Tommy said to give you a message."

"All of us, or just me?"

"Just you."

Evie, Lorna, and Nate took their coffees and moved to a table in the corner by the front window.

"Let's have it."

"Said to tell you that this one was easy. They get harder from now on. Lots harder."

Max took another swig of coffee. "He say anything else?"

"Matter of fact, he did. Didn't make no sense to me until I seen you come in." He flicked a glance at the table where Evie was sipping her coffee, smiling at Nate and Lorna. "Said if you was after a *real* treasure, you might start by looking right under your nose."

As Max walked to the table, he kept his eyes on Evie. Sunshine filtered through the window, casting her profile in silhouette. The old man had called her a treasure, and maybe she was. And maybe that wasn't the problem. Maybe the problem was, he didn't deserve to be rich.

She stared up at me, all innocent and soft. But I wasn't no dummy. I'd seen her kind before. The kind that likes to sucker you in, make you think about things a man's got no business thinking about with a broad like that. Then, wham. She pulls the rug out, see? And you're left flat on your back with a ring in your pocket and mud on your face.

T. E. Heyworth, 1959
The Lady Takes No Prisoners

Everyone was hungry, so Suze came by the table and took their orders. While they waited, Evie sat back in her chair, idly stirring her coffee with a spoon, letting Thomas's words stir around inside her head.

Suze arrived with plates heaped with food and placed them in front of each of them. After she'd departed, Max said, "Any ideas?"

Evie picked up her fork, resting her hand on the table. "I don't know," she said slowly. "I'm still thinking."

Max doused his eggs with salt and pepper then heaped strawberry jam on his toast. "Where is *The Lady Takes No Prisoners* set?"

"Seattle mostly," Lorna offered. She lowered her lashes and blushed. "I read a lot of Mr. Heyworth's books in preparation for working for him. Unfortunately, since he was killed so soon after I arrived, it didn't really do much good."

"But you read this book," Dabney said, as he added ketchup to his hash-browned potatoes. "And it takes place in Seattle. What part?"

Lorna gave a delicate shrug. "All over the place. The villain of the story is a door-to-door brush salesman who approaches housewives, then kills them."

"Does he get caught?"

She nodded. "He falls for an undercover policewoman who sets him up."

They were all silent as they ate their breakfasts and pondered the meaning of the clues. Finally, Evie said, "We might not be able to figure this one out as easily as the first one. If Lorna and I can't decipher our clues, maybe Edmunds can't figure his out, either, and he'll head back to the island."

Max tossed down his napkin. "I think we should go to the library, get a copy of the book, and go through it page by page. Maybe something'll pop."

"Oh, dear," Evie drawled, sending Max a sardonic look. "I think I actually agree with you."

"Hmm. I just may have to note that in my memoirs."

"That might be a good idea," she quipped, "since it will probably never happen again."

"I wouldn't bet on that, sweetheart." Then he winked.

Damn, she wished he'd cut that kind of thing out! Just when she had it in her head to dislike him, he'd do something charming. She wished he'd make up his mind on how to *be*, so she could figure out just how she felt about him.

They finished breakfast and rose from the table. The men paid the bill, then the four of them headed for the door.

Outside, the late morning sun had decided to hide behind a layer of dense clouds. A breeze had come up, carrying the scent of rain with it. Evie stopped at the curb and looked over at Max, who was deep in conversation with Dabney and Lorna. Though she didn't know Lorna very well, it was obvious the woman had developed feelings for the handsome poet, who didn't look like a poet at all—at least, not like any poet Evie had ever seen. He seemed shy and sweet, and very attentive to the equally shy and sweet secretary.

Out of the corner of her eye something caught her attention. A flash of light—then the window behind her shattered!

Evie screamed and lifted her arms to cover her face. Another blast, and wood splinters from the door behind her spiked through the air.

She felt an impact, like a locomotive knocking over a rag doll. The air whooshed from her lungs as she landed hard on the sidewalk, a heavy object covering her body.

Max.

His arms were around her back, her head cradled in his hands so her skull wouldn't slam against the cement.

Another blast, and the sidewalk beside their heads spit pellets into her exposed scalp. She buried her face in his shoulder.

Arms still wound around her, Max rolled the two of them into the gutter behind a parked car. His weight felt solid and secure against her as he shielded her from the gunfire.

A second passed, then another. He reached into his pocket for his cell phone, and his open hand brushed her breast. For a moment she stopped breathing.

He punched a button. "Shots fired!" he shouted into the phone. "Tavvy's, across the street from North Precinct. Location of shooter unknown. Exit precinct with caution. Four individuals on the ground . . . Yeah, affirmative."

She could feel his chest expand and contract with each labored breath. He had one arm around her, the other free to hold the phone, but he seemed in no hurry to let her go, even though the gunfire had ceased.

Sirens screamed around them, voices shouted as police officers swarmed the area, and customers and business owners crowded onto the sidewalk to see what the commotion was.

Snapping his cell phone closed, he looked into Evie's eyes for the first time.

He licked his lips. "You okay?" he panted.

Though her heart was racing and her mouth had gone dry, she managed, "Uh-huh." The bruises on her back hurt like hell. She wanted to cry from the pain but fought it.

She realized her legs had somehow wrapped around Max's and that his groin had settled into hers. With a start, she realized he was engaged in a full-fledged stress-induced erection.

"Tell me you're not hurt, Evie," he whispered, his lips only inches from hers. He looked deeply into her eyes as though he'd be able to see her answer before she spoke. As though he'd see something important there, if only he looked hard enough.

She'd never been this close to a man without kissing him. Did Max want to kiss her? Did she want him to?

"The bruises on my shoulder and back are killing me," she rasped, blinking, breaking eye contact with him. "But I wasn't shot, if that's what you mean."

Seconds passed. No more shots came. He'd be getting off her now, and while parts of her were glad of it, parts of her—everything south of the border—were going to be decidedly disappointed. It felt good to be in a man's arms like this. But it wasn't real. She had to remember that. He'd shoved her out of the line of fire, and that was all it was.

Pushing himself to his knees, Max brought her with him and gently sat her on the sidewalk, her back against the door of the parked car that had probably saved their lives.

"Stay put," he said. His gaze dropped to her mouth. He licked his lips, then raised his eyes to hers.

When he didn't immediately move away, she lifted her chin in silent challenge. *Make the first move, then. Kiss me.*

He tilted toward her. Someone shouted his name. He blinked, breaking the spell that had been spun between them.

In one swift move he was on his feet, his hand inside his jacket, reaching for his weapon.

Suddenly, Lorna was beside her, plopped down by Dabney, who said, "Be right back." In a swift move of his own, he was on his feet and running up the street after Max.

Both Evie and Lorna leaned forward to get a better view. The sight of two hunky men tearing off up the street after a bad guy made Evie's blood sing all the way to her toes.

She glanced at Lorna, who rolled her eyes and fanned herself with her hand. "That's enough to give a woman an orgasm right there."

"Lorna?" Evie gaped. Taking a long, hard look at the secretary, she said, "So, still waters run deep, hmm?"

Lorna raised her delicate brows and she sent Evie a smile. "You have no idea."

A policewoman approached and crouched in front of them. "You two okay?" she said. "An aid car is en route."

Lorna appeared every bit as messed up as Evie felt. Both of them had streaks of blood on their faces and necks where flying debris had pelted them, but it didn't seem to Evie that Lorna had taken a bullet, either.

The aid car arrived and cleaned them up, and a trip to the hospital was deemed unnecessary. The policewoman took their statements, while Evie anxiously watched the busy street to see where Max and Dabney had disappeared to.

She was fine. Unhurt. But she was changed, nonetheless.

Max was her enemy. They both knew it. So why

had she wanted him to kiss her? The heat of the moment? Maybe.

There were so many unanswered questions. Max Galloway was pushy and controlling and rigid. She knew she'd be absolutely crazy to fall for a man like him. So why was she tempted to do just that?

The look in his eyes when he'd asked her if she was hurt had gone straight to her bones. It had been real. He'd looked terrified. Was it because he cared about her a little, or was he simply afraid he'd lose Thomas's money without her help? Or because if she were killed on his watch, his reputation would suffer? She didn't like him and had told him so. Okay, she *hadn't* wanted to like him, but over the last couple of days her dislike had been tempered.

Maybe Thomas had been a little wrong about Max. Maybe there was more here than met the eye. Maybe . . . Oh hell.

She lowered her head, placing her face in her hands. Dammit. Just because he *could* be charming and he *could* be funny, and when he touched her his caress was so incredibly gentle, it didn't mean. . . .

Oh, *hell*.

Besides, she had a bigger problem than simply falling for Max Galloway. Somebody had fired shots at her. That meant the trap in the barn hadn't been meant as a prank or to hurt her. It had been set to kill her, and that changed everything.

Chapter 10

Dear Diary:

Pete isn't going to be my dad. My mom said it's because he suffercates her, whatever that means. She told me that men always want to own her and that when they get too attached, it's time to move on. I told her I liked Pete a lot and that maybe having him own us wouldn't be too bad, but she said, nope, kiddo, we're hitting the road. Someday, I'm never going to hit the road. I'm going to find a good place and stay there forever and ever.

Evangeline—age 10

By the time they were done at the crime scene, it was too late to go to the library. The butler and the psychic had one hell of a head start on him, and if they'd already found Clue Number Three, they may even have found Number Four.

Max stood in the doorway of the precinct captain's office, rubbing his jaw with his knuckles. Even if he knew what the second clue meant—which he didn't—the attack had taken a lot out of Evie and Lorna, and everyone needed some rest.

Especially Evie. She'd been through hell in the last week, and it wasn't over yet. While he'd saved her from taking a bullet, her peace of mind had been shattered. Two attempts on her life in a week. Emotionally, she was trying to hold it together, but she was seriously shaken.

Walking over to where she sat against the wall, he crouched before her chair.

"Evie?" He looked into her face, and saw magnificently suppressed terror. Her eyes were rimmed with red, her cheeks were pale. She held her hands in her lap with fingers twisted together so tightly her knuckles had turned white.

"There must be something you can tell me," he coaxed softly. "People are rarely targeted like this for no reason. Is there *anyone* you suspect? Any reason somebody might want you dead, even if it seems completely far-fetched?"

She blinked, then pressed her lips together. Her hands trembled, so he placed both of his over hers to warm them.

"Have you pissed anybody off lately?" he persisted. "Stolen somebody's husband, stiffed a waiter after an expensive meal? Are you blackmailing anybody? Give me *something* here, honey."

"D-Don't call me that."

"*Honey?*" He shrugged. "Most people consider it an endearment."

"I don't like it," she said quickly. "My . . . my mother's boyfriends used to call me that. They were always around, looking at me, wanting to touch me. 'C'mere, honey,' they'd say. 'How about you climb up here on my lap and . . . ' "

Her voice trailed off. Then, licking her lips she said, "Don't call me honey. I don't like it."

Max was silent for a moment, processing what he'd just heard. Her mother's boyfriends? Son of a *bitch*.

Anger swelled inside him, filling his mouth with a bitter taste. A vulnerable little girl, an irresponsible mother . . . Jesus Christ. What a wretched childhood she must have had.

"I think I understand," he said, trying to keep the edge out of his voice, the fury. "I promise. I won't call you that again."

Running his splayed fingers through his hair, he said, "Look, you thirsty? There's a machine just down the hall. How about a Coke?"

She nodded. "Yes, please. That would be good."

As he dropped coins into the machine, he turned the day over in his mind.

Evie couldn't think of anyone who wanted her dead, let alone anybody who'd set a trap for her at the barn, then follow her into Seattle to take a shot at her. It just didn't make sense.

Of course, it could have been Edmunds. He could have doubled back, waited for the right moment to catch Evie in the crosshairs. But why? And what about the Grovda woman? Was she simply waiting in the car, or had the butler already killed her?

Knowing how Evie felt about Edmunds, he hadn't

even suggested the possibility that the butler might be behind the attempts on her life. He'd just wait and see how everything played out. For now.

A bottle of soda rolled out of the dispenser, and he picked it up, letting his fingers wrap around the cold, damp plastic. As he walked back into the precinct lobby, he let his gaze brush over Evie, sitting with Lorna under the Most Wanted bulletin board.

Dammit. She'd come that close to being killed again today, only this time she'd been under his protection—*and he hadn't seen it coming*. They'd been on a sidewalk in front of a tavern, in broad daylight, on a busy street across from a police station, yet somebody was waiting and took a crack at her. How ballsy was that?

Who in the hell was this guy, and why did he want her dead so badly he'd followed them to Seattle?

The only bullet they'd been able to recover had been dug out of the door frame. Hopefully, ballistics would tell them something. He just wasn't sure what.

His attention fell to Evie's lips, and he remembered how close he'd come to kissing her. She'd been daring him, and he'd almost done it.

For the second time since they met, their bodies had come into close contact. He was beginning to crave the feel of her against him, want more of it. They'd landed on the ground just like they would land in bed, and his body reacted in the only way it knew how—with an automatic, masculine response, straight up, all systems go.

With her head cradled in his palms and the silken feel of her hair tantalizing his fingertips, it had been all he could do to concentrate on the fact somebody was trying to gun them down. Then she'd looked up at him, her eyes shocked and confused, yet somehow trusting. It touched him in a way he'd hoped never to be touched by a woman again, and for one crazy moment he thought maybe she'd come into his life for a reason, that maybe the gods had granted him some kind of reprieve from his own anguish and stupidity.

But he was a jerk. He knew he was. He'd practiced the skill for years at the feet of the master. Just like his old man, he'd ended up hurting everyone he should have cherished, everyone who'd love him unconditionally. He'd already lost one good woman, driven her away. Evie deserved better than a man like him.

As he unscrewed the plastic cap on the Coke, he walked over and took a seat next to Evie and across from Nate, who was having a lot of trouble maintaining his cover, especially under the circumstances. However, judging from the look of rapture on Lorna's face as Nate spoke, things hadn't been shot to hell quite yet.

". . . splintered wood screamed beneath the blast that laid the bodies in the gutter, low. And with that shot, another came, and another yet—"

"*In passion and in pain,*" Max interjected dryly as he handed the soda to Evie. "Yeah, we know. Well, it ain't the Iliad, but who knows, James. In another three thousand years. . . ."

Ignoring his sarcasm, Nate turned to Lorna. "Did *you* like it?"

She beamed at him. "Oh, Dabney. You're simply . . . amazing."

Max slid his foot forward and tapped the toe of Evie's shoe with the toe of his. Her head turned, her brows lifted, her gaze locked with his, and it was as though they'd done that simple move a thousand times before.

He'd done it without thinking, then realized it was a very "couple" thing to do. And here he'd just given himself hell over her . . .

Instead of pulling back, he maintained the position. She could scoot away if she wanted. He'd let her decide. Yeah, that was the ticket.

But she didn't scoot away. Instead, she took a long pull on her soda.

"So," he said, sprawling back in his chair, sliding his leg along the side of hers. "Since there's nothing left to do here, what do you say we either head back to the island or check into a motel? We could all use some R and R. Maybe give the clues more thought and—"

"I have an idea where Thomas might be directing us," Evie interrupted. He felt the heat of her leg against his, and still she made no effort to pull away. "I've been sitting here thinking about those very clues. . . ."

Max leaned forward, resting his elbows on his knees, pressing his thigh against hers, tormenting himself, yet unable to stop. "Good. Let's hear it."

Around them phones bleeped or buzzed or chimed, uniformed and plainclothes police officers talked with each other or took statements from civilians, but Max tuned all that out and concentrated wholly on what Evie was about to say.

"The villain in the story killed most often in

Seattle, but he lived in Tacoma," she said. "We've already discussed the fact that, if you consider Thomas only had time to change the last clue, it's probably at Mayhem. It would make sense, then, that he's leading us back there, that he began the treasure hunt at its farthest point. Then, each clue brings the hunters closer to the island, and back home for the culmination. We began in Seattle, next would be Tacoma. That would leave four clues spread out between here and Heyworth Island. Of course," she sighed, "I could be dead wrong."

"No, no," Max protested quickly. "I think you're right. That way, he can have his grand finale on the island, at Mayhem Manor. A fitting end to his hunt."

"But where in Tacoma?" Lorna said. "It's a big city."

"Look," Nate interjected. "Tacoma's only an hour from here, but it's already nine-thirty. Maybe we could hit the road and talk about it on the way. Maybe check into a motel or something then go after the clue in the morning. I don't know about you, but I'm beat."

Evie and Lorna in one motel room, Max and Dabney in another; somehow, they'd all gotten through the night in spite of the fact they would have had a lot more fun, and gotten even less sleep, if the room assignments had been switched.

It was close to seven in the morning when Evie and Lorna took a table in the busy coffee shop, anticipating that the men would join them soon. Just as they sat down, the double glass doors opened and Max and Dabney walked in.

They'd all had to wear the same clothes as yesterday, yet as Max approached the table, Evie thought he managed to look like he'd just stepped out of a men's clothiers. He and Dabney had obviously found someplace to buy razors, because they were both freshly shaved and looked clean and sexy, a fact that was apparently not lost on Lorna, if the little sigh she gave when she saw Dabney was any indication.

Evie casually perused her menu, but she couldn't help notice that every waitress in the place, and half the women customers, had stopped whatever they were doing to gaze at the two men as they made their way to the table. She had to admit, it was an impressive sight. In blue jeans and jackets, a sexy guy with dark hair and a hunky blond with weak eyes seemed to have every female fantasy covered.

But neither Max nor Dabney appeared to notice their admiring fans. They made a beeline for her and Lorna, smiles on their faces, a trail of disappointed femmes in their wake.

The first words out of Evie's mouth as the men joined them were, "I think I figured it out."

Before Max could respond, the young waitress—beaming like she'd just won the lottery—materialized between the two men, coffeepot in one hand, menus in the other. Lorna's elbow lightly nudged Evie's arm.

Yeah, I know, thought Evie, trying not to roll her eyes. Women probably fell at their feet wherever they went.

After the waitress had gleefully poured coffee, taken their orders and departed, Max said, "Okay, Detective Randall. Let's have it." He grinned at her over the rim of his coffee mug, forcing Evie to try and remember what she'd been about to say.

She liked him. That was so nuts! She hadn't wanted to like him—in fact, she'd been prepared to hate him—but he wasn't at all what she'd expected. Yes, he could be arrogant and pushy and a bit on the alpha side, but there was something about the way he looked at her, something behind the cynicism and wariness in those hazel eyes, that she connected with. Maybe it was because he cared so passionately about what he did, about being one of the good guys, or maybe it was something else.

Should she explore that possibility? she wondered. Probably not. Yet it was tempting . . . it was so tempting.

"Here's the thing," she said. "I started to analyze all the phrases in our clue and I remembered that, after the salesman killed one of the women, he rolled her body up in a rug and put it in his trunk. Later, he dumped her in the mud near a saltwater inlet where he went fishing every summer. Most of the locations in the story are pure fiction, but the inlet is real. Maybe we could start there."

She wasn't certain she'd interpreted the clue correctly, but she hadn't been able to make heads or tails of Lorna and Nate's clue at all, so it was either this or head back to the island to regroup.

They hurried through breakfast, then Dabney and Lorna excused themselves to go to the rest rooms.

"No matter what happens today," Evie said to Max as he walked her to his car, "Tomorrow's Tuesday, and I have an appointment. I'll have to go back to Port Henry."

"What if we find the third clue?" he said. "We'll probably need your help to figure it out."

"I'll do what I can," she argued, "but this is an appointment I made weeks ago and refuse to cancel. It'll only take a few hours in the afternoon. Besides, I would expect the clues to get harder and take longer to analyze. Edmunds can't be having an easy time of it. I called Mrs. Stanley first thing this morning, and nobody on the island has seen or heard from Edmunds or Madame Grovda since they took off on Saturday night."

Max opened the car door for her, then put his hand on her arm to stop her from getting in.

"You okay?" he asked. "Really okay?"

Except for his fingers curled around her arm, the world had gone stone cold. Where he touched her was the only place on earth that mattered. It was difficult to concentrate on mere words when all she could think of was how alive and warm she felt standing a heartbeat away from a man she was growing more attracted to by the minute.

"I'm confused, worried, admittedly scared half to death, looking for murderers behind every parked car and flower pot. I'm a little tattered around the edges, but I'm functioning." Gazing up into his eyes, she said, "Oh, and in case I forgot to mention it yesterday, thanks for saving my life. Again."

A second ticked by, then another. Whatever he'd been about to say, he changed his mind. Without a word, he released her and stepped back. "Here come the others," he said sharply. "Get in. Put on your seat belt." Before she turned away from him, Evie saw his mouth flatten into a hard line.

Well, she thought, feeling a little twinge at Max's sudden change in demeanor. If you don't want my peaches, then don't shake my tree.

For the next four miles, Evie glared at the back of Max's head, hoping he'd see her reflection in the rearview mirror and realize she was upset.

You don't save a woman's life, she thought, buy her a Coke, subtly rub her leg with your own, listen to her speech of gratitude, then turn away and frown. It could give a lady a complex. And she already had enough complexes for five lifetimes.

The body of water they were looking for was a small cove off Puget Sound that offered campsites, a boat dock and small marina, Lola's Quik Mart, a gas station, and Dave's Bait and Tackle.

While Dabney and Lorna took on Lola, Max and Evie headed for Dave's. With any luck at all, retrieving the clues would simply be a matter of asking the right person . . . who apparently wasn't on duty that day, because when the four met back at the car fifteen minutes later, they were each empty-handed.

Evie sighed. "This could be the wrong place," she said. "I'm sorry. I really thought we'd find something here."

Max leaned back against the fender of his car and crossed his arms over his chest, the dark glasses he'd slipped on making it impossible to tell where he was looking. However, if the prickly heat Evie felt on her skin was any indication, he was looking at her.

Dabney and Lorna decided to go down to the marina to see if anybody was on board any of the small sailboats. On a Monday morning in July, several of the slips were empty, but a few boats remained to rock and tilt in the dark green water, pulling against their moorings whenever a speedboat zoomed by farther out on the water.

"What's the name of that book again?" Max asked, sunlight glinting off the dark lenses of his glasses.

Kicking a pebble with the toe of her shoe, she said, "*The Lady Takes No Prisoners*."

"Well," he drawled, raising his arm, "there's a boat down there called *The Lady*—"

Evie sucked in her bottom lip and followed the line of Max's outstretched arm and pointing finger. Before he'd finished his sentence, she took off at a dead run.

Within seconds he was beside her, laughing, grabbing her hand tightly in his, racing with her down the crunchy gravel path toward the docks.

Together, they jumped a short log fence and maneuvered around several boulders, bumping into each other as they tore onto the wooden wharf like two kids running across an open field. Running together toward Clue Number Three.

Chapter 11

Dear Diary:

I haven't written to you for a long time. My mother died, and I didn't know how to tell you it. It was the worst day of my life and I stayed in my room for days. The lady policeman told me she died of an OD. They asked me if I understood and I said yes, because I wanted to go to my room and cry. Even though Mommy wasn't home sometimes, I still loved her. Right after she died, I stayed with some people who were nice to me. Yesterday a man named Thomas came to take me away with him. He says he lives on an island. He says I'll have my very own butler. That sounds ok, but I would rather still be with my mom.

Evangeline—age 11

Edmunds either had a key or knew where one was hidden. The elegant, thirty-five-foot Beneteau Oceanis 352 hadn't been broken into, but somebody had been aboard recently.

Max crouched in front of a countertop. Dust patterns on the tile showed that objects had been moved, and there were bits of damp mud on the galley floor.

Neither Lola at the grocery store, Dave at the bait shop, or anyone else they'd spoken to had seen the distinguished butler or the distinctive psychic, so it was likely they'd boarded early that morning, and not all that long ago, either, since the cabin door had been left unlocked. Had the butler fled when he saw them coming, or had he left the door accessible on purpose?

"Here it is!" Evie shouted from the captain's cabin. "Clue Number Three, under the mattress. I knew 'flat on your back' meant something."

"Sure means something to me," Max mumbled as he ducked his head and entered the small cabin, which was mostly wall-to-wall bed. When Evie turned toward him, he plucked the envelope from her fingers.

She glared at him but made no effort to pluck it back. Too bad, he thought. He would have enjoyed tussling with her in a room that was made up mostly of a big bed with walls around it.

With the blade of his pocketknife, he sliced through the seal and opened the envelope. Lorna and Nate, seeing them run toward the boat, had followed and now crowded in behind Max, their eyes expectant, their hands empty. If their clue was on *The Lady*, they hadn't found it yet.

Max unfolded the paper.

I told the kid behind the soda fountain to gimme a cuppa joe, and make it quick. He didn't say nothing, but he had that look about him that said he was too good to be slinging hash to slobs like me . . . that he was more than just a pretty boy in a greasy apron behind the counter at the five-and-dime.

T. E. Heyworth, 1954
The Last Straw

Max handed the note to Evie. "Ring any bells?"

He watched as her eyes moved over the typewritten lines on the page. Her brow furrowed and she nibbled absently on her bottom lip. Finally, she shook her head and said slowly, "None. I have no idea what this means."

It took another fifteen minutes of searching, but Lorna and Nate finally came up with their clue, hidden inside a sea chest.

Max rubbed his chin with his thumb. "According to these two clues," he said, "our paths are about to diverge. Heyworth has used quotes from two different books, which probably means we split up."

After several calls to the Tacoma Public Library and the larger bookstores in the area, they decided to admit defeat and head back to the car. "The books are too old," Evie said. "Thomas may have written forty mysteries, but they weren't what you'd call classics."

"You mean they sucked," Max offered.

"I think the word you were obviously searching for, yet failed to find, was *uncomplicated*," she challenged. "Thomas's books were meant for the average reader."

He sent her a look of exasperation. "Yeah, if the average reader hadn't dropped all his crayons under his high chair."

She slipped her hands into her jeans pockets and settled her butt against the fender of his car. In the midday sunshine, her hair gleamed like burnished copper. The freckles on her nose gave her that sweet, alluring, kissable country girl, roll-in-the-hayloft look. He slid his dark glasses into place so he could look his fill without her suspecting he was imagining putting his hands wherever his eyes roamed—and they roamed just about everywhere.

"Libraries and bookstores aren't going to have them," she said. "We'll have to go back to the library at Mayhem Manor. I wouldn't be surprised if Edmunds and Madame Grovda have to do the same thing."

"Like a cat that's been chased high up a tree," Nate said solemnly as he shoved his glasses up on his nose. "We've all been stymied by Clue Number Three."

"*Temporarily* stymied, Tennyson," countered Max. It seemed *Dabney* had gotten a little too wrapped up in his role, and for some reason felt the need to spew rotten poetry at the drop of a hat. "I thought you were the kind of poet who didn't rhyme so much. Perhaps you should go back to free verse."

Nate narrowed one eye on him. "Whether I rhyme or not depends wholly on the spot . . . uh, I'm in."

Next to him, Lorna covered her mouth with her fingertips and made a choking snort-giggle sound, but the look in her eyes was one of pure adulation.

"It's gonna take a while to get back to the isle. While the sunshine is glowing, we'd better get going." Apparently reveling in Lorna's admiration, Nate smiled like he'd just been credited with the second coming of *Beowulf*.

As Max opened the car door for the snickering Evie, he looked over at Nate. "Know what I think? Your poems really stink."

Nate opened the door for Lorna and said, "My poetry's fine. You're simply a slime . . . uh, ball."

Max slid behind the wheel and put the key in the ignition. As the engine roared to life, under his breath so the women in the backseat couldn't hear, he said, "Stop with the rhymes and the poems that suck, or I'll pull out my gun and shoot you, dumbfuck."

Nate adjusted his seat belt, then purposefully looked out the passenger side window. "*Some* people," he murmured, "have no appreciation for creative genius."

The ferry ride from Tacoma had them back in Port Henry by dinnertime, and, thanks to a quick call to the island, Earl Stanley was waiting for them at the dock with the runabout.

As soon as they hit the front door of Mayhem Manor, the four of them hurried up the stairs to the second floor, to the enormous library—the same library in which Thomas Heyworth had been shot to death.

Entering the wide double doors, Max was brought up short by a sight he wasn't certain he'd ever see again—Edmunds the butler and a weary, disheveled Madame Grovda. They sat at one of the mahogany tables by the fireplace, huddled over a book. As soon as Max and the others entered the room, Edmunds slammed the cover shut.

"Edmunds!" Evie rushed to the butler and threw her arms around him. The man stood and pulled her into a loose hug, lowering his cheek to her hair. His skin was pale and he was in need of a shave. The lines around his eyes were pronounced, and he lowered his lids as he hugged Evie as though he needed her support or he'd drop.

Madame Grovda didn't look much better. Her white hair stuck out in billowy tangles, her eyes were wide and glassy, she wore no makeup, and her clothing was stained and rumpled. She looked like a fairy godmother who'd been struck by lightning.

"Why did you two take off like that?" Evie choked, still hugging Edmunds. "Are you okay? Until I saw you, I didn't realize how worried—"

"Evie," Max interrupted. "I need to talk to these two."

Pushing herself out of Edmunds's embrace, she flung her arms wide as if to protect him. "You can't arrest him. He didn't do anything—"

"For God's sake, I'm not going to *arrest* him," he snapped. "For one thing, he didn't do anything illegal. For another, this isn't my jurisdiction."

She blinked and lowered her arms, and he felt his

temper rise. Not because she had jumped to conclusions about him, but because she'd been prepared to fiercely defend somebody she loved. Would she be that passionate protecting him? If, of course, she ever loved him?

Tamping down his anger, he said, "How many clues have you collected, Edmunds?"

The butler straightened. "Three, sir."

"Any of them give any indication who might have killed Heyworth?"

"No, sir."

"Why'd you leave early after we had all agreed to wait until morning?"

Up until now the Russian woman had remained silent. With a hearty sigh, she pushed herself up from her chair and said, "I have made him to do it. I have the vision that tells me where to look, so we go." Her bottom lip trembled, her eyes dampened.

"A vision?" he repeated. "Tell me about it."

Dabbing her eyes with a handkerchief she pulled from a handbag the size of Detroit, she said, "I am to come over."

"You are too overcome?"

"*Da*. Yes. Is so."

Max was sure he heard at least one window rattle and a delicate vase on the mantel crack when she blew her nose. Closing her eyes, she lifted her arms in front of her like a B movie sleepwalker.

"I am changing for the bed, you see? I begin to feel dusty."

"Dizzy."

"*Da*. Dizzy. I see it the envelope. My *Tomas*, he means for me to have it," she insisted, her hands still in front of her, as if she were carrying a load of invisible firewood.

"Did your vision tell you who killed Thomas Heyworth?"

She opened her eyes. *"Nyet."*

Lowering her arms, she said, "I would speak to you in the privates?"

Max stared at her, unsure how to answer.

"I think she means *privately*," Evie whispered against the back of his neck.

"Thanks," he mumbled over his shoulder. "I was getting a visual on that you would not believe."

With that, Evie, Nate, and Lorna quickly moved to the far end of the room, out of earshot. Edmunds excused himself to go check on dinner.

When they were relatively alone, Madame Grovda sat once more, bit her bottom lip, and fiddled with her fingers. Finally, she said, "You are a good detective, yes? You are, how it is said, successful?"

He shrugged. "My record for cleared cases is right up there."

She smiled at him, a sad little quirk of her lips. Her deep-set brown eyes looked tired, the color faded. Haltingly, she said, "Madame Grovda, she . . . is not so successful as you. The psychic theory, yes, I can teach. But the practice, eh, it does not work for me all of the time."

He waited while she twisted her fingers around the handkerchief, her head down, her white hair fluttering like feathers as she nodded to herself. "I was not always, ehm, as you see me. I was once young, beautiful. *Tomas* and I, ah, we make the love all the time. But it was not meant to be."

Max understood, or thought he did. "So you're after the inheritance to get your revenge on the lover who spurned you."

Her eyes widened. "*Nyet. Tomas* did not give the spurn to me. Always, we used the condom."

Max took a long, hard breath and held it for a moment. Finally he exhaled and said, "Not sperm. *Spurn*. It means he rejected you."

Her eyes widened even more. "*Nyet!* It was I who give the spurn to him. He wants to marry me, but my father . . ." Her voice trailed off and she looked as though she wanted to go sit in a corner and have a good cry. "Ah," she sighed, slowly shaking her head. "It is so long ago. I was so very young. The love, it is hard thing."

Lifting her troubled gaze to him, she blinked and sucked in her lower lip. With a tilt of her head, she said, "It is not for the money that I come to this place. It is to find who killed my *Tomas*. He deserves this much from me. I come to touch the air with my heart, listen to vibrations of his life with my soul. And, I think, maybe then I will know." She closed her eyes. "But I have failed him once more. I cannot see the face of his murderer. I am sorry, Detective. I—I am not the very good psychic."

He studied the woman for a moment. So, Heyworth had loved her. It was difficult for Max to imagine a man like that having softer feelings, but he'd apparently had them for Evie, so maybe it wasn't too big a stretch to imagine him having loved Ernestina Grovda, back in the day.

The old woman stood, shed of her gloss of boisterous confidence. For the sake of a man she had loved once upon a time, she had let her guard down before a stranger, admitted her failures, bared her vulnerabilities.

Would he be so brave, he wondered, when the time came?

"It, um, it could just be, madame," he stumbled, "that your grief has temporarily clouded your abilities. Perhaps when you have had some rest and your sorrow has passed, you'll, uh, be able to focus again."

She smiled weakly at him, tears sparkling in the corners of her eyes.

Reaching toward her, Max took her hand between his palms, gave it a gentle squeeze, and smiled back.

Across the room, Evie stood alone with a book in her hand, her mind, not a million miles away, but only a mere twenty feet.

She didn't know what they were saying, but the look of compassion in Max's eyes as he spoke to Madame Grovda told the story.

For a badass, know-it-all, arrogant, dictatorial, cynical loner cop, he could be a very nice man. Occasionally, anyway. When the spirit moved him. Like, on a Tuesday in October during a full moon when the tide was out, and he'd gotten enough sleep the night before.

Not for the first time, she wondered why he'd hated Thomas, why Thomas had hated him. Had Max really abandoned his dying mother? He couldn't have been very old when his mother had married Thomas. The next time she got the chance, she would ask him.

She turned her attention to the slim volume she held, silently reading the title. *The Last Straw*. Though it had been published fifty years ago, it was in pristine condition, having been opened only rarely. She'd first read it when she was a teenager, but in the years since it had been placed in Mayhem's library, few guests, if any, had taken it to their rooms for a cozy night's read. Truth be told, her beloved Thomas was a terrible writer, a fact she had been loath to admit to herself for years, and had never mentioned to him.

"What did you find?"

At the sound of Max's voice, she looked up, directly into his eyes. Absorbed in her thoughts, she hadn't heard Madame Grovda leave or him approach. He stood only a foot away, his hands in his pockets, a flirty smile on his lips.

Her fingers tightened around the book.

"I'll trade you," she said, trying to keep her emotional distance, when what she really wanted was exactly the opposite. "I'll tell you what I found if you'll tell me why you and Thomas hated each other so much. You go first."

"My, my, my," he drawled, leaning his hip against a library table. "Quite the little negotiator, aren't we?"

"Not at all. But after the things Thomas told me about you—"

"You expected me to be some slathering, scarfaced Hun with pointed teeth, a crooked nose, and a naked woman tossed over my shoulder."

She gave him the once-over. "You forgot the part about the wooden leg."

"I left it at home. It makes a helluva racket on parquet floors." He gestured to her throat. "That's a pretty pendant. Family heirloom?"

She touched her neck, covering the gold crescent moon with her fingers. "It was my mother's. She said my father gave it to her."

"I see."

Once again she caressed the pendant. "My mother liked to have fun," she offered quietly. "She was the original party girl. Drinking, drugging, it didn't matter. Fun, fun, fun. Eventually, it killed her. No more fun. No more Maggie O'Dell."

"Did you love her?"

"Yes. I loved her very much. I miss her. I miss her every day of my life." When he didn't say anything, she laughed. "I guess I went first after all. Your turn."

"Fair enough." He shrugged. "In a nutshell, Heyworth broke up my parents' marriage. He ruined my family on every possible level. He was greedy and selfish and didn't care who he hurt as long as he got what he wanted."

She knew Thomas was a bit on the rough side, but had never heard of him doing anything so underhanded. "I . . . I can't believe that. Not of Thomas. Oh, Max. How on earth—"

"Until the great Thomas Heyworth came along," he said gruffly, "my parents had a pretty good marriage. My dad was a police officer and my mom dabbled at archaeology. Sometimes, she'd take me and my sister Frankie with her on digs. Every summer she'd go somewhere new. She loved it. We did, too."

He paused for a moment, apparently letting the

memories roll over him, through him, until he seemed saturated with fury. "She met Heyworth one summer my first year of college. Bottom line, the bastard seduced her away from my father. When she divorced my dad, he lost it, started screwing up on the job. He ended up being shot in the back by a suspect he'd just collared."

"No. Oh, *no*. Oh, Max, I'm so sor—"

"After they were married," he rushed on, "Heyworth brought her to this fucking island. Kept her here like a prisoner. Wouldn't let me see her. A few months later she died. It nearly destroyed Frankie."

He pushed away from the table and went to stand in front of the window, his hands on his hips, his face turned to stone. She came up close behind him.

"And you, Max?" she whispered. "Did it nearly destroy you, too?" With trembling fingers she touched her hand to his shoulder.

He turned his head a little. "My mother was . . . special. She was smart and fun. I couldn't believe it when she left my dad like that. But it was *Heyworth*. That goddamn son of a bitch. It was *him*. He promised her things, I guess, and she fell for it. Oh, I don't blame her. I'm sure he was really something back then. I swear to God, I could have strangled him with my bare hands."

Evie removed her hand from his shoulder as a cold feeling surged through her system. She tried to get her mind around it, but her brain had frozen at his words.

"Was it you?" she whispered.

"Was what me? What are you talking about?" He turned to face her.

She took a step away from him and looked up into his eyes, horror and disbelief constricting her heart. Thomas's words came back to her.

One of you killed me ... and I know which one ...

"Did you do it, Max? Did *you* kill Thomas?"

Chapter 12

Dear Diary:

I *love* llamas. There are five of them and they live on the island all the time, and Thomas told me I could take care of them from now on! They're really soft and they hum. Not like people hum, but it's a totally cool sound. Daisy is going to have a cria, that's a baby. Thomas says that if it's a boy, we're going to call him Fernando. He laughed and thought that was really funny, but I don't get it.

Evangeline—age 11

Max looked stunned, as though she'd just slammed a frying pan upside his head. Then she watched as his eyes seemed to turn to green flame.

"Excuse me?" he drawled, anger simmering just under the softly spoken words.

Evie frowned as she said, "I had no idea how much you despised Thomas, or why. Did you hate him enough to—"

"I did not kill Heyworth," he growled. "Not my style. I'm a police officer, Evie. Sworn to uphold the law."

"And nobody sworn to uphold the law has ever murdered anybody."

"You know they have," he snapped. "I'm just not one of them."

Flipping back the edges of his jacket, he shoved his hands into his pockets—to keep from choking her, she was certain.

"Do you think I'm capable of cold-blooded murder, Evie?" His glare was hot enough to melt titanium.

"I don't know you well enough to answer that."

"Look at me. Look into my eyes. Do you see a killer?"

"I'll bet Al Bundy used that same argument."

"It was *Ted* Bundy, and I can't believe you're comparing me to some slimy serial killer."

She shrugged. "I'm just saying that you apparently had a very real motive for wanting Thomas dead. And being a cop, you also had the means. You carry a gun and know how to use it. Thomas was shot by somebody who was an excellent marksman, or terribly, terribly lucky."

She paused for a moment, eyeing him. "However, in spite of the fact you're a lout, I'll grant that even you aren't stupid enough to have put your career and your life on the line just for revenge."

"Wow, thanks," he said sarcastically. "You really know how to pump up a man's ego, sweetheart."

"Your ego is healthy enough to withstand a little deflating."

Stepping closer, he reached up and ran his finger along her jaw, tipping up her chin. "What about opportunity, babe?"

Her eyes widened. He was touching her again. For much of her life she'd been wary of a man's touch, welcoming it only on rare occasions with men she trusted implicitly. But Max's touch seemed the most natural thing in the world, a realization that bothered her and made her extremely nervous.

"Op-Opportunity for what?"

"You said I had means and motive. But what about opportunity?" He slipped his hand around to the nape of her neck and stepped a little closer.

In the coolness of the room, she could feel his warmth pulsing against her, and she stood there and let it wrap around her like a cloak. Her insides balled up. He was leading her down a path of subtle seduction, and to her own surprise, she wanted to go.

"Opportunity," she mumbled. "Well, you could have gotten a skiff, come out to the island, hidden away until the right moment, killed Thomas, taken off again, and nobody would have been the wiser."

"Anybody could have done that. If you think it was me, you don't know me very well."

"I don't know you at all."

"Yes you do." His mouth curved into an extremely sexy smile. "Besides, maybe you killed Heyworth."

She dropped the book and then smacked her open hands against his chest. "What? You moron. You know I didn't do it! I can't believe you would . . ."

Her voice drifted off as he laid his hands over hers and smiled down into her eyes.

She swallowed. More touching. Part of her wanted to run away and hide. Part of her wanted to ease herself a little closer.

Granted, she was a young woman and her hormones were wondering why in the world she never paid them any attention. They had lives, too. They wanted things. Sexual things, love things, relationship things. They kept quiet most of the time, but they certainly made their presence known whenever Max Galloway was around.

She'd had enough to deal with in her mother's boyfriends. A few had grabbed at her, but none had hurt her. She'd seen that look in their eyes, though, and young as she was, had known those looks meant something bad. It had scared her, made her feel unclean, and she'd blamed herself.

Men, especially big men, were to be feared. They could overpower, hurt, take. That one time she'd been cornered, her mother had returned from the liquor store just in the nick of time and smacked the guy. He'd smacked her back.

And now Evie spent much of her life on an island—avoiding men, avoiding intimacy—all the while wanting it with all her heart.

"I—I was at school when Thomas was killed," she stuttered. "I didn't even know he'd returned. As soon as I got to the island, I went down to see the llamas—"

Looking deeply into her eyes, he said, "Hell, everybody knows those llamas would lie for you, Evie."

"Let me go," she said impatiently. "I—I need to go to the barn."

"No you don't."

"I do," she responded. "Lily's close to birthing. She may need something—"

"Llamas have very little trouble birthing. She's just fine." He looked very satisfied with himself. He'd obviously done a little research on camelids, and was feeling pretty damn smug.

"Oh, I see," she accused. "You think you can walk in here, start with the llama talk and have your way with me. Well it won't work."

"Won't it?"

Without another word, he tugged her into his arms and kissed her. And the hunger she'd sensed in him, feared of him, had hoped for from him, overpowered her.

He caught her chin with his thumb, urged her mouth open then thrust his tongue inside. A moment later he pulled back.

"Come on, Evie," he whispered against her open mouth. "You want this, I want this. Let's see how good it can be."

He took her mouth again, this time with every ounce of passion he had. He didn't simply kiss, he conquered. He was greedy, demanding, rough. Her heart went flying, her pulse raced.

She stepped closer, unable to resist his pull. Wrapping her arms around his neck, she brought her body flush to his. He groaned as he tightened his embrace, keeping her hard against him, claiming her, body and soul.

She felt his thighs against hers. His erection, long and thick, jabbed her stomach. It should have terrified her, but it didn't. Instead, the feel of him wanting her excited her, tempted her, made her desperate for closer contact.

Max lifted her off the floor and rolled his hips into hers. She felt him press hard just where she needed it, and a pulse of pure desire shot through her. She wanted to curl her legs around his waist, open herself to him, accept the pleasure she knew she'd find there.

Too soon, too fast, too much.

She broke the kiss, shook her head. *Stop.*

Had she said it out loud or only thought it? Max eased her down and stepped back. His mouth was damp, his breathing labored. He said nothing.

"I don't want to do this," she panted. "I don't want to get involved with you."

"You *are* involved with me," he growled.

She tried to catch her breath, tried to hold onto her sanity while her body screamed for more. His hands on her, yes. That's what she wanted. It didn't even matter if it was his hands. His fingers, his mouth, his tongue, anything, everything, as long as some part of him was in contact with some part of her.

But she wouldn't let it happen.

Shaking her head, she put words to her thoughts. "I'll bet . . . I'll bet you kiss women like that all the time. You're smooth, and hard, and you—"

"You make me sound like a bowling ball."

"You know what I mean, Max! You're *using* me.

I'm . . . I'm the only viable female of the species around, so you thought you'd just spend a little time seducing me. I'm convenient, and nothing more. Seducing me would be just dandy for you, but what about what *I* want? What if where I want to go is *different* from where you want to go?"

"Am I gonna need a map for this?"

Her heart raced. She wanted this to go *exactly* where he did, and it scared her half to death.

"Evie," Max said, "this island could be dripping with naked mermaids and sirens and a thousand other *viable* members of the species, and I'd still notice you. You'd still be the one I want."

She took another step away from him and cursed herself for being functionally frigid. What would be the harm in sleeping with Max? She wasn't a virgin. She'd had sex with a couple of her boyfriends in college, made love thinking she was *in* love, and had awakened to discover that while she could go all way physically, she could only go so far emotionally.

It hadn't been the fault of her boyfriends. They were nice guys looking for more than she was capable of giving. She'd been terrified that if she let her defenses down, she'd go wild and not be able to control herself, or end up hurting people she cared about.

I could just have sex with Max, she thought, a man I barely know. But then she'd be just like her mother, a party girl, indiscriminate, callous, never thinking about tomorrow or the consequences. And what if she stupidly fell in love with him?

"You think too much." His eyes were serious, his voice soft.

"You don't understand," she said, then pressed her lips together.

"Maybe I do," he said, lifting his shoulder in an offhanded shrug. His gaze meandered around the room, then settled on some distant spot outside the window. "For your own reasons, you're afraid of getting close. Well, for my own reasons, I am equally afraid of getting close. But, Evie," he said, looking at her now, "there's something between us. I want to find out what it is. Maybe I even need to."

"Between us, I think we have too much baggage."

"Maybe we could repack it and take a trip. Together."

"You're putting a *lot* of stock in that one kiss."

"It was a lot of kiss."

When she said nothing, he blew out a long breath, then gestured to the book in her hand. "Is that ours?"

Remembering the little volume in her hand, she said, *"The Last Straw."* She held it out to him. "Maybe you should read it tonight. Give you something constructive to do, Detective."

"I'll take it to bed with me," he said, his eyes never leaving hers. "A little *under covers* work. Maybe you could join me." His gaze settled on her mouth. "You *do* still owe me that tongue lashing."

She blinked, then turned to leave. When she reached the door she stopped and looked back over her shoulder. In as bland a voice as she could muster, she said, "Just what kind of sucker do you take me for?"

*   *   *

Tuesday morning showed up clear and hot. But on the western horizon a mass of dark clouds lay in waiting. Given the direction of the wind, Evie predicted a cold rainfall by late afternoon.

She had dressed in her usual island attire—boots and jeans—and a pretty blue and white plaid shirt. As she filled the llamas' trough with oats and alfalfa, a stiff breeze from the sea whooshed up from behind her, lifting bits of hay, tumbling them in the air in a twisting, twirling dance. A butterfly flitted over her head, then dashed off on the wind.

Fernando stood next to her, a sudden gust tickling his long fleece with phantom fingers. His ears went alert as his eyes fixed on something behind her.

She knew what it was . . . rather, who it was. He didn't need to say a word. The hairs on the back of her neck stiffened and her knees went weak. Her heart spurted into a sprint. Her breathing changed and her mind emptied of everything she'd been thinking. She'd either been poisoned or Max Galloway had come to stand directly behind her.

"I knocked on your door last night, Evie." After only a few days the soft rasp of his voice had become familiar. Already her body had learned to anticipate it, want it, maybe even crave it.

Without turning, she emptied the contents of the oat bucket into the trough. "I may have been asleep. I do that at night sometimes."

"I wanted to see how you were doing."

She walked to the barn and set the empty bucket on the bench. It made a hollow sound as metal met wood.

He followed her. "I read the book." There was that soft rasp again. Tiny chills scooted up her spine and down her arms and into every nook and cranny of her body. It was as though somebody had splashed warm champagne all over her naked flesh. "I have some ideas," he said, "but we need to talk about it."

The same electric charge she felt every time he was near zapped her again. He gave off enough sexual energy to power the entire northwestern grid.

"I can't talk about the murder hunt right now," she said. "I'm taking Fernando into Port Henry to the senior center."

He eyed the llama. "Really? He doesn't look that old to me. They have a special wing just for llamas?"

She turned to glare at him, but he reached for her and pulled her into his arms. His move surprised her, but she didn't fight it, just let her body fall against his, limp, unresisting. Her arms dangled at her sides. Eventually he'd get the picture and let her go.

"Put your arms around me, Evie."

Okay, maybe not right away, but eventually.

Into his shirt front she mumbled, "Nrph."

He squeezed her tighter. Her head lay against his solid chest and she could hear the steady beating of his heart, feel the rise and fall of his chest as he breathed, the movement of strong bones under his firm muscles.

"Evie. Put your arms around me."

Dammit. She was weak, and he was so . . .

Slowly, she straightened and wrapped her arms around his chest, letting her open hands feel the strength of his back. He tugged her closer until not so much as a breath could pass between them.

"Evie," he said, nuzzling her neck. "I feel your heart beating against mine. I like that. I feel your breathing against my skin, and I feel how warm you are, how alive, how strong. And more." He lay his cheek on the top of her head. "I hear the sorrow in your voice when you speak of your mother, and see the love in your eyes when you talk about Heyworth, the llamas, Edmunds. Jesus, I thought about you all night, Evie. I couldn't sleep worth a damn. I can't get you out of my mind. When this is over, I want to see what can happen between us. Give me a shot at this, will you?"

He raised one hand and cupped her cheek, tilting her face, gently forcing her to look at him.

She gazed into his eyes, remembering Madame Grovda's prediction. Of course, she'd dismissed it at the time as a silly joke. But ever since, she'd been reluctant to let it go. For some reason, the psychic's words had burrowed straight into her heart like seeds tossed into fertile garden soil. As she stood in the circle of Max's arms, she felt those tiny seeds of hope take root and begin to grow.

He smiled into her eyes, and she realized nobody had ever looked at her like that before.

"I don't blame you for being cautious," he said. "So, let me give you something to think about."

He took her mouth in a hard, claiming kiss. Beneath her breast she felt his heart speed up. He growled, way deep down in his throat, the sound of a famished beast.

His lips were firm and so very talented. He knew

just how to kiss her, nibble at her mouth, slide his tongue along hers, stop to suckle and soothe.

She felt his hand slide up her rib cage and knew he was going to touch her. He moved slowly, giving her plenty of time to protest, back away, haul off and slug him.

But she didn't budge.

His thumb touched the bottom curve of her breast, and she felt the zing of it all the way down to her toes. He curled his hand around her breast, letting his finger glide over her nipple, bringing it to a peak beneath the thin lace of her bra.

Sensation washed through her body, pooling low inside her.

He moved his hand a little and she felt one of the buttons on her blouse pop open. She leaned into him, and he popped another one.

"You are so hot," he whispered against her parted lips. "Jesus, Evie. I've got to see you."

With that, he popped open the last two buttons and shoved the fabric aside. With both hands he undid her bra and pushed it away. Then he simply stared at her, his hazel eyes smoky with masculine appreciation and potent desire.

She felt his gaze touch her naked breasts like a caress, tightening her nipples, making her ache all over. Deep inside, she began to throb.

Lowering his head, he took her nipple in his mouth.

"Oh," she cried, the word barely audible. "Oh, Max . . ."

She cupped his head in her hand and arched into him. Her breathing went wild, her heart tumbled and leaped, as Max flicked the nipple with his tongue, gently bit it with his teeth. His hot breath would have been enough to drive her insane, but the sensation of his mouth on her sent tendrils of delight curling all through her body.

His hands came up to cup her breasts as he suckled first one nipple, then the other, making her want to sob with the need he made her feel.

"We have to stop," he panted, "or I'm going to drag you to the ground and do it in the dirt, right here, right now. If . . . If I don't stop . . ."

His words came in a rush, his eyes never leaving her bare breasts. "I won't be able to, if I don't . . . so, I'm stopping now, okay? Christ, you're so beautiful."

He lifted his sleepy gaze to her eyes. "We *could* keep going. But if you want me to stop, telling me now would be a good thing. Just remember, I'll interpret silence as consent."

His eyes were dark green, filled with flagrant desire. For her.

"Hell, I want you so much," he choked, "I may take no as consent. Maybe you'd better kick me or something."

Reaching up, Evie adjusted her bra and buttoned her blouse. She wanted to speak up, to say it out loud, but she was afraid she'd say the wrong words and her no would come out more like, *Take me now, what's a little dirt?*

"I'm sorry, Max," she whispered. "I'm not trying to be a tease, honest. I—I just need more time. So much is going on—"

"You're right," he interrupted. He put up his

hands. "I had only meant to kiss you. I swear. The rest, well, it was sort of a spur of the moment thing."

"That happens to men a lot."

"Yeah, it does."

She turned to Fernando, who was still waiting patiently. Picking up the grooming brush, she began to stroke his warm neck, trying desperately to bring her breathing back to normal, ease her tight nerves, forget how Max's mouth had felt on her. Common sense warred with common lust as she fought to understand what had just happened, and what it meant, and just why in the hell she was resisting him in the first place when she wanted him so much.

Max shuffled around, undoubtedly trying to do the same thing she was, maybe even wondering the same thing. Finally, he said, "I'm coming with you today."

"No, you're not," she stated. "I don't need an audience."

"Not an audience," he said flatly. "A bodyguard."

Chapter 13

Dear Diary:

I saw them again today. The old people who live in the house by my school. They sit on the porch with blankets on their laps, and stare at me after Edmunds drops me off. Sometimes, they wave at me and I wave back. They smile, too, but I don't think they are happy. I think they hope that if they smile hard enough, somebody will come and visit them.

Evangeline—age 11

An hour later Max turned the bow of the runabout away from the dock while Evie made Fernando sit, or lie down, or whatever in the hell llamas did when they weren't standing around looking superior.

"Kush, Fernando," she ordered. "Kush!"

Fernando did as commanded and went down first

on his knees, then settled his butt, curling his legs beneath him. He looked like a dust mop sitting in the bottom of the boat, neck extended, eyes wide, fuzzy banana ears alert.

Gesturing to Fernando, Max said, "So 'koosh' means sit down?"

"Mm-hmm."

"What do you say when you want him to stand up?"

" 'Stand up' usually does the trick," she replied dryly.

He turned the wheel and adjusted the throttle, sending the runabout through the rolling water at a pretty good clip. The bow knifed smoothly through the froth like a blade through whipped cream.

"If there's a special word for sitting down," he said, "why isn't there a special word for standing up?"

"You ask too many questions."

"In other words, you don't know." He grinned.

Ignoring him, Evie sat next to the llama and cooed softly into its ear.

Max slid on his dark glasses. "Llamas seem to sit down like that a lot. How do they ever have little llamas?"

"If you must know, they do it sitting down. At least the females sit down, just like Fernando is now. The male approaches the female from behind and mounts her."

"You're making me hot."

"Doesn't take a lot."

Max throttled down and adjusted his speed. "So

she just sits there and like, what, watches TV while he—"

"What, do you want me to draw you a picture?"

"Pictures are good. I like pictures."

She laughed a little, then said, "Pretty much, actually. He approaches her, mounts her, and they have sex until she spits him off."

"Sounds like a girl I knew in college."

"This comes as no surprise to me whatsoever." Shaking her head, she accused, "Has it occurred to you that many of our conversations have to do with the reproductive habits of wildlife?"

"Yes it has," he said seriously. "I think it's because you have a one-track mind. Personally, I find it appalling."

Evie rolled her eyes and turned her attention toward the mainland.

Max let his gaze linger on her, suppressing the urge to laugh out loud. Jesus, she was sweet, and feisty, and so easy to tease. She was quite a package. Sexy, smart, and fun. A man looking for a woman to share his life could do a helluva lot worse.

As the boat skimmed across the corrugated sea, its rhythm reminded Max of making love. The steady rolling, the relaxing momentum.

His focus went fuzzy for a moment. He saw her body, naked, flushed with passion, and the rocking went on and on. Lazy and hot, rolling up and over and down, up and over and down, gently, slowly. His hips moving with hers until he nearly came apart.

"You can put it in here."

He blinked hard. "What?"

She frowned at him. "The boat. You can dock it right here."

Oh! They were there, at the dock.

They slid into the runabout's slip, and the security man came out to help tie off while Evie prepared Fernando to stand and leave the boat.

"C'mon, sweetie," she crooned. "Up. That a boy!"

As Fernando lifted his rear and then his shoulders to stand, Max said, "Not un-kush, huh?"

"Well, you can try it, but he'll just stare at you."

"He always just stares at me."

"Hold out your hand," she ordered, and when Max did, she slapped a key into his open palm. "That blue Dodge pickup over there. Bring it around, please."

Max gave her a mock salute and said, "As you wish, ma'am."

A few minutes later the llama was kushed in the bed of the truck. Gesturing to Fernando, Max said, "Isn't he going to jump out?"

"No," Evie replied. "He likes to go for trips in the back of the truck. Besides, I've tied his lead to the cleat in the bed. He'll be fine."

Max flipped up the tailgate and locked it in place, then escorted Evie to the passenger side of the truck.

"I'll drive," he said, opening the door for her.

As he came around and slid in behind the wheel, Evie fastened her seat belt and said, "It's 17 Jefferson Street. The Rhododendron Senior Center. They're expecting us." She glanced out the back window. "Just don't make any sudden turns."

The center was a two-story Victorian, painted in brown and peach tones. He thought it must have been quite a place back in the day, but now the paint was peeling and the garden needed work. Obviously, funds were tight.

Max hopped out of the truck and met Evie at the tailgate, where he unlocked it and pulled out the plank she'd used to load the beast. Fernando stood and looked around as though he did this kind of thing every day.

As Evie led the llama up the stone pathway to the covered porch, the front door opened and a young woman in a pastel yellow uniform stepped out.

"Hello!" she said. Her name tag read CYNNDRAH. She was perky and pretty, with her brown hair pulled back in a ponytail. Her eyes widened when she saw the llama. "This must be Fernando! May I pet him?"

Max glanced at Evie. She'd gone pale and seemed to have tuned Cynndrah out completely. Something was wrong, but he had no idea what.

He wished he could hear what she was thinking, wished she'd turn to him, confide in him, trust him with her fears. He'd known her for, what, a week? And yet he felt as though there had never been a time when she hadn't been in his life. He wondered, was seven days enough time to connect with a woman to the point that, if she vanished, a man just might never get over it? Over *her*?

He'd always been polite to women and treated them well—he wasn't a total SOB—but underneath, he had scorned them. Years of training at his father's side had left him feeling cynical and often cold. He never showed that side of himself to anyone, certainly not to a woman he wanted to take to bed, but it had been there all the same.

Had been there. Evie had somehow managed—without managing at all—to change that.

"Evie?"

She blinked. Her cheeks flushed and she smiled at Cynndrah. "Sorry. I, uh, where do you want us?"

As they entered the parlor, he was surprised to see a dozen or so residents eagerly awaiting the arrival of Evie and her llama. Even the nurses and orderlies were grinning and looking like a group of children happily anticipating a visit from Saint Nick.

Llamas were just fluffy camels, as far as he could tell. Couldn't do any tricks that he knew of. Perhaps Evie would have done better to bring a dog, or maybe even a horse or donkey. What good bringing a llama to an old folks' home was, he couldn't begin to guess, especially when it looked like what the place really needed was an influx of cold, hard cash.

A haphazard circle of chairs had been placed in the middle of the room, every chair occupied by an elderly resident. Each lined face was set with a smile, and in each person's eye there was a gleam that Max would have bet a bundle didn't appear there very often.

"Are llamas camels?" This from a woman with frizzy gray hair, thick glasses, and a tan polyester pantsuit.

"No," explained Evie. "Camels are descendants of llamas. Llamas are camelids and are from South America."

A cracked voice spoke up. A man in green pants and a plaid shirt. "Do they bite?"

Evie smiled at the gentleman. "They rarely bite, but llamas do spit when they're aggravated."

Or sexually satisfied, thought Max.

A woman in a wheelchair began to clap her hands like a child at a play. "Closer," she begged, her voice high and thin. "Please? Closer."

Max moved the chair in a little and the llama turned to look at her. He pricked his fuzzy ears and plodded forward, lowering his head in an obvious bid for a petting.

With palsied hands, the woman reached out and lightly touched the llama's ear. "So soft," she mewled in a thin voice. "Hello, lovie. You're beautiful."

Evie crouched before the wheelchair and said, "Fernando is a North American llama, which means he was born here and not imported from South America. Did you know that llama wool is warmer than sheep's wool? The fibers are hollow."

The woman ran her crooked fingers through Fernando's fleece, beaming all the while like a young child at a petting zoo.

For the next two hours Evie and Max walked the llama around the place, introducing him to the people who were too old or too sick to leave their beds. Wherever they went, the beast was a big hit. Better than a dog, or a horse, or a donkey. Maybe even better than cold, hard cash.

As they waved good-bye to Fernando's admirers, the woman in the wheelchair patted Evie's arm and looked up at her with milky blue eyes. "Thank you, dear," she said softly, her feeble voice raspy with emotion. "Thank you."

Evie nodded curtly but said nothing. Her lips were pressed tightly together even though she smiled down at the woman. Leaning forward, she pressed a kiss on the ancient lady's wrinkled brow.

"We'll come back another day," she promised quickly, then stood.

They walked out to the truck in silence, Fernando plodding along next to Evie. When they reached the tailgate, Max put his hands on Evie's shoulders and turned her to face him.

She refused to look him in the eye.

"Evie?"

She swallowed. "Um, we have to go. Clue Number Four—"

"Evie. Look at me."

She shook her head.

Max cupped her chin between his thumb and palm, lifting her face. Though she kept her lashes down, he could see the tears welling in her eyes.

"Evie?" he probed quietly. "Is it always like this? Are visits to senior centers always so . . ."

She swallowed. Nodded.

"Why in the hell do you do it?" he demanded gently. "That was one of the most painful things I've ever seen in my life. The looks on some of their faces. Shit, Evie . . . why?"

She sniffed, dabbing her nose with the arm of her sleeve. "Why do I do it? Because they're alone. They're called elder orphans. It's one of the terms we've created in the modern world in an effort to make sure everybody's labeled properly." Her voice was mild, but her words bitter. She stuck her hands in her pockets and shrugged.

"Their husbands and wives are dead. Their children, if they ever had any, are gone, too. Do you know what it's like to be *completely* without family?" she whispered. "Have you any idea how lonely it is? All my life, even when my mother was alive, I was alone. And then one day, even she was gone. I loved Thomas and I love Edmunds, but it's not the same thing, Max. I used to wish with all my heart that Thomas was my real father, and that was why he'd come to get me. I wanted so much to have *somebody* I could point to without hesitation and say, this is *my* family. I am *not* alone."

He ran his thumb over her cheek, brushing away a hot tear. "Why you, sweetheart? Why do *you* do this when it reminds you—"

"Me," she interjected, "because maybe I'm one of the few people in this world who really, truly, and honestly understands what it's like to be by yourself. Don't you see? *They* are *me* a few years down the road. Nobody behind them, nobody ahead."

Her mouth quirked into a sardonic grin. "Maybe I'm hedging my bets. Building up a little good karma so that someday, when I'm at the end of this very same road, some stranger will bring a llama by so I can touch it and pet it, and remember."

"Evie," he whispered. "Evie, stop it. You're killing me here."

Max folded her into his arms and pulled her close.

He felt her chest expand and contract with each

breath. As the moist heat of her tears saturated his shirt, something inside him he'd kept under tight control cracked and began to give way. Something he'd surrounded with bricks and iron and walls of stone and mortar and steel, and arrogance and detachment and fear.

Oddly, the image of his father forced its way into his head. *I don't want to think of you now, Dad. I don't want ever to think of you.*

But something about Evie's softness conjured up his father's rigidity, and how he himself had adopted that attitude. He'd admired his dad and had wanted to love him, but the man was harsh and distant, and because of that, for too long a time he'd believed that was how men were.

He'd let someone in once. Melissa. And just look how that had turned out. In response, he'd boarded up his heart behind an even tougher wall, and had kept it fiercely guarded since then.

Until Evie.

Pushing away from Max, she sniffed, then turned and faced the patient llama, reaching up to stroke his coat.

"As long as we're in town," she said, "I need to stop at the drugstore and get an allergy prescription refilled. It won't take long. You can stay in the truck and babysit. I doubt he'll give you any trouble."

"Sure," Max said.

Evie turned back to him. Arching a brow, she said, "I was speaking to *Fernando*."

Max laughed and shook his head as he helped Evie load the beast into the bed of the truck, then she headed down to the pharmacy on Water Street.

Sitting in the nearly empty parking lot of the Olympic Pharmacy, Max glanced out the back window of the truck. Evie had told him the llama would be fine, but he felt uncomfortable about it, so he climbed into the bed and sat with the creature, enjoying the mid-afternoon sunshine.

When Evie was gone more than ten minutes, he began to seriously crave caffeine.

He glanced at the door of the drugstore, told himself she shouldn't be much longer. He could hang on for a few more minutes.

"Fernando?" The llama stared at him, blinked, and flicked its ears. "You need to take a leak, buddy?" The llama stared at him, blinked, and flicked its ears.

"In case she asks," he told the llama, then glanced at the pharmacy again, "I tried to make this about your needs, but it's really all about me. I need some coffee. There's a walk-up just down the street. And since I can't leave you here . . ."

He let his voice trail off and shook his head when he realized he was explaining his motives to a llama.

Standing next to the fluff monger, he commanded, "Fernando. Un-kush!" The llama stared at him, blinked, and flicked its ears. So much for theory. "Fernando, stand up, you miserable piece of carpet lint. Up!"

The llama blinked languidly and slowly rose to his feet. He looked a little pissed, if Max was any judge.

Unlocking the tailgate, he lowered it and jumped to the ground. Muscling the plank into place, he tugged on Fernando's lead rope. "C'mon, buddy.

I'm a desperate man. Maybe they have llama lattes. My treat."

Fernando plodded onto the plank and down to the ground, his head high, his eyes alert. He turned toward Max, neck stretched, nose up and ears back. His body had gone erect and his tail was raised. Uh-oh.

"No!" Max shouted, raising his hands in a defensive gesture. But it was too late.

The llama coughed, and a giant spiderweb of green slime emptied onto Max's hair, hands, shirt, and pants.

"Oh, God!" he yelled as he backed as far away from Fernando as he could. "God, what is that *smell*?"

"Max?" It was Evie, standing in the doorway of the pharmacy. Rushing forward, she went to Fernando and put her arms around his neck in a protective manner.

"What did you do to my llama!" she demanded.

Max shook his head and held his hands away from his body. "What did I do to your llama? Look at me," he shouted. "I'm covered with toxic waste, and you ask *me* what I did to *him*? The little fucker threw up on me!"

He glared at her, and she began to laugh. Covering her mouth with her fingertips, she giggled until tears formed in her eyes.

"You look really disgusting," she choked, then laughed some more. The llama stood with its mouth hanging open, as if to air out a smelly garage.

When Evie calmed herself, she said, "It's called

spitting, but it's not saliva. It's partially digested stomach contents. You must have made him really *mad* for him to do that."

Max raised his head. "Yeah. I offered to buy him a latte. I can see how that might have offended him. How do I get this crap off of me?"

"There's only one thing that will eradicate the odor," she said as she headed for the driver's side of the cab. "You two hop in the back. I'm taking you to my house."

It was less than a ten-minute drive to Evie's cottage. Of course, in Port Henry, he realized it was less than a ten-minute drive to most anywhere.

She pulled up in front of a pretty yellow rambler with a white picket fence covered with white roses. Parking in the short driveway, she unloaded the creature and tied it to a post at the side of the house by the kitchen.

As she unlocked the door to let Max in, she said, "Don't touch anything. Go directly to the bathroom and take off your clothes inside the tub."

He stepped closer to her just to watch her nose wrinkle in disgust.

"My hands are sticky," he said in his most sincere tone. "I may need your help undressing."

Pushing open the door, she went to a drawer and pulled out a plastic bag. "Here," she said as she dangled the bag in front of him. "Put everything in this and I'll wash it while you're in the shower."

With his clean two fingers, he took the bag and walked through the small kitchen and into the hallway.

"Last door on your left," she yelled after him.
"Leave the bag on the toilet seat and I'll grab it
while you're showering."

He wanted to take a look around her house, but
there'd be time enough for that later. Right now he
needed to get the spitball from hell out of his hair
and off his hands and face.

Toeing off his boots, he stepped into the tub and
stripped, then shoved his clothes into the bag. He set
it on the closed commode, yanked the clear plastic
shower curtain shut, and turned on the water. As
steam rose around his body, he rubbed honeysuckle
scented soap all over himself. Out of the corner of
his eye he saw the door open an inch or two, a hand
reach in, and the bag disappear.

He lathered his hair, grinning to himself. She
wasn't the type to just march on in, take a look, and
stride right out again, or, even better, join him. No,
Evie would need an invitation to look at his naked
body . . . an invitation he was going to make damn
sure she got.

Chapter 14

Dear Diary:

Living on an island is really fun! You get to ride on a boat every day to go to school and stuff. And sometimes Edmunds takes me over to the mainland in the runabout just so I can see my friends or when I go to a birthday party or a sleepover. I like the boat rides a lot, except for when it gets windy and cold and the waves are gigantically huge, even in the summer! Then I get scared and living on the island isn't so fun anymore.

Evangeline—age 11

Under his capable fingers, the keyboard's rapid taps and clicks sounded like music. On the screen, the tune came alive in the form of numbers and names, cities, countries, and very impressive totals.

And it was all his.

It hadn't always been this way. He'd grown up poor, and worked like a demon to make his way in the world. He owed his success solely to himself, and if the world at large thought well of him, he deserved their adulation, had earned it, and intended to keep it.

While Tommy Heyworth had frittered away vast sums on food and drink and women and stupidity, *he* had kept his nose to the grindstone. He'd played along, been friendly, but not a friend.

For all his family's wealth, Heyworth had been a cynic, and a suspicious one at that. It had taken forever to get the bastard to trust him, but in the end patience had won out. Patience, and greed, and luck. Not the kind of luck that was happenstance, but the kind of luck he had *made* happen.

As he closed one spreadsheet and opened another, he chuckled to himself. Trust was such an elemental thing between people. Once it was firmly established, a dishonest man could use that trust to pilfer and plunder and take his revenge in any number of ways. And Heyworth had never suspected; at least, not until just before his death. As long as he'd had all the money he needed, the bills were paid on time, and he could continue with that ludicrous writing career of his, Tommy Heyworth seemed not to care at all what happened to the rest of the Heyworth millions. And with no heirs to muddy the waters, nobody ever would.

He jabbed the keyboard, anger rising from deep within him at the injustice of it all. At how, out of the blue, the stupid son of a bitch had decided it was time to acknowledge his heir. His heir! Some brat gotten off some slut maid thirty years ago could step in and take it all away? Not bloody likely.

Heyworth wanted to change his will, wanted to acknowledge the little bitch, open the records and make an accounting of his holdings. Well, *that* was out of the question.

Tommy had to go, and go he had gone. Too bad the first attempt had been botched. This murder hunt business was tiresome and stressful, and the sooner he found the last clue and destroyed it, the better.

The phone rang and he answered it.

"She's in town. I seen her with her boyfriend."

"She doesn't have a boyfriend," he drawled. "It's probably Galloway. Where are they now?"

"Her house. A little quality time in the sack, I bet."

He sighed. "Knowing her, I sincerely doubt it, but feel free to imagine whatever you wish as long as it costs me nothing extra."

"You got it. So, we still on for tonight?"

"Yes. Call me the minute they leave so I can establish my alibi. Then head for the boat. You know what to do."

"You sure you want me to do this tonight? She won't be alone."

"Listen, Sam," he snapped, losing patience with the incompetent ass. "It doesn't matter whether she's alone or not. It has to be done, and soon. Your little barn accident was a total failure. Take care of it this time, and stop asking stupid questions." He closed the file and shut down his computer. "I'll consider your getting rid of Galloway payback for having failed to eliminate James, *and* for screwing up the first attempt at Heyworth. If not for that, we wouldn't be engaged in this asinine game. Finish her tonight, or I'll find someone who will, and I'll pay *him* your ludicrous fee."

"Hey, don't threaten me, pal. I know where all the bodies are buried. Remember?"

"And I know who *put* them there, so shut up and do your job."

When Max came out of the bathroom, a pink-and-white-striped towel wrapped snuggly around his hips, Evie was gone. Instead, the seductive scent of brewing coffee lured him toward the kitchen. A note on the small oak table said: *Be back in a minute. Keep an eye on Fernando. E.*

She'd left him a note. Why he felt that was something special and intimate between them, he couldn't have said, but he liked it nonetheless.

He picked it up, examined her handwriting. It was lovely, just like her. Not small and scratchy, not big and blousy, just neat little swirls and curls, and the prettiest initial E he'd ever seen.

Grinning at the piece of paper like a total idiot, he traced the E with his fingertip, then folded the note in his hand and went looking for his clothes. On the enclosed back porch, the washer was still going, so he figured he was a good hour or so away from clean, dry clothes.

He wandered through the small house, his bare feet slapping against the cool hardwood floors. A kitchen, a single bath, two bedrooms, nice and cozy. Max imagined her here on winter evenings, correcting spelling tests and grading papers, a small fire crackling in the fireplace as she sipped a mug of spicy tea.

It was mid-July. School wouldn't begin for over a month. Maybe he'd come back one cold autumn night, bring a bag of Chinese food, coax her out of her flannel nightgown and make love to her by the warmth of that fire.

He looked out the window to see Fernando kushed and staring off toward the town, his lead rope still securely tethered to the post. Good thing. There was no way he was jogging down the street after a runaway llama wearing only a pink-striped bath towel.

A blue truck pulled into the driveway. *Evie.*

As he entered the kitchen from the hallway, she pushed open the door and set groceries and a department store bag on the table. Tossing her purse down, she smiled at him, and he realized he was very glad his impromptu kilt was made of such heavy terry cloth.

"Sorry I was gone so long," she said. "On my way back from getting groceries, I drove by Harbisson's department store. They were having a great sale. Bras and panties half off . . ."

"I prefer them all the way off, myself."

". . . and I realized you wouldn't have anything to wear until your clothes were washed and dried."

"But I don't wear panties and bras anymore," he chided. "Not since I got caught that time—"

"Shut up." She picked up the plastic bag and

threw it at him. "New clothes. Put them on. Your presence in my kitchen in nothing but a towel is . . . perverted."

He caught the bag and peered into it. "Thanks. But you weren't initially going to say perverted, were you?"

She pulled a container of mushrooms out of the grocery bag. "If you don't shut up and get dressed right now, I'm not going to feed you."

She was going to cook for him? For that he would promise never to speak again.

Tucking the bag under his arm, Max went to the coffeemaker and poured himself a mug. Without another word, he backed out of the kitchen and went to the spare bedroom to change.

He had coffee, and she was making him dinner. He didn't stink anymore, and he had new clothes. Life just didn't get any better than this.

Well, he grinned as he let the towel fall to the floor, it might get a *little* better if, say, he could eat Evie for dessert.

Evie checked the meat loaf and adjusted the heat under the potatoes. While she'd been busy preparing dinner, Max had spent the last hour in the back bedroom at her computer. As she turned to set the table, she bumped straight into a wall of solid muscle.

His arms came around her, keeping her from falling, pulling her close to his body.

"I didn't hear you come in," she choked.

"Mea culpa," he said. "I didn't want you to hear me."

"Why not?"

Lifting his shoulder in a shrug, he said, "So I could scare the hell out of you so you'd bump into me and trip and lose your balance so I could grab you to keep you from falling so I could pull you close so I could do this."

He lowered his head and took her mouth.

Dear God, the man knew how to kiss. Did it come naturally to him or was it something he had cultivated over the years? She quickly decided she didn't care.

He pulled back, and their lips clung for a moment, so he nibbled them free.

"Thanks for the new duds," he said. "But I didn't mind the towel."

"You, um, you have a very impressive chest."

"Likewise, I'm sure." He chuckled, bending, taking the lobe of her ear gently between his teeth.

"Dinner's nearly ready," she said, closing her eyes as he nuzzled her neck. "In the meantime, I—I have some ideas about the clue. . . ."

"Such as?" he murmured, obviously not giving the hunt the attention it deserved.

"Such as, I think our next stop is Olympia."

"I know it well." He trailed his tongue along her collarbone, and she just about lost her mind.

"It's the southernmost part of Puget Sound," she said as his hand slid up to cup her breast. "I'm w-willing . . ."

"My favorite words," he growled. "You're willing to what?"

". . . t-to bet Clue Number Four sends us up the west side of the Sound, back toward Port Henry."

"You're probably right." With his free hand he

cupped her other breast, then gave them both a little squeeze.

"How do you like them, regular or mashed?"

His hands stilled. "Excuse me?"

"Potatoes," she said, flicking a glance at the bubbling pot on the stove.

With a laugh, he kissed her quickly, then released her. "Mashed would be great."

He walked to the kitchen window. "Assuming the next clue is in Olympia, where do we look? The passage refers to a five-and-dime, and to my recollection, there aren't very many of those around anymore."

Taking the meat loaf from the oven, Evie said, "I have an idea about that. I want to look at the book again tonight. There's a particular passage I'm thinking of that might answer that question."

"It's getting a little misty out there. We should probably hurry if we want to get back to the island before the storm hits."

But they didn't hurry. They lingered over dinner, Evie talking about what it was like to grow up on an island, Max discussing the finer points of wood shop, and the nutcracker he'd made one Christmas for his mom.

"It wasn't very good," he said, leaning back in his chair. "In fact, it broke the first time she tried to use it, so I made her another one, and another one, and *another* one, until she had a whole collection. The last one even works." He grinned across the table at her.

She liked it when he spoke of his mother. His eyes

softened and his mouth turned up on one side when a particularly funny memory came to him.

"Did you make anything besides broken nut-crackers?"

He laughed and tossed his napkin on the table. "Yeah, woodworking became a hobby after that. I made my coffee table at home, a couple of clocks from burls I found on hikes. I even carved a set of chess pieces I'm rather proud of."

And he was. She could tell by the lift in his voice as he described designing each piece, finding the right kind of wood for it, then slicing away the excess until he had just the form he wanted.

They talked so long, by the time they finished dinner and reached the dock the sky had dimmed from lavender to murky indigo and a layer of mist hovered above the rolling water. Overhead, the cloud cover broke here and there to reveal a velvet sky scattered with glistening bits of starlight. A slice of moon hung low on the horizon like a golden hook descending to pull a mermaid from the sea.

The wind had steadied, forcing the water to peak into whitecaps, creating an endless sea of waves crawling over each other to reach the shore.

Gauging the conditions, Max said, "Looks a little iffy to me, but there are other boats out there and nobody seems to be in trouble."

Looking out across the water, Evie said, "It's only a twenty-five-minute boat ride, and I've made it in much worse weather than this. I wouldn't risk Fernando's life if I thought for a second it was too dangerous to cross."

"Fernando's life? What about *mine*?"

She smiled up at him. "Jealous of a llama, Detective?"

As she walked back to the truck to get Fernando, she heard Max mutter a soft, "Maybe."

Once Evie and Fernando were settled in the runabout, Max punched the starter and the motor roared to life. He flipped on the running lights and tossed the line, easing the boat away from the dock.

Fernando was in his kush position in the bottom of the boat and seemed intent on ignoring him as much as possible, which was fine with him, if having a relationship with the beast meant being slimed whenever the damned thing got pissed.

Max swung the bow toward open water, the distant lights of Heyworth Island weakly penetrating the fog like stars through smoke. Keeping an eye on the twin lights that marked the entrance to the cove, he throttled forward, sending the runabout churning through the choppy waves.

Evie sat next to Fernando, idly letting her fingers sift through the animal's soft fleece. He wondered if she was thinking about him, about them. He knew that he was having a hard time thinking about anything else.

The wind blew steadily from the north, but that didn't explain why the back of his neck began to itch. A feeling of uneasiness poked at his gut. Something wasn't right.

"Evie?" he shouted over the sound of the motor. The mixed scents of salty water and fuel exhaust swirled around them. "You doing okay?"

"I'm fine," she yelled. "Anxious to get back."

In twenty more minutes they'd be on the island. Things were going smoothly. So why did he have a feeling low in his belly that something was about to happen?

That's when he heard it. An engine. Nearby. Coming toward them.

"Evie!" he shouted. "Can you see a boat?"

She half stood and looked around. "I hear it, but I don't see anything."

Behind them Port Henry's waterfront twinkled in the dark like a string of tangled Christmas lights. In front of him the silhouette of Heyworth Island was dim, blending into the night like spilled ink on a black carpet. Around them all was mist and shadows.

"Evie!" he yelled above a sudden blast of wind, the noise of the engine, the thundering of his own heart. "Can llamas swim?"

"I—I don't know!"

He reached down and yanked open the storage bin, grabbed a life jacket and shoved it into her hands. "Put this on," he ordered. "Now!"

Their running lights were on. They could be seen, even through the fog. Anybody heading toward them would adjust their course.

The wind shifted direction and he heard the engine again, louder now, closer. He could take evasive action, but what if that turned him right into the oncoming boat?

Pressing the horn, he blasted it in rapid succession, warning the approaching vessel to veer away.

The throb of the engine grew louder, its roar just a few feet to starboard.

Blasting the horn again, Max yelled to Evie, "Hang on!"

And it was on them.

He jumped back as the blade of the bow pierced the runabout, slicing it in half.

Wood screamed and shattered, water exploding around him, sucking him down, covering him in a massive backwash.

He tried to call her name, but his mouth filled with cold seawater and he choked and went under. When he surfaced, the boat was disappearing to port, into the mist. Not stopping, not even slowing down.

Max smashed at the water with his hands, trying to grasp something large enough to hang onto. Finally, a piece of the runabout was within reach. As he grabbed it he yelled, "Evie!" He took another breath. "Evie! Answer me!"

His heart pounded, his eyes stung, his throat tightened.

"Evie!" Her name was a harsh rasp on his lips. His lungs felt like they were on fire. Yet he called her name, and called it again, called it until he couldn't draw another breath.

The wind whipped across the water, teasing the rolling waves into hands that slapped his face and tried to force him under.

But he didn't go under. Instead, he found his breath and called her name again as he thrust himself forward through dark waves. His clothes weighed a ton, threatening to drag him under, to drag him to his death, but he kept his arms moving in the hope he might accidentally come upon her. All around him, he could see debris, vague shapes rolling and bobbing in the black water.

He didn't know how much time had passed before he heard the sound of a horn. Across the peaks of water, a light, steady and bright, moved toward him. Over the thrashing of the wind, he heard the sound of an engine. But would the boat see him, or would it too run him down?

Or had whoever it was come back to finish the job?

A shaft of light reached out, illuminating the wreckage of the runabout. Shards of wood, a floating seat cushion, part of the stern.

But no Evie.

The oncoming boat slowed and he heard a man shouting.

"Over here!" Max lifted an arm and waved just as the light touched his fingertips. In minutes the boat slid close to him and a rope ladder uncurled over the side, splashing into the heaving water.

As Max clambered up the ladder, he shouted, "Turn the beam back onto the water! Turn it back!" Twisting on the rungs, he yelled, "Evie!"

"Dave!" the stranger yelled to someone behind him. "Get that light out on the water. And radio the Harbor Patrol!"

Behind the man, Dave moved the light across the surface of the water, and for the next hour the three men searched for Evie. When the Harbor Patrol arrived, more lights flooded the area, but much of the debris had already been scattered by the wind and the storm waves.

Max considered it a positive sign that no bodies

floated amidst the debris. No llama. No woman. It wasn't a whole lot of hope, but it was better than nothing.

The tide was going out. The storm waves could have carried her a mile out to sea by now.

They searched all night. At daybreak, when the wind had calmed and the sea flattened, Max wiped the veil of mist from the lenses of his binoculars and continued scanning the horizon. The empty horizon.

Chapter 15

Dear Diary:

Today I found out that Mayhem Manor used to be called Heyworth's Folly, but that Thomas changed the name when he inheritted it and wrote mystery stories. All of the bedrooms are named after famous detectives in books, like Hercueles Parrot and Miss Marble or somebody. Edmunds told me that there are secret passageways in the house, too, but I haven't found any yet. They sure are hidden! I am going to look like crazy around the manor to find them. I know I'll find at least one! That may be scary if I find one though, because I bet they're all filled with spider webs and skeltons!

Evangeline—age 11

The Harbor Patrol was very sorry, but the young woman—if she had even survived the impact, which was doubtful—couldn't have had much debris to hang on to. Fully clothed in a tumultuous sea, an outgoing tide, not to mention the llama . . . well, ugly as it was, with each passing hour and no sign of Evie Randall, the truth simply had to be faced.

In all likelihood, they said, her body would be found within the next few days on one of the many islands dotting the sound. They would continue to search, of course. But, hell, if she'd caught a good current, she might just end up on Vancouver Island. Canadian turf. And wouldn't *that* be a nightmare of paperwork.

As a police officer, Max understood where they were coming from. He didn't like it, but he got it.

As a man, it tore him to shreds.

It was Wednesday afternoon, and still no sign of Evie. His head pounded from stress and lack of sleep, but no amount of urging from the authorities or anyone at Mayhem could get him to take more than a short break to eat or grab some coffee.

He hadn't shaved since Monday morning and had only taken time to eat to keep his strength up. He looked like shit and didn't care. Only Edmunds looked as bad, if not worse.

Max wouldn't have thought the old guy had it in him, but Edmunds proved a strong and tenacious partner. He appeared decidedly unbutlerish in damp jeans and a sweatshirt, his gray hair uncombed, his face haggard. His eyes were bloodshot, and deep circles under them made it look as though he'd gone a nasty three rounds, and lost.

Since the boat was being refueled, Max poured another mug of coffee and meandered over to the kitchen window, letting his tired mind have its way. He gazed through the glass and thought of his mother. Had she stood musing out this window in her short stay at Mayhem? She'd only lived a few months after coming here. Had she found solace in the tall trees and quiet of the place?

Reaching into his pocket, he found the coin she'd given him and gripped it tightly in his hand.

Another sip of coffee. Regrets. Yeah, he had 'em, in spades. Maybe he shouldn't have listened to his father, shouldn't have let his parents' divorce cleave his relationship with his mother. He hadn't seen it back then, but he saw it now. He'd been a fool—a young, headstrong, know-it-all fool.

Turning his back to the window, he let the buttery sunshine warm his shoulders, but his thoughts remained as dark and cold as the sea that encircled the island.

"I'm sorry you feel that way, Maxfield," his mother had said the day before her marriage to Heyworth. "It's just going to be a small civil ceremony. I do wish you'd come."

He'd been nearly nineteen, filled with the self-righteous arrogance of youth and the pernicious delusions his father had poisoned his brain with since he'd been a kid. At that age, his world had been black and white and right and wrong—all absolutes, no shades of gray, no subtleties, and no room for forgiveness or compassion.

"I wouldn't breathe the same air as that son of a

bitch," he'd snapped, and saw the hurt in his mother's eyes. But she hadn't argued with him.

"Perhaps when you're older," she'd said softly. "When you know a little more of the world and men and women, you'll forgive yourself for what you just said." She paused for a moment, lowering her eyes. "You idolize your father, Maxfield, and there's nothing wrong with that. He is a good man, a very good man. But idolizing him as you have, it's been difficult for you to see that he and I . . . well, the way he has treated me over the years has put some stress on our relationship."

"What are you talking about?" he'd ranted. "He takes care of you, doesn't he? Pays for everything? Nice house, good cars. He's never cheated on you, never raised a hand to you!"

She bit her lip and continued to avoid eye contact with him. "I can only tell you my side, Maxfield. If you want to know your father's side, you'll have to ask him, though I doubt he'll be honest with you. Now, before you go off half cocked," she rushed on, forestalling another accusation on his part, "I had already planned on leaving your father. Thomas simply gave me a reason to speed up the process. These last few years have taken a lot out of me, and I'm tired, Maxfield. I'm very tired. Thomas lives on an island. It's peaceful, and I need that. He understands me in a way your father . . . well, never mind. It sounds too clichéd, even to my ears. Even though it's the truth."

She had looked at him meaningfully, but at the time, he'd missed it. His anger and selfishness blocked her real message, and he missed it completely.

"But what about Frankie and me and Dad?" he'd spat out. "What's going to happen to us?"

He realized now just how childish that had sounded, but his mother hadn't chastised him for it. Instead, she smiled wearily and said, "It's no use discussing it further, Maxfield. What happens to you is up to you. I am hoping that, someday, you'll meet someone, and she will be unlike any other. She'll be special, and you'll see it. You'll know you can be happy with her. But because of your father's influence and your own stubbornness, I don't think it will happen for you for a long time yet, but it will. Eventually, when your father's poison has worn off . . ."

He'd simply glared at her.

"That's my fault, I suppose." She'd set her teacup on the table and folded her hands in front of her. "I should have left him years ago, taken you and Francine with me, rather than let his attitudes become your own."

Looking into his eyes, she said, "You don't respect women, Maxfield. Oh, you're not mean. You would never hurt a woman or mistreat her, but you've learned from your father that women are interchangeable, like auto parts or ink cartridges. Use one up, change it for another. Someday, dear, you'll discover women are not ink cartridges. And when you do, I hope you'll think back to this moment and remember my hopes for you. And remember, too, how much I loved you."

He'd stormed out, and she married Thomas Heyworth, and eight months later she died.

And she'd been right. Close to sixteen years had passed, and he came to realize just how right she'd been.

. . . you'll meet someone, and she will be unlike any other.

"Evie." Closing his eyes, he whispered, "Where are you? Come back to me."

With his fingers wrapped around his mug of coffee, he wandered through the manor, letting the kinks out, while Nate and Edmunds finished refueling Heyworth's yacht. As he entered the library, Lorna raised her head and looked at him with hope in her worried eyes. But it faded when she realized he had no news.

Madame Grovda sat in a large chair near the fireplace, her eyes closed, her hands crossed over her ample belly.

Setting his coffee on one of the mahogany tables, he walked over to her. "Can you find her?" he demanded.

Keeping her eyes closed, she whispered, "Poor man. Poor, poor man—"

"Can you find her?" he repeated. "If you can, now would be a real good time."

She shook her head, setting her earrings swinging. "I have tried, but nothing." Her eyes still closed, she put a hand to her throat. "I see the water, black, deep, and hear the screams of the wind—"

"I don't need a weather report," he barked. "I need Evie!"

"*Pozhalujsta*. Please. Have the patience."

He rubbed his tired eyes with the back of his hand. "I'm sorry. I'm . . . sorry."

"I feel sand," she murmured. "Hard sand, so? Yes? Under my fingers. But she is, eh, lost. Very lost. Tired, hungry. . . ."

"Lost? Like on an island? Can you tell which one?" His anxious heart began to build speed, his throat went dry.

Madame Grovda shook her head as deep furrows lined her brow. "*Nyet.*" Her round face flushed, her eyes moistened. "That is all that comes to me."

He nodded. "We're going back out in a few minutes. We'll be gone until dark, unless we find—"

Behind him there was a sound. The library door had slowly creaked open. Lorna made a choking noise and Madame Grovda squealed. Max turned . . .

In the middle of the doorway stood an exhausted-looking, sand-encrusted, wet, bedraggled Evie Randall, and a giant sand flea with fuzzy banana ears.

"Guess what?" she rasped. "Llamas can swim."

Before she could move, he was there, his arms around her, pulling her into the room, into his embrace. She let her body go limp against him and tried not to think about the first emotion that had struck her when she'd seen him standing there.

He was unshaven and his hair was a mess. If she hadn't felt like a battered piece of driftwood, she would have thought he looked ruggedly hot.

"Oh, God, Evie," he muttered against her hair. "Thank God. I thought I'd lost you. I thought . . ."

He shoved her to an arm's length and his eyes raked her, head to toe. "How did you . . . where have you . . . are you all right?" His voice cracked over the words as though he was having trouble containing his emotions.

She looked up into his hazel eyes and placed her trembling fingers on his cheek. "You made it," she whispered, fighting the sharp pain she felt in her throat. "I knew you would."

He led her to the nearest chair, sat her down, and sent Lorna scurrying to the kitchen for some water. Madame Grovda patted her hand, asking if there was anything she could do.

Max kneeled at her feet, touching her face, her arms, her thighs, her shoulders. "Are you positive you're all right? You're a real mess."

"Well," she sighed wearily, "I would have taken a bath on the boat but I preferred to wash up on shore."

He laughed at that, showing his straight white teeth. He really did have a stunning smile and sexy laugh, and she was grateful to be able to witness both again.

Lorna returned with the water, then excused herself to go get Edmunds and Dabney.

"Do they know who did it?" Evie asked, clutching the water tumbler between her hands. It was déjà vu all over again.

He shook his head. "We'll talk about that later. First, we need to take you to the hospital."

"No!" she choked, then let her body relax into the chair. "No hospital. I didn't drown and I'm not injured. Just bone-tired and filthy and hungry. But I'll tell you, these life-threatening mishaps are really beginning to *piss me off*."

Max grinned at her as if she'd just told the world's cutest story. God, it was good to see his face. She couldn't stop staring at him. She liked everything about the way he looked . . . and more.

"What day is it?"

"Wednesday," he said.

"Wednesday. That means we only have ten days left to find the other clues."

"We'll worry about that after you've had some rest."

Turning her head, she saw Fernando kushed down in the middle of the library. "Would somebody please bring some water for my llama?"

"I'll take care of it," Max assured her as he reached into his pocket and pulled out a cell phone. "I need to notify the Harbor Patrol that you've been found."

"Actually, I found myself."

He grinned again. "Actually, you did, Scout."

While Max called and then went to get water, Madame Grovda inched nearer.

"I am so pleased, so pleased," she all but sobbed.

Before Evie could reassure the psychic she was fine, the library doors burst open again.

"Evangeline?"

Edmunds. Pale as snow, looking a hundred years old, he rushed through the doors and into the room, his eyes wide with obvious exhaustion and relief.

Kneeling at her feet, he leaned forward and gathered her into his arms in a hard embrace.

"Thank God," he choked, his spent voice barely audible. "Oh, my child. My dear, dear child. How frightened we were when we couldn't find you."

He pulled back and looked at her, as though to reassure himself that she was there in the flesh, and she looked at him.

When on earth had Edmunds grown old? For years he had been her friend and confidant, her chauffeur and occasional rainy day playmate. He'd attended tea parties with her dolls and pushed her on the swing that hung from the ancient maple tree behind the house. He had always been so energetic and vital, so much younger than his years.

But today every line in his face seemed etched that much deeper. His eyes, always so alert and intelligent, appeared faded. His spine and shoulders, normally erect and squared, were bent.

He was no longer the Edmunds who had greeted her at the door fifteen years ago, a strawberry lemonade in his hand and a sparkle in his eye. Time had passed, had worn him away, and she simply hadn't noticed.

Evie put her hand on his cool cheek. Her eyes filled with tears and she did nothing to wipe them away.

"Hello, darling," she whispered. "Thank you for worrying about me, but I guess I'm made of pretty stern stuff."

He blinked at that, and his smile wavered for a fraction of a second. Then he said, "Can I get you something to eat, my dear? You must be half starved."

"In a minute," she replied. "I just want to sit and enjoy your company. For a while, there, I was worried I'd never be able to do that again."

Max returned then and placed a big bucket of water in front of Fernando, who began to drink greedily. Next to the water bucket, he set a large bowl of oats.

"The search has been called off," he said, "but the police are going to continue the investigation. Detective McKennitt wants to talk to you, but he's stuck on something in Seattle and may not be able to get back up here until tomorrow."

Edmunds said, "Where have you been, Evangeline? We searched the island and found no trace of you."

"Fernando must either have known which direction our island was or we lucked out," she said wearily. "When I woke up, we were in a kind of cave behind a jumble of rocks and driftwood, which may be why you didn't find us. I kept phasing in and out of sleep, so I don't remember hearing anybody or anything."

"Evie," Max said, "when we were hit, did you see any markings on the boat? Did you get a glimpse of the pilot? Anything?"

"I heard the engine," she murmured. "Heard you blast the horn. Then, this huge bow just appeared out of the fog. I jumped back, yanking Fernando with me. The runabout split in half and we went into the water."

She took another sip from the tumbler. "It didn't have any lights on, and I didn't see any markings." She shook her head as chills of fear overtook her once again. "It all happened so fast."

"So that overgrown dust bunny saved your life?" Max said, glancing back at Fernando.

"We sort of saved each other," she corrected him. "Oh, and one more thing."

"Yeah?"

"As I was fading in and out of consciousness, it came to me."

"What came to you?"

"It," she said. "The location of Clue Number Four. It's actually quite brilliant."

Max narrowed his eyes and flattened his lips. "I must say I'm impressed," he said dryly. "Despite a third attempt on your life, you swim to safety during a storm. Then you go comatose for several hours, yet, in your lucid moments, you have the wherewithal to decipher an ambiguous clue penned by a lunatic which may or may not lead to millions of dollars and the identity of a murderer." He took a breath. "Tell me, while you were comatose in that cave, did you happen to hit on the solution to the unified field theory?"

She scowled at him, then said, "You want to know where the clue is, or not?"

"Okay, Scout," he said, a glint of mischief in his eye. "Shoot. Where is Clue Number Four?"

She leaned back in the chair and took another drink of water. As Edmunds wrapped a warm blanket around her shoulders, she set the tumbler on the table next to her, closed her sore eyes and said, "Get ready for a *big* shock, Detective. Unless I miss my guess, Clue Number Four is hidden somewhere . . . in your house."

Chapter 16

Dear Diary:

My class went on a field trip today to Olympia, the capitol of Washington. We saw where they make the laws, and the governor's house, which is truly beautiful! Edmunds came on the trip as a chaperone and he was in charge of me, Lindsay, Sarah, Amanda, Barbara, and Theresa. We sat on the steps and ate sack lunches. Amanda accidentally spilled Cream Soda all over Edmunds' suit, but he didn't get angry at all. Edmunds is wonderful!

Evangeline—age 12

Even though his brain was on fire with the possibility that Thomas Heyworth had somehow hidden something inside his own home, Max was skeptical as to how the old guy might have managed it. He was a cop, he had a security system, a good one. It

seemed unlikely there'd been any way in hell someone could have clandestinely planted anything of
any kind inside his house. Yet Evie felt convinced,
and so far she'd been right about nearly everything.

But Max was stuck with the others who'd been
instructed not to leave the area while the police
investigated—and either cleared or implicated—one
of the guests or staff of Mayhem Manor.

Until the collision that had nearly drowned both
Evie and him, Max had been forced to take a minor
role in the investigation of Thomas Heyworth's
death, but with this newest threat to Evie's life, he
felt that reading official reports was no longer good
enough. It was time to get his hands dirty.

He checked his notes, then went to the kitchen
where Mrs. Stanley was busy preparing Saturday's
dinner. The room was filled with the fragrant scent
of spices and roasting meat. His stomach began to
growl.

"Mrs. Stanley?" She nodded and continued to
peel potatoes as he looked on. The cook was a slender woman in her mid-fifties. Her curly gray hair
had been pulled away from her face into a loose
knot at her nape. She had probably been a knockout
in her youth and was still a fine-looking woman,
with clear skin and bright gray eyes. "Do you mind
if I ask you some questions?"

She sent him a quick look. "Already told the police everything I know."

"Then you won't mind simply repeating what
you said to them." He gave her his most charming
grin. "It won't take long."

Forming her mouth into a long frown, she said,

"Fine. So long as it don't interfere with my work."

"Where's Mr. Stanley?"

Her eyes darted for a second to the back door, then she said, "Around someplace."

Max picked up a bite-sized carrot stick from a tray on the counter and popped it into his mouth. She scowled at him and set the tray out of his reach.

"How long did you work for Mr. Heyworth?"

A potato in one hand, peeler in the other, her work never slowed as she said, "Close to eleven years."

"How did you feel about him?"

She shrugged as she plopped the naked potato in a pot of water. Picking up another, she began attacking its peel. "Meat and potatoes man," she said. "Nothing fancy. Chocolate cake, plain. Suited me fine."

"Did you ever overhear anybody threaten to kill him? Did he ever argue with anyone that you can recall?"

She dropped the peeled potato into the pot and grabbed another. "Argued with everybody."

"What about?"

"Everything."

Well, this was a lot of help. "Tell me about the rest of the people at Mayhem."

Never looking up from her potato peeler, she said, "Edmunds, he's the sandwich sort, corned beef on rye, pickle on the side, glass of milk. My Earl, he's stew and dumplings. Lots of gravy." Tossing the potato into the pot, she reached for another. "Miss Whitney, she's chicken and rice, you see. Delicate, the tea and petit fours type."

"And Miss Randall?"

"Evie?" Another quick glance at the back door, then, "I'd, uh, I'd say she's more of a smorgasbord."

Max fought hard to suppress the image of Evie's naked body stretched out on a linen tablecloth for him to sample.

Swallowing, he said, "Smorgasbord?"

The cook raised her shoulder in a shrug. "None too picky. Little of this, little of that. Variety, see? Takes what she likes, ignores the rest."

"Can you think of any reason somebody would want to kill her?"

"Nope."

Plop, in went another naked potato.

"When Heyworth was killed, were you on the island?"

"Nope. In town. Groceries."

"What about Tuesday night?"

"Home. Watching the TV with Earl."

"What do you think of Felix Barlow?"

She reacted with several rapid blinks, then said, "That tall, skinny lawyer? I figure him for champagne and watercress sandwiches. Elegant. Real expensive."

"Do you have any idea who might have killed Heyworth, or why?"

She quickly denuded the last spud then tossed it into the pot, added some salt, set the kettle on the stove and turned on the burner. "Can't say I ever thought much about it."

"Your employer was murdered right here in the house, somebody tried to kill Evie in the barn and in a boat on the way to the island, and you haven't given any of this much thought?"

"Told the police all I know," she said, turning to the sink to wash her hands. "It's their job to think about it, not mine."

Flipping his notebook closed, he said, "Thanks for your time." As he turned to go, he said, "Mrs. Stanley?"

She looked up from the sink.

"How do you figure me?"

Narrowing one eye on him, she said, "Game hen. Plump, juicy. Breasts and thighs. All the trimmings. That'd be my guess."

"Evangeline?"

"Over here," she said, guiding Edmunds with her voice through the tall racks of dusty bottles in the wine cellar.

As he came around the last rack to where she stood, he said, "Is there something I can help you find, my dear?"

Evie smiled at the butler, then stared at the wine rack in front of her. Picking up a bottle, she held it in her arms, as one might cradle an infant.

"I just wanted something nice for after dinner," she explained. "This sherry ought to do it. Were you looking for me?"

"Detective McKennitt called to say we are all free to leave the island in the morning if we wish."

"They didn't find *anything*?" Disappointment furrowed her brow. "This is all so incredibly frustrating." She let go a long slow sigh. "I have to admit, though, I can't imagine anybody here on the island wanting to kill me, nor do I think any of us murdered Thomas. But there must be *some* kind of evidence *somewhere* that points to *somebody*."

She leaned against the cream plaster wall and lifted a brow. Clutching the bottle a little closer to her bosom, she said thoughtfully, "Edmunds, you know I've always trusted your opinion."

"Thank you, my dear." He frowned. "They say a burden shared is a burden eased, so, if that remark is a prelude to an emotional liberation of some kind, please feel free."

The man was such a darling. Since the day she arrived at Mayhem, he'd made sure she was always cared for, always comfortable, never wanting for anything. He would have been like a second father to her, had she ever known the true identity of her first one, that is.

She turned and walked to the large oval mirror hanging on the wall at the end of the row. Reaching up, she smoothed away the thin film of dust to see her own reflection in the thick glass. Meeting the butler's gaze in the mirror, she said, "May I ask you a question? It's about my mother."

Though he didn't react overtly, there was a subtle shift in his demeanor. He didn't blink or clear his throat. He didn't move at all, but his normally rosy cheeks seemed to pale.

"I believe I've told you all I know of her, Evangeline," he said. "However, I'll be happy to help in any way I can."

Turning to face him, she set the bottle of sherry on the table next to the mirror then looked into Edmunds's eyes.

"How well did you know her?"

"What do you mean?"

"Well, you were here when she worked at Mayhem."

"Yes."

Evie crossed her arms over her stomach. "Did you get to know her at all?"

He made a slight shrug. "Very little. I recall she was beautiful, young, headstrong. She stayed on the island for a time working as a maid, then became restless to leave. One day, she simply flew away, I suppose you'd say. Mayhem never shone quite so brightly after that—until you came here, my dear."

Evie turned again to the mirror, her own reflection and Edmunds's behind her, watery images in the ancient glass.

"I have so many questions," she said. "What kind of relationship did my mother have with Thomas? She never spoke of him or her time here at Mayhem, yet he came for me after she died. Whenever I tried to broach the subject with Thomas, he put me off with some excuse or other."

Edmunds took a step toward her. "Evangeline," he said, his voice low and solemn. "The year before you came here, Mr. Heyworth's only wife had died—"

"Max's mother."

"Yes. He loved her deeply, I believe. After her death, I sensed in him a great change, as though he were sorry he'd waited so long to wed. When he brought you back with him, I was quite surprised. I was not aware Maggie had . . . a child." He shrugged. "I was glad he'd brought you, though, since he was not usually a man given to public displays of altruism."

Evie laughed a little at that. "No, he wasn't. You know," she said, taking a deep breath, "for a long time I thought he was my real father. Since he was an unmarried, middle-aged man, I figured he must have been my real father, otherwise, they wouldn't have let him have me."

The butler cleared his throat and advanced another half step. "You were earmarked for foster care, but Mr. Heyworth was an extremely persuasive man."

"You mean, he bought somebody off."

"Exactly. You were eleven, in all likelihood too old for anyone to adopt you, give you the kind of home you needed. An alternative was the foster care system, which Mr. Heyworth denounced, as he felt you would have been shuffled from one place to another. You'd had eleven years of that already. He didn't want that for you, and since he knew he would never be allowed to adopt you outright, he saw to it that your paperwork, er, became lost in the system, so to speak."

Evie's eyes widened. "Why that scoundrel!"

The lines around his eyes deeply creased with worry, Edmunds said, "Have you been unhappy at Mayhem, Evangeline? Was it a mistake for Mr. Heyworth to bring you here?"

"Oh, no," she said quickly, placing her hand on his arm. "God, no. I've been insanely happy with Thomas and with you, and of course the llamas. I adore you all. Living on the island has been like a fairy tale."

Edmunds shifted his gaze away for a moment, then, "If I may say it, you've grown from a compassionate, shy little girl into an exceedingly lovely young woman, yet there exists a dearth of suitors at your door which I do not comprehend. Perhaps an island isn't the best place for a beautiful and intelligent young lady who is seeking a marriageable gentleman."

Evie picked up the bottle of sherry. Focusing on the label, she said, "I have my own house and live in town during the school year. And I have friends, and—"

"Detective Galloway seems quite taken with you."

She lifted her head and locked gazes with him. "He does? Do you think so? Did he say something? Do you like him? I used to dislike him . . . well, hate him, but lately, I've . . . oh, damn. I'm babbling, aren't I?" Her cheeks heated in embarrassment at her girlish silliness.

"He does. I do. He has not. I do. I know. And yes, you are." He winked at her and tapped her on the tip of her nose with his finger as he had all those years ago when she'd first come to Heyworth Island. Leaning forward, he whispered, "Ain't love grand?"

Her heart skidded to a stop. "Who said anything about love?"

"Nobody," he replied, straightening his shoulders. "But I imagine the topic will come up soon enough, of its own accord."

Evie felt her cheeks warm as chills skittered down her arms. If falling in love made you feel like you were on the verge of a nervous breakdown all the time, then she was definitely headed in that direction.

                              *   *   *

The white dress Evie chose to wear to dinner was
soft and silky, and hugged her body without being
obvious. She wore her hair down around her shoulders because she figured *he'd* like it like that. Besides, the feel of it against her neck made her feel
sexy.

When she entered the dining room, Max was in
the corner talking to Edmunds. The two men
stopped and turned toward her. Edmunds smiled
and she scrunched her nose at him. He gave a little
wave and headed into the kitchen.

As for Max, he seemed to freeze in place. His
gaze raked her from head to toe, and she was certain
by the flush of his cheek, his blood pressure had
gone up a notch or two. His eyes took on a smoky
quality.

He stood there a moment longer, then slowly
crossed the room to her. Without saying a word, he
took her arm and escorted her around the corner
and into the office, where he closed the door firmly
behind them.

Turning, he took her by the shoulders and pushed
her against the closed door.

"Nice dress," he murmured, letting his eyes de-
vour every inch of her. "If I said you had a luscious
body, would you hold it against me?"

He didn't say anything else, just stared into her
eyes. She watched as the muscle in his jaw worked.

"I suppose that's your idea of a good pickup
line?"

He glared down at her, his eyes hot with interest.

Leaning forward, he put his hands on either side of her head. His hard chest teased her suddenly sensitive breasts. "It's no line, Evie—"

With that, pressing her against the door, he took her mouth, thrusting his tongue deep.

She made a soft crying sound at the back of her throat as she moved her hands up his chest and around his neck. His hands moved down, to glide over her sides, over her breasts, down the curve of her hips until his splayed fingers gripped her bottom. Pleasure pooled deep inside her as he began to slowly rub himself against her.

He broke the kiss, turned his head and slanted another kiss over her mouth, stealing her breath way. Through the fabric of her soft dress, he gripped the globes of her bottom, edging his fingers underneath, closer to her center.

She pushed him away. "Somebody's going to come—"

"Damned straight," he growled as he lifted her skirt and slipped his hand into her panties. Without deciding to, she simply eased her legs apart to give him better access.

His gently probing finger found its mark. She cried out against his open mouth as heat and tension and desire swirled through her body like ripples on a warm pond. Her nerves tightened, her knees went weak.

With his thumb, he moved the fabric of her panties aside until his finger was on her again. He found his mark, gently rubbing until she became slick, until her body felt like it was locked in a vise. She couldn't move. All she could do was stand there while he made her feel so good. . . .

Max, she tried to say, only the sound never formed. Her lips moved but she was too paralyzed with pleasure to speak.

He slid the shoulder of her dress down, taking with it her bra strap, leaving her breast nearly bare. Instantly, his mouth was on her flesh, kissing the rounded top of her breast, urging the fabric to fall away until her nipple popped free. In a heartbeat he was on it.

Her body felt like a living flame. She panted, tried to catch a breath, but his tongue on her nipple, his finger moving, circling, all combined to drive her insane with pleasure.

"Max . . . oh, God, Max . . ." Her neck arched and she closed her eyes, letting the sensations overtake her.

"Come for me, baby," he rasped. "Let it happen, Evie. Come against my hand."

With that, he slid his finger inside her and she clamped around him, nearly delirious with the need for release. Her back arched and she thrust her hips against his palm.

"That's it, Evie. A little more. A little more. God, you are so hot."

He leaned down and softly bit her nipple, and pleasure shot through her, sending her over the edge. Her climax burst hard, pulsing through her body as wave after wave of sensation rushed over her skin, through her muscles, clenching and releasing her insides until she thought she would die from the pleasure.

"Oh, God . . . oh, Max," she sighed as her hips writhed against his hand.

Barely able to breathe, she leaned against him for support, hanging on until her head stopped spinning.

Reason eased its way into her brain, and she realized Max was putting her panties back in order and gently lowering her leg. He tucked her breast into her bra and straightened her bodice. Her back was flat against the office door and he was still pressed snuggly against her.

When her breathing had steadied, he lifted his hands and cradled her face in his warm palms. Then he kissed her as though he were kissing a shy, timid girl. His lips were tender as he moved them over hers. He made no demands, just held her in place while he soothed her hot mouth with his gentle kiss.

When he pulled away, she sighed. "Did that just happen?"

He gazed down at her for a moment, then whispered, "The look on your face when you came was . . . Jesus, Evie. You're the most beautiful woman I have ever seen."

"D-Don't you want to . . . I mean, what was in this for you?"

He smiled into her eyes, and her knees went so weak, she thought she'd drop right to the floor.

"More than I bargained for, I think," he said sardonically. "Definitely more than I deserve."

"Tell me what you mean," she said quickly, then frowned. He'd run hot and cold since she'd met him, a nice guy one minute, distant and cynical the next. His remark opened the door and, by God, she was going to walk through it.

"Who are you, Max? Who are you really?"

His lips flattened. "I'm the man who just made you come."

"That's a knee-jerk response," she accused. "With the emphasis on jerk. It's a defense. Maybe even a decoy. You're smart and funny. You carve pretty things for your mom. You get choked up at an old folk's home, and you're often heroic. You're pushy and controlling and sullen and snappish, and you despise somebody I loved without even considering you might be wrong about him. How can you be all those things, all those people, Max? Or do you just wear a variety of emotional masks so you can keep others from seeing who you really are?"

"Don't try to psychoanalyze me, Evie," he growled. "I'm exactly who I appear to be. I'm selfish and self-involved. Me first. *Always*." He glared down into her eyes, and she almost believed him. If she were smart, she thought, she would.

She laughed, but there was no humor in it. "It's funny," she said. "I've always been the one to shy away from relationships, afraid of letting anybody too close. And now that I'm finally coming to terms with it, when I might welcome it, I find I'm attracted to a man like you, a man who doesn't want what I'm offering."

"Depends on what you're offering." His voice was gruff, his eyes dark, smoky green, his lids sleepy.

She gazed up at him and felt her heart tear into little shreds.

He cocked his head to one side. "Have you had your say, or is there more?"

If only you knew . . .

She was falling in love beyond anything she had ever imagined, and she wanted to tell him so. Maybe if he knew how she felt, he'd decide she was worth the risk of opening up to her.

And maybe not. She didn't think she could bear to see that kind of rejection in his eyes. It would hurt so much, and the tiny spark of love she felt for him right now would be doused—and she did not want it doused. She wanted it to grow and warm her whether he knew it existed or not.

So she didn't say a word.

Chapter 17

Dear Diary:

I got my period today! My first one! Sarah and Lindsay already got theirs and they said it was very messy and not quite what they expected, but I didn't think it was so bad. I asked Mrs. Robely, the cook, how many periods I would ever have, and she looked at me like she was really tired, and said I would have one every darned month for the next forty years (except she didn't say darned). That is so cool! I can hardly wait for my next one!

Evangeline—age 12

Max pursed his lips. "We, uh, we need to go in to dinner."

Evie had grown quiet. She'd straightened her clothes and stood now with her back to the door while she concentrated on not looking at him.

She wanted to know who he was, who he really was. He knew he could tell her, and then she'd leave him alone. That *was* what he wanted, wasn't it?

Yeah. Maybe. Maybe not.

He reached for her and brushed a stray lock of hair from her face. What in the hell did you say to a woman you just brought to orgasm up against a door only a few feet away from a room full of people searching for a murderer? A woman you'd known less than two weeks who had already made inroads to your soul others hadn't been able to make in a lifetime? A woman who challenged you on every level, including being unwilling to accept your bullshit?

If this were any other woman, she never would have had a chance to confront him. He'd have been half out of his clothes by now and had her naked and flat on her back on the desk. End of conversation.

He hadn't intended to haul her off into a dark place, shove her up against a door, lift her skirt, and engage in heated sexual foreplay only moments before dinner. He liked to think he had a little more going for him than that.

But when she'd walked into the dining room and he set eyes on her, something inside him had shattered into a million pieces, stopping his heart, piercing his throat so he couldn't breathe, tearing at his muscles until they ceased to function—unless it was to put his hands on her.

And when he had finally touched her, some frozen thing had melted inside him, some iron barrier turned to dust.

Was it conceivable he could simply shove aside his

father's toxic thoughts and replace them with purity and truth? Was it possible to fall in love in a breath and a heartbeat? Or had he been falling for her all along?

He gazed down at her. Evie, with her big blue eyes and her tender heart, her smelly llamas and indomitable spirit, her tears for old people she didn't even know. He'd often heard that the love of a good woman could change a man. His mother had been a good woman, but his father had changed not at all. Maybe that said something about his father; he hoped it said more about him.

Perhaps the love of a good woman could change a man, if that man wanted to change.

A rap on the door startled him.

"Dinner is served." Edmunds? He knew they were in there? Jesus, he'd never intended to embarrass her like this.

She closed her eyes. "Great. Damn." Running her fingers through her hair, she gave a little sigh. "Well, so much for open communication. Let me know if you ever—"

"Evie, listen, I . . ."

The words were on the tip of his tongue, but courage failed him just as he was about to speak.

Then he remembered Madam Grovda and her admission that she was a lousy psychic, that she had wanted to find her former lover's killer but failed. He remembered the tears in her eyes, and the pain, at having to confess that to a stranger.

"Evie," he said, "I, uh, I think we should talk later. Maybe I can explain a few things, and maybe you can tell me a little more about Heyworth. I'm not saying I'll agree with you that he was a great guy, but, uh, I'll listen. You know, if you want to tell me."

"Oh, Max," she whispered. "Would you?"

He gave a sharp nod. "After dinner. We can, uh, you know, just talk."

She smiled up at him. "We'd better go now before Edmunds breaks the door down."

"I'll go first," he said. "You can come when you're ready."

Without missing a beat, she reached up and curled her fingers around the knot of his tie.

"Apparently," she murmured, her mouth curved into a flirty smile, "I can come even when I'm not."

". . . and finally, keep in mind," Felix Barlow announced, as though everyone at the table was not already acutely aware what day it was, "you have until midnight seven days from now to capture the final clue, or Mr. Heyworth's estate, in its entirety, will be forfeit. Any questions?"

"I have one," Nate said. In an apparent attempt to look the part of the urbane poet, Detective Darling had somehow managed to find a velvet jacket and a blue silk ascot. Unfortunately, his build and rugged looks made him appear more like an undercover cop unsuccessfully trying to look like an urbane poet, but Max had to give him points for trying.

"According to the will," Nate said, leaning forward in his chair, "Heyworth claims he left no heirs. But what if he did? Would the winner still get the estate?"

"The question is moot, Mr. James," Barlow said politely, "as Mr. Heyworth left no heirs."

Nate pressed on. "But what if *there* . . . were an *heir*? Would the outcome be *fair*, I *dare* . . . uh, say?" He adjusted the ascot and flashed a grin at Lorna.

Max drowned his laugh in a giant gulp of water while Lorna sent him a smile dripping with adoration.

Barlow put his hands together and tented his fingers, a detached look on his face as he considered Nate's question.

"The original treasure hunt was based on Mr. Heyworth's belief that no heir existed. Should an heir be discovered, and be able to prove without question a blood relationship to the deceased, the terms of the hunt would become void, and the heir would undoubtedly be awarded the estate."

Next to Nate, Lorna looked thoughtful. "But how would a person prove they were related? Mr. Heyworth is dead, so—"

"Documentation," interrupted Barlow smoothly. "Certificate of birth, sworn affidavits, and most tenably, DNA testing."

"But how could anybody do that if Mr. Heyworth's dead?" she asked.

"To prove a relationship," he explained, clasping his hands in front of him on the table, "DNA samples must be collected from both parents. As his death was the result of a homicide, the authorities have no doubt maintained a sample of Mr. Heyworth's DNA. Anyone purporting to be an heir would have to provide a sample of his or her own

DNA, and a sample from the birth mother in question. Without the mother's DNA, too, the only definitive result would be that paternity could be ruled out."

"So," Max said, "with only the suspected father's DNA, you could prove he was *not* the father, but you could never prove that he was, without DNA from the kid's mother."

"Correct." Barlow shoved his dessert plate away and poured himself another goblet of wine. Lifting the glass to his lips, he said, "Edmunds tells me he and Madame Grovda are in possession of their third clue and will venture to the mainland tomorrow in search of the fourth."

At the end of the table, the Russian psychic examined Barlow as though she were trying to see him through an aquarium filled with darting fish. Finally, her eyes seemed to focus and she slurred, "This is so." Setting her empty wineglass on the table, she stood. "I go now to punch the straw."

"Hit the hay," Evie corrected.

"Da." With that, the woman wobbled her way out of the dining room and disappeared down the hallway that led to the stairs.

Nate stood and grabbed Lorna by the hand. "We have work to do. Good night."

Lorna's eyes brightened for a moment, then she softly said good night to all and followed the ersatz poet from the room.

Turning to the lawyer, Max said, "I'd like to have a word with you, Mr. Barlow. Are you staying the night?"

"No, no," he said with hearty enthusiasm. "Edmunds is waiting at the dock to take me back to the mainland. Much to do, much to do. I'm running late. Can this wait for another time?"

"It'll only take a few minutes," Max assured him.

Before either man could say anything else, Evie interrupted. "I should go. It's getting late and we have a big day tomorrow."

Barlow's brows lifted. "Are you on to your next clue, too?"

"Good night, gentlemen," she said, not answering Barlow's question.

As soon as Evie was gone, Max turned back to the lawyer. Without prelude he said, "Where were you the night Thomas Heyworth was killed?"

"Excuse me? Oh, well, I was at a fund-raiser, Detective." Barlow tossed down his napkin and rose from the table. "The police have my full statement."

"I know. I read it. Any witnesses?" Max swallowed a last gulp of wine, set down the empty goblet, and stood.

"About forty or fifty I should think."

"You own a boat, Mr. Barlow?"

The lawyer flattened his mouth. "Yes, as do hundreds of thousands of other people in the Puget Sound area."

"What kind of boat?"

"It's a Sea Ray Sundancer. Thirty-one foot."

"Yeah? Nice boat. Big. Expensive. What kind of horsepower you get on that? About three hundred?"

"Sounds about right. Not that speed matters. I use it mostly for fishing."

Max considered this. "Did you go fishing Tuesday night?"

Barlow's brows shot up. "See here, I—"

"Where were you, sir?"

The man sent Max a look of pure antagonism, then shrugged. "Dinner. With a friend."

"Male or female?"

"Female. A client. I can give you her name, but I beg you not to disturb her."

Max smiled. "Only if I have to."

Barlow whipped out a business card and wrote down the woman's name and address, then shoved the card across the white tablecloth to Max.

As he tucked the card into his breast pocket, Max said, "Where do you keep your boat docked, Mr. Barlow?"

The man made an elaborate gesture at his watch. "I *must* leave immediately or be late for a very important teleconference." Pushing back his chair, he turned to go.

"Sorry," Max said to Barlow's back. "I didn't mean to keep you so long. Just tell me where your boat is, and we'll be done."

Buttoning his jacket, Barlow faced Max once more.

"I loaned it to a friend for his honeymoon. A week ago. He'll be back in two weeks."

"A friend's honeymoon," repeated Max. "What an altruistic thing to do. Must be a very good friend."

"He is. Are we finished?"

"Just about. How did you meet Mr. Heyworth?"

Barlow eased his hands into his pants pockets. "He and my older brother were friends. I tagged along."

"Ever tag along to Heyworth Island when you were a kid?"

"On occasion."

"Where's your brother now?"

Barlow straightened his shoulders, then relaxed a little. "Killed," he said softly. He pursed his lips, as though being asked to remember his brother was uncomfortable. "He was barely nineteen, you see. I understand it was a land mine. Korea. A long time ago."

"I'm sorry," Max said. "The Forgotten War."

"Forgotten, Detective?" he said, his voice weary, edged with bitterness. "Not by my mother who mourned for him. Not by my father who wept over his ashes. And not by me, Detective." His shoulders rose and fell on a deep sigh. "Never by me."

In the darkened room, sitting cross-legged on her bed, Evie let her head fall back against the headboard. She could still feel Max's fingers against her flesh, pleasuring her, making her want so much more of it, so much more of him.

His hands and mouth on her body were one thing, but it had been the look in his eyes when he asked her if she wanted to talk that she couldn't forget. For the first time since she met him, he'd looked vulnerable, even shy. He'd stammered and been uncertain, but in the end had said the words. He was willing to talk. Better, he was willing to listen.

Such a simple thing, yet it had given her something valuable and very precious—it had given her hope.

But Barlow had droned on, and dinner had gone

late, and she returned to her room and waited, but so far Max hadn't knocked on her door.

Frustrated by that, she shoved the quilt off her legs and went to the enormous armoire that stood against the common wall her bedroom shared with the one next door—Max's, as it happened. Quickly undressing, she slipped into her nightgown.

By the light of the summer moon, she regarded the lovely armoire and her ghostly reflection in its oval mirror. The ancient piece of furniture was nearly as large as the wall itself, and so heavy it was immovable. Having been designed in a time before closets existed, it was wide and deep, able to hold a person's entire wardrobe.

As she began to close the door, a glint of something near the back caught her eye. With only the moon to guide her, she shoved the clothing aside and bent to investigate. A small piece of wood had apparently come unglued and fallen to the bottom of the armoire, revealing a brass knob about waist high.

Her fingers closed around it and she tugged. Immediately, the back panel of the armoire silently slid open.

Well, would you look at that. She straightened and stared at the narrow doorway, just wide enough for her to step through. Evie's heart began to beat wildly as excitement tightened her nerves.

When she first came to Mayhem Manor and Edmunds told her about the secret passageways, she'd tried to find as many as she could. Though she'd come across several, they all seemed to lead no farther than the adjoining room, which was not all that exciting for a little girl—no skeletons, no treasure, no ghosts—so after a while she lost interest and stopped searching.

But she wasn't a little girl anymore, and there was treasure, and then there was *treasure*. If her theory held true, this particular passageway would lead to . . .

A flashlight. Did she have a flashlight? No, dammit. Okay then, a candle?

Quickly, Evie stepped back and hunted through the desk drawer for a candle. *Ah, there.* She found a book of matches, struck one and touched it to the wick. The acrid smell of sulfur nipped her nose.

She held the candle in front of her, one hand cupped protectively around the flame. Stepping into the armoire, she peeked through the hole, holding the candle as far in as she could reach. Peering inside, she held her breath.

The passage was narrow, made of wood and brick. It seemed to follow the line of her bedroom wall for as far as she could see. Beyond the reach of her candle flame, all was blackness.

The temptation was too great. She'd seen all those movies where the nightgown-clad heroine was lured into a secret passage and then set upon by the villain or ghosts or killer birds or something. But this was different. She wasn't going to go more than a few feet.

Gingerly, she stepped through the panel and into the secret passage. *Nancy Drew would be so proud.*

Instantly, the panel closed behind her.

She turned, thrusting her hand toward the opening, trying to stop the door from shutting, but her movements were too quick. The flame on her candle flickered and danced and sputtered and died, leaving her in utter darkness.

"No!" she cried. "Damn it, I *hate* it when that happens!"

Reaching out, she slammed her palm on the wood. She felt around the edges for the knob to reopen it, but found nothing. Doubling her fist, she pounded on the panel.

Options . . . options . . . options . . . Well, she could stand there and pound on the panel until somebody heard her, came into the room, figured out what had happened and let her out, but that could take all night, maybe longer.

She let the candle fall to the floor as she placed her open hands on the tunnel wall. The air in the passage was warm and stale, and she figured if she didn't get out of there soon, she might suffocate.

Moving slowly to her right, she shuffled along the narrow corridor until she reached another wall. She felt around in the dark for a knob or a loose board, something that would trigger the mechanism that opened the panel to the adjoining room, but her fingertips were met only with smooth wood.

"Max!" she yelled. "Max! Help!"

Doubling both fists, she pounded on the wood and brick, but the thick walls seemed to absorb her yells, and she began to worry the tunnel was soundproof. She tried not to panic, but the air seemed to be getting awfully thin.

"Max? Help me!"

She pressed her palms against the wall, feeling her way in the darkness. The wood was rough under her fingertips, but nothing she touched felt like any kind of knob or handle, nothing that would open a secret door.

Panting, her heart frantic in her chest, she doubled her fists again and pounded, screaming her head off. Then one of her punches did something. A panel slid open and she fell through, right into Max's waiting arms.

Chapter 18

Dear Diary:

We learned about sex at school today. How gross!
It's disgusting! They say that's the only way people
can get babies, and that it is just how life is formed,
but still! I guess I'm never going to have a baby because I will never, ever, ever, never, ever do that with
a boy! Yuck!!!

Evangeline—age 12

"What did you do with the gun?"

"Right here." Sam Ziwicki produced the Smith
& Wesson .357 Revolver that had once belonged to
the late, highly unlamented T. E. Heyworth. "I'd
like to keep it, if it's all the same to you. Thanks for
the memory, and all that."

"Give it to me. Is it loaded?"

Sam grinned as he handed over the gun. His customer was so testy tonight.

"I only spent a few bullets. Waste not, want not, my grandma always said. She lived through the Depression, you know, and they all say that."

"Where's the boat?"

Talk about a one-track mind, Ziwicki thought. Christ, lighten up. "It's all snuggled safe inside a very out-of-the-way boathouse over on Whidbey, just like we discussed."

There was a pause, then, "Was there any damage to the hull?"

"Yeah, the bow got smashed up a little. After things simmer down, you can get it fixed."

No response.

Since he'd gotten out of the army a few years back, he had done a lot of custom work for this guy, but he had frankly never enjoyed it. The pay was healthy, and it sure put the sharpshooting skills he'd picked up in the service to good use. Highly decorated, that was him. After his mother had died, her sister had raised him; his aunt had all his medals tucked away in a drawer somewhere.

She was real proud of him, too. Showed them off to all her old crony friends whenever the spirit moved her, even though she never let on it was still how he made his living. She told them he was a successful entrepreneur, and sort of left it at that. Yeah, popping people off was pretty lucrative, all right.

"I'm not happy with you, Sam."

Uh-oh. Pissed off again? Some people were just so friggin' hard to please.

"Why not?" he protested. "I done the jobs. Hey-worth's dead, ain't he?"

"But you failed to eliminate that annoying poet."

Sam shook his head. "Now, see. I don't know what happened there, because I had the guy in my sights and I just do not see how I could have missed."

"The fact that he's alive and well and showed up for Heyworth's idiotic game proves you were sadly mistaken."

With a shrug, Sam said, "We all got our off days, you know? Now, the thing at the tavern went down bad, that's true. But I finally got her with the boat. She's—"

"Alive."

Sam's brows shot up. "No shit," he drawled as he casually unwrapped a stick of gum and folded it into his mouth. Spearmint, his favorite.

"No shit. Honestly, I can't afford any further screwups. I have so many loose ends to tie, then move on before the cops begin to probe too deeply. Your incompetence has added to my stress, Sam, not to mention putting me in jeopardy."

"Hey," he laughed. "That's my aunt's favorite show. 'I'd like Potent Potables for five hundred, Alex.'"

Sam chewed his gum, letting its minty sweetness tickle his tongue. "Look, I followed them from her house and waited until I seen them leave the dock. No running lights, just like you said. It was getting foggy so I stayed close behind, but not so close so's they'd get freaked. Then, when the time was right, *whammo*! They never seen me coming. And the boat's hid so good, it'd take a fucking psychic to find it. Just like always, nothing ties any of this to you. See?" He smiled. "What say I try again tomorrow? No extra charge."

The location for their meeting was nice—a windswept cliff above Port Henry where you could see the whole town, the harbor lights, the bay, and all the way out to Heyworth Island, Whidbey Island, and, on a clear day, clear on up to Canada. They'd met here before, several times. It was private property. Nobody would bust in on them, so, while his grumpy employer stood a few feet away, Sam decided to simply enjoy the view.

"I don't know, Sam. I'm just not happy about any of this." He rubbed the barrel of the revolver with his thumb.

Sam shrugged. "Hey, it'll be okay. Besides, if you're worried, just give me what you owe me, and I'll, you know, like, disappear."

A second passed, then another. Slowly, the barrel of the gun shifted until it pointed directly at Sam's heart.

"Interesting choice of words, Sam."

And then Sam disappeared.

"Well now," Max said. His voice was filled with husky appreciation; his hands were filled with Evie. "Will you look at what popped out from behind Door Number One?"

As he hugged her to him, her fingers curled over his very broad, very naked shoulders. Against her breasts she felt the smooth muscles of his chest.

Against her belly, the taut muscles of his stomach. Against her hip, okay, that was no muscle, but it was definitely worth noting.

"In the armoire in my room," she said. "There's a secret door and . . ." Her words dwindled away as she realized they might not get much talking done tonight after all.

Moonlight washed his room in silvery tones, grazing his cheekbones and sensuous mouth with its light, illuminating the side of his strong neck, the curve of his shoulder, the rounded muscles of his pectorals.

He looked over her head to the large mirror behind her, open now like a door. He peered inside, then pushed it closed.

"I wondered what all the racket was," he said. "I figured it was either you or a steroidal mouse. I was beginning to think I might not have enough bullets to bring the sucker down."

He ran his fingers along the mirror's frame. "So a panel in your room leads to this mirror in my room. Intriguing. It probably made secret assignations much easier that way."

"Pr-Probably," she stumbled. "You're naked."

"Pretty convenient, huh." He chuckled. "I was just getting changed to come to your room, but unimaginative traditionalist that I am, I was going to use the door." His arms tightened around her a little more. "But this works. This definitely works."

Against her breast she felt the rapid beating of his heart. Deep inside and low, she tightened. *Oh, yes. Naked. Making love. With Max. Oh, yes.* Her eager body remembered him fingering her sex, sliding into her, bringing her incredible pleasure, leaving her wanting so much more. And tonight . . . oh, yes . . .

He was silent a moment, then murmured, "Busy day, wasn't it?" His hand glided to her hip.

She nodded.

"You're probably beat." His hand moved up her rib cage.

She nodded again.

"Way too tired for any kind of strenuous activity." His thumb grazed the bottom of her breast.

Her breath caught. She swallowed.

"Guess that leaves it up to me." His thumb brushed across her taut nipple.

Oh God . . .

He slid his hands under the shoulder straps of her nightgown.

A little cry escaped her throat as the silky fabric slipped down her breasts to catch on the peaks of her upturned nipples. He shoved the bodice down to her waist as though he were too hungry to wait, too impatient for patience.

"Jesus, Evie," he panted as he stared at her bared breasts. He bent, took one nipple into his mouth and sucked.

Her high cry mingled with his groan of satisfaction. Pleasure swirled through her with every lick of his tongue. Cradling his head in her hands, she ran her fingers through his soft hair, learned the shape of his skull, the strength of his neck and shoulders as she held him to her breast.

He grabbed the edges of her nightgown and tugged it down over her hips until it pooled at her feet. Immediately, his hands were on her bottom, gripping, kneading, tugging her against his loins.

She muffled a small cry, and he stopped.

"Did I hurt you?" His low voice was edged with concern.

"Sorry," she whispered, lowering her head. "It's the bruises. They're still terribly painful."

"Oh, Jesus, Evie," he rushed. "Did I hurt you before, too? Why didn't you say something? Maybe we should wait—"

"No!" Her head came up and she put her fingertips to his mouth. "Don't say that, don't even think it. If you don't make love to me tonight, I'll . . . I'll . . ."

Suddenly, his hands and mouth were everywhere, making her body sing with delight. His touch was tender and he was careful to stay clear of the bruises on her shoulder and hip.

Then his arm went under her knees and he lifted her, taking her to the bed. He laid her there, pushed her knees apart, and settled himself between her thighs, taking her open mouth in a lusty kiss. He lifted her arms over her head, dominating her, keeping her body completely available to him and to whatever he wanted to do to her.

Evie arched against him, rubbing his erection until he moved his hips and the head of his penis slid into place . . . there. *Right. There.* She wanted to scream from the pure sensation of it, but she was breathing too hard to catch enough air.

Breaking the kiss, he pulled out of her and grabbed for the nightstand. A packet tore open, his hips moved, then he was poised over her again.

Panting, he said, "Jesus, Evie . . . you're like a candy store, and I want a bite of everything I see. I want it all."

She wrapped her legs around his hips and lifted herself to him. Her eyes closed, her back arched, she whispered, "Then take it."

She felt every inch of him as he slowly entered her. Kissing her neck, he put his mouth next to her ear and panted, "Good?"

Dear God, yes. He thrust into her again.

Sensation reached every corner of her body as he gently thrust in, then pulled out. She felt the heaviness of his muscles and bones on her, the strain on his arms as he held himself a little away so as not to crush her. The movement of his smooth chest against her breasts increased the pleasure a hundredfold.

She slid her hands down his taut stomach and flattened her palms over his hips. The movement pushed her breasts together, allowing him to lick each nipple in turn.

Her body went rigid and she couldn't catch even the smallest breath. Mounting pleasure shut down her brain, and it was all she could do to hang onto him while her orgasm swelled. One last thrust, one last lick, one more lusty kiss, and she cried his name, clenching around him over and over as the pleasure of her climax caught her and would not let go.

The world disappeared. There was only Max and his heat and the feel of his skin under her palms, the harshness of his breath against her neck, then the taste of his mouth on her tongue.

He groaned and made a low-pitched choking

sound, slamming into her until the force of his own release had him cry out.

Wrapping her arms around him, she held him close, feeling the lovely beating of his heart against her own. Simply being near him had made her feel sexy and feminine, special in a way she had never known. Kissing him had set her body on fire. Now, making love with him brought her to a new level of awareness, of satisfaction, of finally feeling whole.

He remained inside her. She contracted her muscles, squeezing around him a little, and he laughed against her neck.

"Give me a sec, okay?" His body was hot, his forehead damp.

"A sec?" she purred.

He shifted and looked into her eyes. "Okay. Two. Tops."

"Wow. I *am* impressed."

As he brushed a stray lock of her hair off her face, his eyes grew serious. "Stay with me tonight."

She smiled tentatively. "Of course I will. Why? Do you usually send your women packing as soon as you're done?"

There was silence for a moment, then he whispered, "Yes."

Oh. I see. . . .

"Well, it all depends," she said softly, trying to shove her fears aside. "How many condoms do you have left?"

Max generally awoke slowly of a morning, but he was rarely disoriented. He always knew where he was, what he'd been doing, who he'd been doing it with, and where he'd left his gun.

Though he avoided putting himself in that position anymore, he was still aware that the morning after a long night of first-time sex was often fraught with emotional peril. So he'd mentally prepared himself to feel what he usually felt when he accidentally ended up spending the night with a new woman—the urgent desire to thank her for a great time, then beat a hasty retreat.

But not this morning.

No, on this particular morning he wasn't done doing what he had been doing and hadn't done nearly enough of, and if the sleeping woman in his arms could be made to see reason, he'd be spending the next several decades refining the details.

Evie's butt was nestled snuggly in his crotch, her smooth back pressed against his chest. He frowned as anger heated his blood.

Even with the room still veiled in shadows, he could see the deep purple of the contusion on her shoulder, evidence of her near fatal fall in the barn. Silently, he renewed his vow to get the SOB who'd done it to her.

Her injuries were part of the reason he hadn't made love to her last night as much as he'd wanted to, part of the reason he was both sated and yet hungry for more of her.

The honeysuckle scent of her hair blended with the musky aroma of sex, flaring his nostrils like a wolf scenting his mate. He inhaled deeply, then bared his teeth and tenderly bit her unbruised shoulder. Ending the attack with a kiss, he found himself enthralled once more by the incredible softness of her skin.

She stirred and released a long, satisfied sigh, and he grinned smugly to himself. He knew he was responsible for it, and he wanted to waken her so he could be responsible for her making it two or three dozen more times.

Lifting his head, he checked the clock. Goddammit. They had to get a move on if they were going to get to Olympia before noon. Never in his life had duty and his personal agenda collided so irritatingly, but lying here with Evie in his arms was worth every bit of angst his brain could dish out.

Her breathing changed. He knew the second she came awake.

"Hey, sleepyhead," he whispered in her ear. She turned in his arms, bringing their bodies close. He felt the tight points of her nipples against his chest.

"My breath," she said, without moving her lips. "I want to kiss you, but . . ."

He laughed. "You can't have morning breath if you haven't been asleep," he said, and kissed her. But the simple kiss immediately turned hot and urgent as Evie shoved him back against the pillows and thrust her tongue inside his mouth, sliding her open hand down his belly to wrap her fingers around him.

When they were spent, they lay together, panting, recovering, touching here and there, slowly sliding their legs against each other's. With the leisurely drag of a finger, the warm press of a palm, they explored each other's bodies. Evie laid her head on his chest and listened to his heart; he placed his hand on the soft curve of her neck and measured the beat of her pulse. They kissed tenderly, caressed constantly, laughed and giggled and shared.

The sun had risen enough to catch the edges of the furniture, the ornately cut rim of the mirror, the handle of an antique water pitcher. On the nightstand, Max had emptied his pockets the night before. In the center of the cluster of everyday coins, keys, and his pocketknife, the singular coin he always carried glinted in the morning light like a beacon.

Evie reached over him and picked it up. "This is beautiful," she said, awed by the image on the metal disk. "It's not quite round, is it? And it's heavy for its size."

"It was my mother's," he said, scooting up behind her. The mattress dipped as he spooned around her warm body.

"It's lovely," she said, turning it in her fingers. "I'll bet this coin has a story."

"It's my good-luck piece," he said, his voice still a bit rough from sleep, or lack of it. "It's more than that, actually. It's hard to describe. My mother found it on a dig one summer in Britain. Turns out, that same day she found she was pregnant with me. She gave it to me when I turned sixteen and told me she hoped it brought me as much luck as it had brought her."

"Is it Roman?"

"Probably. Dates from about 10 B.C." Even though he'd never shared the story of the coin with any other woman, save for Melissa, the words formed themselves, and he found himself wanting to tell Evie all about it. All about everything.

"It must be very valuable," she said.

"Only to me. Monetarily, it's probably worth about fifty bucks, but it's the only thing of hers I have that meant something to the both of us. Carrying it around," he said with a shrug that was more casual that he felt, "sort of takes me back to when I was a little kid and she first told me about it. Maybe because I was different back then. Innocent, I guess. Before I realized what a bastard my father could be and how I was turning out just like him."

She shifted toward him, confusion on her face. "Why do you say that?"

Soft! His father's often repeated words rang in his ears like a bad tune that stayed with you. *Letting yourself love a woman makes a man soft. Weakens you. Don't be an ass, Max. Take, but only give back what you can afford. Don't be stupid.*

Max lowered his head until his forehead touched hers.

"Max? What's wrong?"

He debated, then decided. "My father didn't *like* women," he said. "He raised me to believe that women were made for men to use, but that caring for a woman made a man an idiot."

"Oh. I see."

He raised his head and locked gazes with her. "No, you don't. You couldn't. Even I didn't see it for years, and I lived with him. He was every stereotypical cop you've ever seen. Dark glasses, swagger, locked jaw, attitude. And when he came home, he didn't turn it off. But I worshiped him. I wanted to be just like him. I *am* just like him."

She nodded, and it cut him that she didn't disagree, couldn't disagree. After all, he'd given her no reason to.

"He treated my mother badly but I either didn't see it or was too stupid to realize it. I'm only just now beginning to see how I mistakenly idolized the wrong parent." He swallowed. "I, uh, I want you to understand something about me, Evie. I need you to."

"Okay." Her eyes were worried as she placed her warm palm against his neck. Gently, she urged, "You can tell me."

"I did a bad thing," he confessed, unable to look her in the eye. "When my mother left my father to marry Heyworth, I condemned her for it—and Heyworth—when it was my father I probably should have condemned. I had been conditioned for years to think women were simply to be used, that one was just like the next. My mother tried to tell me, to warn me, but I didn't listen. I was naïve and arrogant, and stayed locked into that kind of thinking for a very long time. I was a know-it-all punk with an attitude." He blew out a harsh breath. Softly, he said, "I wish I could have told her. . . ."

"Oh, Max," Evie whispered. "You were so very young then. You're older now, wiser. It's unfortunate your mother died before you had a chance to work it out with her, but I'm sure she wouldn't be happy if she knew you were filled with guilt and remorse."

He shrugged.

She tilted her head and seemed to consider him. "If she was as good a mother as you say, as lovely a woman, then she knew, Max. She understood without you having to tell her. She undoubtedly forgave you the minute the words were out of your mouth. I don't think she went to her grave hating or blaming you."

"Maybe not," he growled. "But I've got enough hate and blame for the both of us."

"I'm sure you do," she soothed, "but it won't do you any good to keep carrying it. Do you think she would want that for you? She was your mother. She loved you."

He moved away from her and sat up, pulling the sheet over his lap. "We need to get going. It's a long drive to Olympia."

"Olympia isn't going anywhere," she said, sitting facing him. "Tell me more. Did you love your father?"

"No. Yes. No. I mean, I did, and then I didn't."

"That's unusual," she quipped dryly. "I'll bet you're the only person on earth who's ever had mixed emotions about a parent."

He grunted a laugh, reached over and tucked a lock of hair behind her ear, then tugged on her earlobe.

"I don't want to talk about my dad right now," he said. And he didn't dare talk about his growing feelings for her. They were new, fragile, and he was afraid if he scared her, the developing bond between them would be broken, and the thought of that happening bothered him a lot.

"There's more," he said. "I, uh, I was married. Her name was Melissa. I treated her like shit and she left me."

Examining her fingertips for a moment, Evie lifted her head and said, "Did you love her?"

He sat forward, bending to place his elbows on his knees. "I thought so at the time." Pausing, he shook his head. "Yes. Yes, I loved her." And he had, and to deny it would be to deny what Melissa had given him, or had tried to.

"I'm afraid I was still operating under the Rules of Relationships as written by Martin Galloway. When she'd finally had enough and left, my father gave me the mother of all I Told You So lectures. He even slapped me. He convinced me Melissa's leaving had only been a matter of time and that I'd been a fool to waste any emotion on her. I bought it. I was hurting, and I bought it."

"Of course you did," she said gently. "Your father had warned you to never love a woman, and you went against his wishes, which says a lot about your needs, no matter how you've tried to deny them. You probably punished yourself doubly for it—once for defying him, failing him, in a way, and another time for losing Melissa. Your father set it up so you couldn't win, Max, no matter what you did."

He reached over and took her hand between his, curling her fingers over his palm. "You must hear confessions all the time," he teased. "Little boys probably want to crawl up on your lap and tell you their life stories."

Evie stuck out her lower lip. "True," she said. "The good news is, most of them are only eleven or twelve, so it's a pretty short story."

As Max tugged on her hand to pull her back into his arms, there was a knock at the door, then a muffled, "Pardon, sir. Detective Galloway?"

Evie wrapped a blanket around her body and tiptoed to the bathroom door, closing it softly behind her. Clutching the sheet around his hips, Max opened his door a couple of inches. "Yes, Edmunds?"

The butler's hands were clasped in front of him, a look of distress on his face. "Detective McKennitt is here to see you, sir. There seems to have been another murder."

Chapter 19

Dear Diary:

Thomas is so wonderful to me, and he came to get me and everything when Mom died, and he treats me just like he's my father. And I've been thinking. Maybe he is my father, my *real* father! This morning I asked him about it, but he coughed and said I needed to finish my homework and feed the llamas. His response made me even more curious. If Thomas is my father, why would it be a secret?

Evangeline—age 12

Detective McKennitt was as Evie remembered him, tall, good-looking, and charming, too. But unlike Max's mesmerizing green-hazel eyes, McKennitt's were a startling blue. In his early thirties, the detective's athletic physique was complimented by a well-tailored charcoal suit. As he scribbled in a small notebook, his left hand moved over the page, causing his thick gold wedding band to toss off a glint of early morning sunlight.

Hunky as McKennitt was, Evie thought, he was hardly an effective detective. It had been nearly two months since Thomas had been killed, and the police still had nothing. Thomas Heyworth had been a famous, wealthy man. She would have thought they'd put somebody *better* on the case.

Looking up from his note pad, McKennitt smiled and said, "Galloway. Ms. Randall. Nice seeing you again."

"Do you know yet who killed Thomas?" Evie all but snapped as she took a chair in front of the massive fireplace in the library. "I've called at least a dozen times over the last few weeks, and they continue to tell me you're working on it but have no new leads."

McKennitt presented her with a relaxed grin, but his eyes grew serious. "I know you're anxious, Ms. Randall. We're following up on all leads as we get them, but it's true, there haven't been any new developments worth mentioning. I'm sure something will break very soon."

"Edmunds said something about another murder," Max said. "Who was it?"

McKennitt set his notebook on the carved oak mantel. Pushing back the edges of his jacket, he slid his hands into his pockets.

"Let me begin by stating a few facts," he said. "Heyworth owned a registered Smith & Wesson .357 revolver, but a search of the house after his murder turned up nothing. The bullet that killed him was also a .357. Same gun? It's likely, but until we secure the weapon, we won't know. However, as luck would have it, the bullet dug out of the doorway of Tavvy's Tavern is *also* a .357 and matches the one that killed Heyworth."

"Well, what do you know," Max said. "Our killer does get around."

Evie's brain went a bit numb. "The same person who killed Thomas is trying to kill me?" She shook her head, leaning forward in the chair. "Why? I just don't see—"

McKennitt held up a hand. "You haven't heard the best part. Late last night a couple of kids looking for a secluded rendezvous practically tripped over a dead guy. One Sam Ziwicki, a suspected contract killer. Guess what caliber bullet they dug out of the deceased, and guess what other two it matches?"

Max went silent for a moment as he walked over to the large bookcase on the interior wall. Running the tip of his finger over the dusty titles, he said, "So, Heyworth is killed by a hired gun, maybe Sam Ziwicki, while everyone connected with the estate has a solid alibi. Then, three attempts are made on Evie's life, one involving the same gun. Sam again, or is there more than one person on active duty here?" Turning to McKennitt, he said, "Any word on the boat that rammed us?"

McKennitt shook his head. "The harbor patrol salvaged as much of the runabout as they could find. We've got a team going over it, looking for particles of fiberglass or paint, something that will give us a lead."

Max roamed over to one of the bay windows.

"What about the two guys that pulled me out of the drink? They see anything?"

"According to the witnesses, the pilot aimed right for you. And, there were no running lights."

"So it was no accident," said Max.

"Nope."

"You get a description of the boat?"

"Said it was too far away from them, and because of the storm, details were hard to make out. Big, though. White or gray, maybe light blue."

Moving away from the window, Max came to stand a few feet from Evie's chair. "Evie," he said thoughtfully. "Where did you find Heyworth's body?"

"What? Oh, uh, right over there, near where you were standing before, by the big bookcase."

"Did you hear the shot?"

"No. But I was busy with the llamas, and the wind was blowing hard from the north. If I did hear it, I may have dismissed it."

"When you got to the library," he said, "tell me what you saw. Was there anything odd about the room? Did you notice anything out of place or different? Anything unusual?"

Evie put her hand to her forehead. So many images to sort through. So much had happened in the last two months, but not so much that she couldn't recall every second of that horrible afternoon.

"I came into the house and headed directly to the library."

"Why did you come here?"

She gave a small shrug. "Looking for a book.

Thomas was due back later in the evening, so I was surprised when . . . you know. When I saw him lying on the floor."

She swallowed and tried to maintain her composure, but it was hard. Thinking about that day, talking about it. It was still so fresh.

"You okay?"

When she nodded, Max said, "What happened then?"

"Well, I walked in, and there he was, just lying there on his back, st-staring. There was blood on his forehead." She softened her voice. "Only a little."

She'd known the moment she saw him that he was dead, but she hadn't wanted to believe it. Her brain had not been able to absorb such a harsh reality. Rushing to him, she'd kneeled at his side, not knowing what to do, what to think.

"If anything was unusual or out of place," she said quietly, "I didn't notice. I couldn't take my eyes off Thomas. . . ." She tangled her fingers in her lap and frowned. "I—I think I must have gone into some kind of shock. I was checking for a pulse when Edmunds came in with a tray of iced tea. He's the one who contacted the authorities."

"The autopsy stated Heyworth probably hadn't been dead for more than an hour, maybe two, before you found him, yet nobody claims to have heard a shot. You didn't see anybody running out of the house?

"No."

"Where was everyone that day?"

"Um, Edmunds and Lorna were down at the

dock, going over a maintenance list for the Hatteras. The Stanleys had gone home. The Stanleys," she explained, "don't live on the island. Mrs. Stanley is the day cook, so, after dinner, they go back to the mainland. They have their own boat and pretty much come and go on their own schedule. Whenever Thomas threw a party, he hired caterers."

Max ran his fingers through his hair and frowned. "I've been trying to talk to Stanley," he said to McKennitt, "but he's apparently a hard man to pin down. Mrs. Stanley says he's around, but I haven't seen him."

"Come to think of it," Evie offered, "I haven't seen him for a couple of days myself. That's not really unusual, though. It's a big island and he's often off somewhere trimming or raking or mowing or repairing, or in town picking up supplies."

Max and Detective McKennitt exchanged another meaningful glance.

"Ms. Randall," the detective said quietly. "Until she died, I understand you had just the one parent, your mother. What do you know about your father?"

"I had one. It's a biological necessity." Her heart rate increased, her palms dampened. She felt suddenly defensive, but wasn't sure why.

"Did your mother ever talk about him?"

She pressed her lips together and let a moment or two pass while she decided exactly what she wanted to say. Finally, "She told me she was married to a man named Randall, but he left before I was born. He was most likely my father. However," she said, working to keep her voice calm, "ever since she died and Thomas came to get me, I've wondered whether he was my real father. There were times I was almost certain he was, but he never said." Her throat tightened. "And if I am his daughter, that makes me his sole heir."

"It does," McKennitt said. "In law enforcement, we have a name for that kind of thing. It's called motive."

Max watched Evie's cheeks pale. "What? You think I . . . I didn't kill Thomas!"

"Evie," he interrupted before she gave McKennitt a set-down that would end up with her in handcuffs. If anybody was going to put her in handcuffs, it was going to be him. Tonight, if good fortune smiled down on him, and, hell, even if it didn't. "Detective McKennitt's not accusing you, he's merely stating that some might consider that a strong motive for murder. You have to understand how it looks—"

"How it *looks*?" she snapped. "*Him*, I would expect to accuse me, but *you*?"

"I'm not accusing you," Max nearly yelled. "But the fact you may be Heyworth's daughter and heir could raise a few eyebrows. It gives you about thirty million reasons for murder."

Her mouth flattened. "Do you think I killed him?"

"No, I absolutely do not think you killed him."

"Then why are you taking *his* side?" she said with a nod in McKennitt's direction. "Why are you defending him and not me?"

"Goddammit, Evie, I'm not taking his side. And you need defending about as much as a Marine with a bazooka."

They locked gazes and stood toe-to-toe while Evie's cheeks flushed. She lowered her lashes.

"Sorry. I guess I'm a little touchy this morning. I don't know what came over me."

Maybe she didn't know, but he did. He'd made love to her, and they'd shared a special night together, and she felt betrayed that he didn't immediately jump to her defense. What she didn't realize was, she didn't need defending. Only evidence would convict Heyworth's killer, and since Evie hadn't killed the old man, there was nothing that could implicate her in his murder.

Max watched her for a moment, then said, "A simple DNA test would have proven whether Thomas was your father, Evie. Why didn't you ever have one done?"

"Because I never came right out and asked him to, that's why. I should have, but I was afraid."

"Afraid of what?" McKennitt's voice interrupted, but not ungently.

"I *wanted* Thomas to be my father," she said roughly. "Maybe I *needed* for him to be. If I'd gone to him and forced him to do the test, and found out he wasn't my father after all, that would have meant my real father was probably some one-night stand my mother couldn't even remember. I just couldn't accept that."

Max heard the pain in her voice and wanted to take hold of her and comfort her, ease the burden from her shoulders and onto his own. But he couldn't. Not with McKennitt watching their every move. He'd already seen too much.

"I guess that makes me a coward," she said shakily, "but I just couldn't face the possibility that somebody *other* than Thomas was my father." She shook her head slowly. "Not knowing seemed so much safer. That way, I could pretend. I never thought it would go unresolved forever. I honestly thought one day we'd have that conversation, cross that bridge. But time passed and then . . . well, now it's too late."

"Unfortunately," McKennitt said, "it doesn't matter, in terms of motive, if Heyworth was your father or not. If you believed him to be, that's damaging enough right there."

Her brow furrowed and she looked up at him. "Detective McKennitt, do you really think I killed Thomas Heyworth?"

He gave her a soft smile. "No, ma'am. I don't. I am concerned, though, that somebody else perceived you were Heyworth's heir and had a problem with it."

She cut a quick glance to Max, then back to the detective. "Who?"

"I can't say just now, but we are following other leads. Please don't speak to anyone about the case except for Detective Galloway here. That's all I can share with you for now."

McKennitt checked his watch, then shoved his notebook back in his pocket. "Thanks for your time, Ms. Randall. Walk me out to the boat, will you, Galloway?"

When the two men reached the runabout, Edmunds was already in it, starting up the motor.

McKennitt stopped and turned to Max. With his hands in his pockets and a scowl on his face, he lowered his voice and said, "You mind telling me what's going on here, Galloway? Just what in God's name do you think you're doing?"

"What in the hell are you babbling about?"

"Look," McKennitt said quietly, so the butler couldn't hear. "Believe me when I say I'm totally sympathetic, but you've obviously allowed yourself to become personally involved in this case."

"I *am* personally involved," Max shot back. "I was invited to participate, remember?" Shifting his weight, he crossed his arms over his chest. "We're on the heels of the fourth clue. With any luck, we'll get to the seventh before anyone else. I'm hoping like hell Heyworth left something in that clue we can use."

"You and me both. We've been watching and waiting, but so far our guy hasn't done anything provocative. If he killed Ziwicki—and we think he did—the son of a bitch snuck his way around our surveillance." He blew out a long breath. "How's Darling doing?"

" 'Dabney James' is keeping an eye on the secretary, and Edmunds is joined at the hip with the psychic. We're a happy bunch, but the sooner we get something on our guy, the better I'll feel about Evie's safety."

"Evie."

"Yeah, *Evie*. Want to make something of it?"

There was silence between the two men for a moment, then McKennitt blew out a rough laugh.

"Look," he said, "it's not like I don't know what you're going through. Before Betsy was my wife, she was a stalking victim."

"You married a woman you met on a case and you're warning *me* off?"

"It was different. I met her before I was on the case."

"If this were my case," Max said, "I wouldn't even consider becoming involved with her. I do understand professional ethics, and, contrary to popular belief, I abide by them. However, I'm not only a suspect myself, I'm an invitee to the game. I'm helping you out, but officially I'm a nonentity. So when it comes to Evie, keep your trap shut."

McKennitt glanced toward the waiting boat then back at Max. "Okay, then. I'm outta here. We're pregnant and I promised I'd stop by the store on the way home and get Betsy some orange juice."

"Pregnant? Congratulations, buddy."

McKennitt snorted, then a huge grin spread across his face. "Yeah. It's great. She sure wants to eat some weird stuff, though. Yesterday it was barbecued ribs, sauerkraut, and marzipan."

As the detective was boarding the runabout, Max said, "So, uh, how do you like being married?"

"Wouldn't have it any other way."

"Yeah?"

"Yeah. Funny thing, though, about committing to a woman for the rest of your life, especially a woman like Betsy." He lifted his shoulder in a shrug. "You get this protective thing going. I don't know how to describe it. I only know that if anybody ever hurt her, I'd rip the guy's balls off and stuff them down his throat. I never saw myself married, but now that I am, it's, uh, well hell, it's everything."

Max shoved his hands in his pockets but didn't respond.

As seagulls squawked and wheeled overhead, McKennitt said, "Evie Randall's a pretty woman." Then he grinned again. "Watch out for them cute ones, pal. One false move and you just might wind up living happily ever after."

By the time Max pulled into his own driveway in Olympia, he was ready to explode. Turning off the ignition, he quickly got out of the car and moved around to the passenger side. When Evie opened her door, he reached in and pulled her straight into his arms. Then he kissed the hell out of her.

"What was that for?" she said breathlessly.

"That was for being so adorable."

"No, really," she said seriously. "What was it for?" He detected a glint in her eye, so he kissed her again.

When he pulled away this time, she was laughing, and he said, "Actually, it was for being so adorable, *and* for being so smart."

Smacking him on the shoulder with her doubled fist, she said, "Well, it sure took you long enough to realize it."

He tugged her a little closer. "Yeah, well, I'm kind of slow sometimes."

Her blue eyes went dreamy. Lifting herself on her toes, her mouth came to within a kiss of his lips.

"Be slow now," she whispered, then touched his bottom lip with her tongue.

Desire shot through him like the blast of a flamethrower. He kissed her again, very slowly, and very thoroughly. As he ended the kiss, out of the corner of his eye he saw a curtain flutter in the window of the house across the street.

"We have witnesses," he said. "We'd better go inside before they start sending out wedding invitations."

Evie glanced around. "They must have seen you bringing home hot babes before now."

"No," he said. "They never have. When you're a police officer, you are subject to close scrutiny by everyone you meet. Your neighbors watch you constantly to make sure you're being good, whatever that may mean to them. Bringing home a string of hot babes would be detrimental to my image in the community."

She scowled. "That hardly seems fair."

"It isn't fair. It's just the way it is. That's one of the reasons the divorce rate for law enforcement officers is so high. Your private life is rarely really private, and that can be tough on a marriage."

"Then why did you kiss me? If you hadn't, your neighbors would have assumed I was no more than your stunning second cousin from Podunk."

"I kissed you because not kissing you was killing me," he said. "And now we're going into the house. I think it's only fair to warn you, I may kiss you in there, too."

"God," she muttered under her breath as she

locked gazes with him. "I hope so." Louder, she said, "Have you figured out yet where the clue is? And have you also figured out how it got into your house?"

Unlocking the back door of his neat little two-story, post-WWII brick and clapboard home, he sent her a satisfied grin.

"Yes, I have," he said. "And, yes, I have."

Chapter 20

Dear Diary:

I have her picture in my room now. My mom. It was in the junk they sent to Thomas from the last house we lived in, where, you know, she died. She was so beautiful. The picture was taken when I was a baby, because she's holding me in a pink blanket and smiling. Her hair is long and shiny and red, just like the desk I have in my room at Mayhem. Edmunds says it's cherry wood, and it's the exact same color as her hair. I miss my mom a lot. I often cry for her. I think I always will.

Evangeline—age 12

So, hunky Max Galloway never brought women home, thought Evie as she looked around his place. He didn't want the neighbors to get the wrong idea. But he'd brought her home, and had even kissed her out there in the driveway. Twice. Why? To, what, give the neighbors the *right* idea? Did he maybe like her more than he'd let on? Or had he simply gotten to the point where he didn't care what the neighbors thought?

As soon as they'd entered his house, Max had run upstairs, leaving her to wander through the kitchen and living room, absorbing what she could of his estrogen-free sanctum sanctorum. He had good taste in furnishings and artwork, and didn't seem at all anal about cleanliness. The place was neat, but not fastidious, comfortable without being sloppy, masculine without animal heads on the walls and gun racks over the mantel and empty beer cans strewn about on sticky-paged issues of *Playboy*.

She walked to the large coffee table and recalled him telling her that he'd made it. It appeared to be constructed of oak, and was inlaid in a herringbone design using lighter and darker woods, and it was gorgeous. Running her finger along the top, she marveled at the smoothness of the wood, so finely crafted she couldn't even feel the seams in the design. It was almost like touching silk.

In the middle of the coffee table sat a chess set, the one he'd made, certainly. She picked up one of the pieces, the white queen, so beautifully carved it nearly took her breath away. The lines of all the pieces were elegant, almost lyrical, and Evie felt her heart teeter on a very high precipice.

A man who could create such beauty with his mind and his hands had to be a man of deep feelings. She held the queen closer to study her face; the lady was smiling.

Setting the queen down, she looked around the spacious room.

Next to the fireplace stood an enormous bookcase, heavy with volumes on every possible subject, as well as a few classics and a best-seller or two. But what drew her attention most was the photograph.

Max's mother had been such a pretty woman, possessed of a generous smile and sparkling eyes. Those dark good looks had been handed down to both her children, who stood in front of her, grinning proudly, each holding some ancient artifact in their short, grubby fingers.

Back at Mayhem, a portrait of this same woman hung in Thomas's room, but the woman captured in oils appeared much changed from this one. Not just older, but weary, and quite fragile. Evie assumed she died within months of its being painted.

She touched the photo on the shelf. Max couldn't have been more than ten. He'd been a rugged, sturdy little guy. Would his own sons look like this? she wondered. Impish grin, wide, hazel eyes bright with pride and awe, tanned little arms stretched out to show off his prize. Her heart tossed in an extra beat at the thought.

Next to him, his sister, devoid of her two front teeth, and perhaps a year or two younger, had inherited her mother's elegant bones. She was smiling like she'd just won a million bucks.

"That was taken on a dig one summer in New Mexico."

Evie turned to see Max standing at the foot of the stairs, an enormous cardboard box in his arms. As he set it on the coffee table, he said, "Frankie and I found some pottery shards. It was the first time I'd actually dug up anything, and I was so excited, it was like I'd just discovered King Tut's lost tomb. Practically wet my pants."

She glanced back at the photo. "You were really cute." Strolling toward him, she said, "I recognized your mom from the portrait at Mayhem. You have any pictures of your dad?"

"Nope." He took out his pocketknife and sliced the tape that held the box closed. Lifting away all four flaps, he stood looking down into the box.

When he said nothing, she gestured toward it. "Christmas decorations?"

"Nope."

He edged back to sit on the black leather couch and proceeded to carefully remove items from the box. Dropping into the wing chair on the other side of the coffee table, Evie reached forward and lifted one of the flaps, to read the mailing label.

"Oh my God," she practically choked. "The Trojan Horse."

"Yep." He took out a sheaf of papers, then an old book, a photograph album, and a couple of tarnished trophies. Setting the items aside, he rummaged around in the box. "I got to thinking," he said.

"Well, they say there's a first time for everything."

Ignoring her wit, he said, "There was no way anybody could get into my house without my knowledge, but if you were right, and the clue is here, then there was only one way it could have gotten in, and that's if I brought it in myself."

"And judging from the postmark on this box," she said, "six months ago the post office delivered it to your doorstep. And you brought it inside."

"Exactly." Max took out a few more things, obviously mementos from his childhood his mother had kept and Thomas had used to disguise his clue. "At the time, I wondered why I was getting all this stuff now, but I just figured somebody at Mayhem had done a little house cleaning and decided to send it to me. I went through it all the day I got it, but I don't recall anything that could be considered a clue in a treasure hunt."

"But six months ago," she said, "you weren't looking for one. You were only seeing what Thomas wanted you to see."

They sat, peering into the now empty box.

"Nothing," he sighed. Shaking his head, he said, "I can't be wrong about this. It's the only way . . . hang on."

Evie watched while he reached down into the box and edged his finger under the square piece of cardboard fitted snugly on the bottom. It could have been placed there to add stability and strength for shipping, or . . .

"Well, goddamn," he whispered. "Will you look at that."

He lifted the square sheet of cardboard, and there it was. An envelope. Across the front was scrawled, *So you finally found it, you stupid son of a bitch.*

"I see it's addressed to you," Evie said. Then, as excitement overtook her, she clapped her hands together, "Hurry up. What does it say?"

Slicing open the envelope, he removed the single sheet of paper and handed it to Evie.

He paced in front of the fireplace and reread her note. Finally, he crumpled it into a tight ball and tossed it into the flames. She was gone, she'd left him. Taken off with some grease monkey with a better set of shoulders. He'd had her pegged, though. Had known right from the start she wasn't the kind to stick around. But what did he care? One dame was pretty much like another.

T. E. Heyworth, 1953
Strike Me, Spare Me

"Oh, God," Max groaned. "I remember this one. It was so bad."

Evie silently read it again. "Right. This is the one where the villain of the story was a professional bowler who met women at tournaments, then killed them. Bludgeoned them with a bowling pin."

Max relaxed back into the buttery leather of the sofa. "I'm sensing a trend here."

She laughed and handed back the clue. "I'll admit, Thomas did have a rather fill-in-the-blanks approach to his plots."

"Do you remember where *Strike Me, Spare Me* takes place?"

Evie rubbed her eyes, then looked over at him, sitting sprawled on the couch, in jeans and a dark T-shirt, pound for pound the sexiest thing she'd ever been in the same room with, let alone the same bed.

In a low voice, she said, "Before I answer that, can I ask you a question?"

His eyes grew serious, maybe even apprehensive. She knew that when a woman who was sleeping with a man said to him, "Can I ask you a question?" the man had to be thinking it was a question he probably didn't want to hear and was in no way prepared to answer.

His eyes narrowed on her. "Shoot."

"Do you know who killed Thomas?"

Ha, ha. Fooled you, she thought.

Something flickered in Max's eyes, and for a moment it almost looked like disappointment. He pursed his lips and sat forward, placing his elbows on his knees.

"We have a theory."

"How long have you had this theory?"

"Several days."

She lifted her hands in a display of confusion. "Then why haven't you made an arrest?"

"It's not that easy," he said. "There's no hard evidence, and until we can prove probable cause, we can't do any searches or subpoena any records. The same laws that protect the innocent against false accusations are the same ones that protect the guilty. We have to work within the boundaries of those laws, or we risk losing a conviction at trial."

"And this person is responsible for the attempts on my life, too?"

"Yes. Either personally or through a possible accomplice, possibly now deceased."

Evie stood and picked up one of the trophies sitting on the coffee table. Running her fingertip over Max's name engraved on the brass plate, she said, "I never figured you for track. Football, baseball, maybe even basketball."

He stood and came around the table. "Not beefy enough for football. I played some baseball, but never won any trophies. Not tall enough for basketball. But track? I am very fast when properly motivated."

Taking the trophy from her hands, he set it on the coffee table.

"Just now," he said. "I thought there was something else you were going to ask me." He looked into her eyes, and she slid her glance away. "Or was I mistaken?"

Oh, sure. I'm going to blow it now by asking if you have feelings for me after a handful of days and a little sex? Only a foolish and insecure woman would be stupid enough . . .

"I'm falling in love with you," she said softly. "Do you mind?"

He slipped his hands around her waist and kissed her. And, oh, what a wonderful kiss it was. Or would have been if she'd been able to keep her mind from wandering, wondering whether this was the kiss of death. The kiss-off. The long good-bye. It's been swell. Hey, you were dynamite in the sack, but I gotta keep my options open. . . .

When he pulled back a little, he said, "Does that answer your question?"

She gazed up at him. "No," she said flatly. "But it will do until you come up with a better one."

He grinned down into her eyes. "Don't take this

the wrong way, sweetheart, but we have to get to the next clue. We'll have to finish this discussion later."

She nodded. "Yes. We will."

"Okay," he said, stepping away from her. "We're at the southernmost part of Puget Sound. If we're going down one side and up the other, as you suggested, our next stop will be north of here, Port Orchard, Bremerton, maybe Silverdale—"

"Bremerton!" she rushed. "That's right. God, it's been so long since I read that one. The killer was retired from the navy and he owned a bowling alley in Bremerton."

Max grabbed her hand and headed for the door. "I hope this clue isn't out of our league."

She scowled. "Is that a bowling pun?"

"Don't you mean bowling pin?"

Evie rolled her eyes. "Like the man says, spare me. . . ."

He pressed the button a second time, and the panel slid closed, sealing off this day's work from prying eyes. It would be a long time, if ever, before this particular panel was discovered.

Tugging his gloves on more securely, he looked around. Christ, but he hated doing the dirty work himself, yet ever since he killed Sam, he'd had no choice, and that pissed him off even more, because he hated having no choices.

He'd been at it for hours, and his temper had worn threadbare. The seventh clue just had to be on Heyworth Island, inside Mayhem, but so far no place he'd thought to look had reaped him any rewards.

And now this. Goddammit. Here he'd thought everyone was gone, but no. Well, that's what happened when you turned up at the wrong place at the wrong time. He'd hoped not to have to kill anyone else—not that he minded the killing, but when he had to do it himself it was just so messy.

His freshest victim already forgotten, he headed for the hallway. Mayhem was huge, three stories, a score of bedrooms, maybe more, three parlors, two offices, and an enormous library, not to mention a variety of bathrooms and other incidental rooms. However, as a kindhearted lover had once said to him ages ago, size doesn't really matter—and in terms of Mayhem's enormity, at least, it didn't. He knew how Heyworth's moronic mind worked. Tommy would have hidden that envelope in an obvious place just to taunt him. It was a mind game, pure and simple, but one *he* intended to win.

In spite of the challenge finding that fucking envelope posed, he was a smart man, smarter than all of them. All he needed to do was second-guess Tommy Heyworth, and hell, he'd been doing that for years.

His stomach burned. What he should do, what he should *really* do, was pack it in right now, cut his losses and head for Canada. But he had a life here, a place in the community. He was well-respected, and he was loath to give it all up until he was good and ready.

That Randall bitch. He'd still love to get rid of her. Her mere existence had screwed everything up for him. She should pay, she really should.

Reaching into his pocket, he pulled out the small

bottle of blood pressure medication. This whole fiasco was infuriating, and his health was suffering for it. Just one more thing he should make Evie Randall pay for.

As he went into a bathroom and filled a glass with water, downing his medication, he thought about finding a way to end the game. But with the butler and that nutso Russian woman off somewhere, and the poet and the secretary gone, not to mention Galloway and the bitch, he had to wait until they all came home to roost, and then . . . well, wouldn't it just be awful if they all died somehow? What would happen to the treasure hunt then? Time would run out, and he'd take control of the funds, just like he'd always planned. He'd make sure to destroy whatever clues they had found, effectively ending the game. The last clue would never be discovered. Tommy could point his dead finger straight at him and it wouldn't matter.

He ran his shaking hand over his meager strands of hair. This was all getting too, too complicated. He wasn't thinking straight. He could never pull something like this off. *Go back to town, grab what you can, and get the hell out.*

Setting the empty water glass back on the counter, he crossed his arms over his chest. Yes, what he needed was a good, solid mass murder.

As his medication kicked in and he began to breathe normally once more, his gaze meandered around the room. Crystal mirror, imported Italian tile, marble floor. Such opulence was disgusting. Turning to flick off the light switch, his gaze came at last to rest on the water glass, and he smiled.

* * *

By six o'clock, they had hit every bowling alley in Bremerton. Nobody had any envelopes, and most had never even heard of T. E. Heyworth or his shitty mysteries. Max was dead on his feet, and Evie looked like she could curl up in a corner and nod right off.

"Maybe we should head back to Mayhem," he said as they returned to the car. "This isn't getting us anywhere and I'm fresh out of ideas."

Evie slid into the passenger seat and let her head fall back against the headrest. Closing her eyes, she said, "This is Sunday night. Six days left. Three clues to go. Thomas's original intent was for us to have fun, so he couldn't have made the clues so hard we couldn't follow them."

Max fastened his seat belt and turned the key in the ignition. A steady rain had begun to fall somewhere between visits to Barney's Bowl 'n' Grill on Devon Street and The Alley Katz on Meeker, leaving fat raindrops on the windshield. Flipping on the wipers, he checked out the view. Across the wide road, the naval shipyard hosted an array of magnificent vessels. Closest to the docks, an aircraft carrier lay at anchor, its sharp angles in contrast to the plump clouds rolling across the sky.

"If Heyworth had wanted us to have fun," Max said, frustration adding bite to his tone, "why in the hell didn't he just hand over the money and let everybody go shopping at the Mall of America?"

Turning toward Evie, he took in her profile, her long lashes fanned across her flushed cheeks. He reached for her, running his finger along her jawline. She rolled her head in his direction and opened her eyes. Sleepy as they were, those big blue eyes nailed him to the wall. Every time.

"Maybe we're in the wrong town," she offered. "Maybe it wasn't Bremerton." Releasing a long sigh that must have started at her toes, she said, "I'm so tired, I just can't think."

Max shifted into first and cranked the wheel, taking them out onto the busy highway. "Before we give up, let's drive around a little. Maybe something will jump out at us."

For the next hour, they drove up one street and down the next until all the single-story businesses and post-WWII bungalows began to look alike.

As he headed back down to the highway, he said, "Okay, we gave it our best shot. Might as well—"

"There!"

He glanced over at Evie. She was sitting straight up, her arm pointing at something on his side of the street.

"I've been to that house," she rushed. "I . . . my mother . . . we lived there when I was really little. I'm almost sure of it."

Max pulled to the curb and studied the tiny home. It was an old house in sorry shape, a single story, gray clapboard with a small chimney poking through the haphazardly shingled roof. The yard was overgrown with weeds, and the white picket fence that had once surrounded the miniature patch of grass was now sticks of blistered wood barely hanging together.

Something inside Max's heart caught, and he swallowed.

"You lived here?"

Her eyes still glued to the run-down cottage, she said, "We lived in lots of places. I don't remember most of them, but I remember this one because I had my own room. The, uh, the sailors who visited my mom, they, uh . . ."

"You don't have to explain," he said as gently as he could. "How old were you when you lived here, Evie?"

Finally, she pulled her gaze away, concentrating on her fingernails as though they held some new fascination. "I was five."

He glanced back at the obviously vacant house and frowned. "Clue Number Five. You don't think . . . Heyworth couldn't have . . ."

"If he did, he must have had a reason, though how he knew about this place, I can't imagine."

"Do you want to wait here?"

She shook her head as she reached for her door handle. "Nope," she said, taking a deep breath. "I'm a big girl now. And if the clue's in this house, I think I know where it is."

To a child of five, the house had been small. To a grown woman who'd seen something of the world, the house was too dinky to be believed. She stood in the doorway, Max right behind her, his hand on her back, warm, gentle, steady. If she collapsed into a puddle of tears, he would be right there to offer his shoulder.

She wasn't going to collapse, but for his gallantry, and for the many intoxicating things she was discovering about him every day, she slid into love with him a little more truly, a little more madly, a little more deeply.

It had taken all of two seconds to pop the lock at the back door. Ignoring the general state of wretchedness in the kitchen, she moved into the living room and stopped in front of the fireplace.

She pressed her palm against the bricks. They felt grainy and rough. Running her gaze over the eroding mess, she said, " 'He paced in front of the fireplace . . . he crumpled it into a tight ball and tossed it into the flames.' "

Stepping around her, Max said, "Let me check. This masonry is old and crumbling. If the thing falls, I'd rather it fell on me than on you." He waggled his brows. "Sometimes I *need* a brick wall to fall on me."

Evie eyed him for a moment, then said solemnly, "I suspect that's true."

While she watched, Max slowly ran his fingers along the outside of the fireplace, testing each dusty brick. When his hands froze, she knew he'd found it.

Pulling on the brick, it came away easily, revealing a hidey-hole. He pulled a penlight from his pocket and shined it inside, clearing away the cobwebs. With two fingers, he reached in and tugged out an envelope identical to the others, with Thomas's familiar scrawl plain to see.

Evie—I wanted you to come back here to face your demons. What once was, will never be again. I bought this house—it's yours now to

*do with what you will. Your past is past. It's
time to move on, my dear.*

When she lifted her gaze to Max, he looked
blurry. That was probably because of the tears
brimming in her eyes.

Okay, maybe she was going to collapse after all.

Chapter 21

Dear Diary:

Tony Carrillo sits next to me during Music, and sometimes he smiles at me, but he rarely talks to me. Well today he ran up and kissed me on my cheek and then ran away so fast it's like he was hit by lightning. Jessica and Ashley said it was because he likes me, and that made me feel wonderful. But then I saw Tony talking to some boys and they were laughing and pointing at me. I figured he only kissed me because it was a dare or something horrible like that. I know it's because I'm ugly! My nose is too big and my freckles are horrible, and I'm just ugly! Nobody will ever want to kiss me for real!

Evangeline—age 12

Max and Evie had read the fifth clue a dozen times, and it still didn't make sense.

*He hated love stories. Love stories were for
dames. His tastes ran to hard-hitting crime dra-
mas and books about how real men won the
West. The kinds of stories where a fella packed
heat and a gal knew her place. But for purity's
sake, for the essence of all things right and true,
hell, nothing beat a good encyclopedia.*

T. E. Heyworth, 1960
Door-to-Door Death

Max shook his head as he stuffed the envelope
into his shirt pocket. This one was going to take a
bit of work.

Glancing at Evie, he decided maybe she needed a
bit of a break. Seeing the old house she'd lived in
with her mother had hurt her, brought back a
bunch of memories he was sure she'd rather have
forgotten. She was quiet now, her eyes sad, maybe
even a little damp.

Pulling into a gas station, he said, "You want to
use the rest room before we head back?"

Without saying anything, she nodded and got out
of the car.

As he waited for her, he rolled the window down.
The rain had petered out and the clouds looked like
broken slabs of slate tossed in heaps across the sky.
Boats anchored in the marina next to the shipyard
tipped and rocked, their flags snapping in the salty
breeze like bits of bright confetti against the bleak
horizon.

Flipping open his cell phone, he punched in his
partner's number.

"Yeah, Darling here."

"You're slipping," Max said. "That didn't even rhyme."

"Listen, Galloway, I could outrhyme you with half my brain tied behind my back."

"Doesn't leave you much to work with, does it?" He glanced in the sideview mirror. Still no sign of Evie. "Where are you?"

At the other end of the connection, Nate crunched down on something. "We're at a coffee shop in Silverdale. Lorna's getting a newspaper, then we're heading back to Port Henry."

"You talked to McKennitt today?"

Another crunch, then munch, munch, munch.

"Yeah," Nate finally said. "The transmission wasn't very clear, though. He was at the hospital because his wife's having trouble with some guy named Braxton Hicks and—"

Max burst out laughing and slammed his palm against the steering wheel.

At the other end of the line, there was silence. Then, "Okay. I give."

"Braxton Hicks isn't a person," Max scoffed. "It's Braxton hyphen Hicks. They're contractions women get in the third trimester of pregnancy. False labor. At least, that's what I read in a pamphlet once."

"You can read?"

"Always the comedian. What's your last clue say?"

Max heard the crackle of paper as Nate unfolded his clue. As he read it, Max kept a lookout for Evie's return.

Nate made another crunching sound, then a slurping sound, then the paper crinkled again. "We don't know what it means," he said, his mouth obviously stuffed with something. "We're hoping to take a look at the novel back at the house and see what we can come up with. I talked to Edmunds about an hour ago. They're on their fifth clue, too, and should be back the same time we are."

"Where are they now?"

"Gig Harbor."

"How's Madame holding out? She had any more visions?"

Nate chuckled, then slurped. "Only of sugar-plums. Edmunds said the woman has hit every pastry shop from Seattle to the Canadian border."

Max rubbed his jaw with his knuckles. "I've got to hand it to Heyworth. He sure knew how to throw a treasure hunt. This might even have been fun, if it hadn't morphed into a search for a killer." Leaning back in his seat, he said, "You still got the Whitney woman convinced you're Dabney James?"

"Into the fray we track our prey, yet take time to play along the way, and munch buffet at the café which is not passé but quite risqué, I hear you say—"

"Stop!" Max ordered. "Jesus Christ, Darling. You're like a dog with a bone. A *stupid* dog with a bone. So she hasn't got any idea what happened to the real James?"

"As far as I know, everybody thinks James is still alive, even the killer."

"So our suspect never met James. It's like we thought, he hired it done."

"Sam Ziwicki."

"The *late* Sam Ziwicki. So, unless our guy has more than one hit man in his employ, he'll have to do his own dirty work from now on."

Nate cleared his throat. Under his breath he said, "Here comes Lorna." At the mention of the secretary's name, his tone had changed.

Max settled the phone against his ear. "So, how are you two getting along?"

"Hunky-dory," Nate said in a way that declared, *Let's just leave it at that.* As Max listened, Nate greeted Lorna with a soft hello. She said something Max couldn't quite make out, to which Nate replied, "Oh, it's just my, uh, decorator. Always trying to furnish me with something I don't have."

"Like a personality," Max muttered.

"Say, Bruce, I've written a new poem."

"Christ, shoot me now."

"What's that? You'd like to hear it?"

In the background, Lorna said something and clapped her hands together enthusiastically.

"Good-bye," Max said.

"It's something a bit unusual for me," Nate persisted. "It's about a detective of my acquaintance."

"I'm warning you, Darling."

"Max Galloway, Max Galloway. Your sour face is here to stay. While your dour disposition is such an imposition, and it seems this is related, that you're sexually frustrated, methinks you're such an angry pup, because you cannot get it—"

"Up until now," Max interrupted, "I thought you were pretty funny."

"Thanks, Bruce. Your good opinion means so much to me."

"Yeah, I can't wait to see you, either. Good-bye, *Darling*."

As Max shoved the cell phone back inside his pocket, the passenger door opened and Evie slid in. Without a word, she fastened her seat belt, then turned away from him to study the distant clouds.

He didn't understand a whole lot about women, but he could generally sense when something was wrong. Her cheeks were pale, her body posture stiff. Crossing her arms under her breasts, she pressed her knees tightly together and continued ignoring him. He'd taken Closed Body Positions 101; she was showing all the classic signs.

Obviously, the visit to her childhood home had depressed her more than he'd thought. Reaching across the seat, he touched her shoulder. She recoiled and shifted away from him until her body hugged the door.

What the hell? He yanked his hand back as though she'd just bitten it. "Want to talk about it?" he asked as he turned the key in the ignition.

"Nothing to talk about."

Uh-oh. Releasing the brake, he pulled out into traffic and headed north. "Thinking about the next clue?"

"No."

Okay. A few miles went by, then he decided to try again.

"Are you still upset about going back to your old house?"

"No."

Perhaps he should try for questions that involved

a more comprehensive reply, not just a simple yes or no.

"Tell me what you're upset about."

"No."

Well, hell. Max punched the button on the CD player. Sultry jazz curled through the air, relaxing him a little but getting him no closer to answering his questions about what was bothering Evie.

They drove on in silence, while Max turned over the events of the day in his head. She needed rest, that was all. The day had been full of activity and surprises. Yes, she needed rest—and a man to make love to her. And he knew just the man for the job.

When they reached the secured lot, he parked and locked the car, while Evie headed down the dock to the new runabout. Without speaking to him, she sat, put on her life vest, then turned away from him to look out to sea. Twenty-five minutes later they were docked on Heyworth Island, and he'd had just about enough of the silent treatment.

Before she could take two steps off the dock, he grabbed her arm, turning her to face him.

"What is wrong?" He made each word its own sentence.

Her mouth flattened. Brushing her gloriously tangled hair off her face, she averted her eyes. "Nothing."

"Bullshit. What have I done?"

She lifted her chin. "What makes you think you've done anything?"

"I haven't," he snapped. "But *you* think I have. Out with it."

"You're imagining things."

Grasping her shoulders, he forced her to look up at him. "What did I do?"

She scowled, then shook his hands free. "I don't want to talk about it."

"Ah, so you *do* think I've done something."

In a tight little voice, she said, "You can run your life any way you want. It's none of my business. You can see whomever you wish. It's no concern of mine."

He closed one eye, tucked in his chin and frowned. What in the hell was she talking about? She'd been fine back at the gas station, but when she came out of the rest room, he'd just been finishing his conversation with Nate . . .

I can't wait to see you, either. Good-bye, Darling.

His own words rang like a gong inside his head. She'd *heard* him. She'd heard him, and she thought . . .

He looked into her accusing eyes and tried not to laugh.

Feigning anger, he said, "Did you eavesdrop on my phone call?"

Her beautiful mouth tightened into a rosebud and she looked away. "You might have mentioned you were involved with someone before I . . . before we . . ."

"Well, I'm not terribly involved," he said in an offhanded way. "It's what you'd call a new relationship, and it's a little unsteady. I'd even call it competitive."

"Whatever," she said in a light, breezy tone.

He was having trouble keeping the laughter from his voice, but the look on her face, the glint in her eyes, the stance of her delectable body, fed his desire to play with her a little longer. He'd make it worth her while, though. He'd make it very worth her while.

"Listen," he said with a shrug. "About that *other* relationship. We have never slept together, and I think it's safe to say we never will. Totally not my type, sexually." He grinned. "Evie. I love it that you're jealous."

Her head came up, her mouth opened, her eyes widened. "I am *not* jealous! I could not care *less* who you sleep with or don't sleep with or—"

"Darling," he said.

"Wh-What?"

"Darling. Detective Nate Darling. He's my partner, Evie. That's what you heard. But I love it that you thought—"

Before he could react, she doubled her fist and punched him in the stomach.

"You son of a bitch!" she huffed. "How dare you make me think . . . you bastard! And here I . . . and you didn't . . . I felt like such a—"

He stopped her tirade with his mouth. Crushing her lips with his kiss, he thrust his tongue inside. Against his chest, her breasts tormented him. He wanted to rip open her blouse and take them in his hands, make love to her here, right here on the dock, revel in her body, listen to her cries, capture her heart for his own.

Instead, he wrapped his arms around her and

pulled her tight against him, holding her so very
close, thankful for her existence, for the energy and
vitality that was Evie. Beneath his hands, her muscles were firm and warm, and he felt giddy from the
joy of holding her like this once more.

And then she kissed him back, wrapping her arms
around his neck, clinging to him, taking possession
of him, telling him with her lips and her body that
she was his, and more, that he belonged only to her.
And, damn it if it wasn't true. He *did* belong to her,
and with sudden clarity he realized he liked that
idea a lot.

Against his mouth she whispered, "I still think
you're a rotten son of a—"

He kissed her again, cutting off her damning
words, holding her close until he felt her body con-
vulse in repressed laughter. She pulled away an
inch, licked and nibbled his bottom lip and murmured, "I am so going to make you pay."

"Can we eat first? I need to keep my strength up."

"And that's not all," she teased.

He took her hand and they walked off the dock
and up the stone path leading to the mansion. All
the lights were on, welcoming them home like
prodigal wanderers. As they reached the front door,
Evie tugged on Max's arm.

"Hang on a minute," she said. "I want to ask you
something."

Leaning back against the stone archway over the
massive front door, he slipped his hands around her
waist. "Anything."

With her palms resting lightly on his forearms,
she said, "If you were me, would you do the DNA

test? I mean, without my mother's DNA, we can't prove whether Thomas was really my father, but if the results exclude him, then that'll be more than I know now."

He considered her words, wondering what it must feel like to forever question where you came from.

"Why now, Evie, after all these years?"

She laid her head on his shoulder and let her body go slack against his. "I guess it's time. I guess I'm ready to know."

"Well, that being the case, having the test would be one solution." He waited for her reaction.

"*One* solution? There's *another*?"

Max tipped her chin so their eyes met. No time like the present to throw somebody's life into total chaos.

"Sure there is, Evie," he said softly. "There always has been. You don't really need a DNA test at all. The truth is right in front of you. If I can see it, I'm sure you can."

"I—I don't know what you're talking about."

"I think you do. If you search your heart, I think you'll realize that you've known the truth all along. You know it now, right this minute. Don't you, Scout?"

Chapter 22

Dear Diary:

Today I wore the moon necklace that used to be my mother's. I showed it to Edmunds and he said it was the prettiest thing he had ever seen. Then he said my red hair was just like Maggie's. He always calls her that. He said she was beautiful and that she was a free spirit. I think that means she had lots of boyfriends. Then he asked me if I wanted some hot chocolate with marshmallows. I don't want to make Thomas feel bad, so I've never told him how much I love Edmunds. He is truly a wonderful and gracious man.

Evangeline—age 13

Evie straightened and distanced herself from Max as much as his embrace would allow.

"What are you talking about?" she whispered,

her mouth gone completely dry. "If I knew the truth, why would I keep asking?"

"Evie," he said quietly, "I don't want to hurt you, but I think you have to face the facts. Heyworth was not—"

"Yes he *was*," she rushed. "I found proof, but he died before I could ask him about it."

Max cocked his head, suspicious, apprehensive. "What kind of proof?"

She swallowed. "A couple of days before Thomas was killed, I was in his office going through the files. Mrs. Stanley had asked me to find the warrantee for the stove. Anyway, I found a piece of paper that had fallen between two hanging files. It was a copy of the second page of a letter Thomas had written."

"Go on."

"The letter asked for information about his . . . his daughter."

"His daughter?" Releasing her, Max absently rubbed his chin with his knuckles. "Jesus."

She nodded. "He'd had a brief affair with a maid on his staff, and he wanted to know if she had given birth to a child. If so, he wanted to bring her to Mayhem and acknowledge his heir."

"How long ago was it written? Who was it addressed to?"

She lifted her shoulders. "That's the problem. The first page was missing. No date, no addressee, only his signature on the second page. I looked through as many files as I could, but I never found it."

"What did you do with the letter?"

"I didn't think I should keep it. Thomas might

have thought I'd been snooping around in his personal correspondence. So I put it in a folder and closed the cabinet, intending to broach the subject with him once and for all when he returned from his book tour. But the day he got back, he was murdered."

"Did you tell anybody about the letter?"

"Yes," she said. "I told the Port Henry police about it when they confiscated Thomas's files, but when I asked them about it later, they said it wasn't there."

"Who had access to that cabinet?"

"Me, Lorna, Mrs. Stanley. Maybe others. This is an island, you know. We don't get a lot of transients out here."

"That would certainly provide motive for the attempts on your life," Max murmured absently. He stared off into space for a moment, then said, "And you're sure it was *you* he was referring to?"

Anger stabbed her belly. Why was he *not* getting this?

"My mother was a maid who left here and had a child," she argued. "And Thomas sought me out and brought me to Mayhem to live with him. What more proof do you need, Max?"

"Positive proof," he said calmly. "But I'm not the one who needs it. You do. Sure, he brought you here, but he never submitted to any paternity tests, and more importantly, he never admitted he was your father. It doesn't add up."

She toyed with the crescent moon dangling at her throat. "I thought maybe, once he'd seen me, he'd just known I was his. I don't know why he never told me. But my father was *not* some faceless, name-less sailor my mother couldn't even remember! He *wasn't*!"

Still angry at Max for being so dense, Evie slipped into her nightgown and tried to turn her thoughts to the game.

It was Monday night. Time was getting short, and so, apparently, was her temper. She knew she shouldn't have been so defensive with him earlier, and had reacted to his comments without thinking things through.

Closing the armoire, she rested her forehead against the wood and groaned at her own stupidity. She'd have to find a way to apologize. . . .

Tapping. At her door. Her heart gave a little jump.

She and Max were alone in the house. Edmunds and Madame Grovda, Dabney and Lorna, had still not returned. The Stanleys must have left hours ago.

At the mere thought of Max standing outside her door, her heart rate increased, her skin became sensitive, her breasts tightened. Her body knew what it wanted, craved, expected to get. She was utterly exhausted, but the thought of lying in Max's arms tonight sent a wash of adrenaline through her system that made every nerve in her body come alive.

"Tired, Scout?" he said as she opened the door to him. His hair was disheveled in a very sexy way. He needed a shave, and his shirt collar was open, revealing his strong neck. She wanted to put her mouth there.

She nodded. "I could use some sleep . . . eventually."

He let his gaze travel down her body. "You still mad at me?"

"Yes," she lied.

"Good," he said, grinning in that sly way he had that drove her nuts with desire. "Come with me, and bring your quilt."

Evie went to the bed and gathered the patchwork quilt into her arms. When she turned to face him, she expected him to kiss her, so when his warm hand clasped hers, she was surprised.

"Follow me," he said softly as he guided her out the bedroom door. He slipped his arm around her waist as they strolled toward the atrium, the quilt bundled in her arms.

"Where are we going?" Evie asked as they moved through the garden.

"To a romantic spot where I can make love to you tonight."

"I'm still mad at you, remember?" she said in a flirty way.

"But you want to kiss-and-make-up, right?" he said as he ran his finger down her cleavage. "And makeup sex is the hottest sex there is."

Evie's blood simmered up another couple of degrees as he led her along one of the winding paths through the palm trees and orchids to the waterfall. He took the quilt from her arms and moved away from her.

She stilled for a moment, watching as moonlight bounced and glimmered off the ribbons of water splashing down the rough edges of the rocks. Trying to quiet her thundering heart, she focused on the rhythm of the water, watching as a fat drop plopped onto a broad green leaf and shattered like bits of glass.

While she inhaled the mingled scents of roses and wild flowers, Max spread the quilt over the thick carpet of grass, stained silver by the floating moon. Straightening, he pulled off his shirt and kicked off his boots.

Moonlight loved him, caressed him as she wanted to do. His broad shoulders and muscled chest moved with each breath he took. His face seemed carved by light and shadow, the high cheekbones, the bridge of his nose, the sensual line of his upper lip.

He came to her, not saying a word. She felt his fingertips under her chin as he raised her face for his kiss. The tip of his tongue licked her lips, slid inside.

Her breathing came hard now, and so did his. She felt the pulse of his breath against her open mouth, until he lowered his head, closing the gap, sealing their mouths together in a heated blast of sensation.

In the back of her throat she felt a moan, a dull sound that vibrated through them both. He broke the kiss.

She felt his fingers on her waist, his hands under her gown, his palms on her breasts. In one swift movement he tugged her nightgown up and off.

"Evie," he whispered as he looked at her in the moonlight. "Your body was made for lovemaking. For my hands on you, my mouth . . ."

He bent and kissed her collarbone, then ran his tongue across her skin and down one breast until he reached her peaked nipple. He suckled it until she wanted to scream.

She eased her hands over his hard chest and down until she reached the top button on his jeans. Popping it open, she let her hands move inside, shoving the fabric along as she went. Reaching around, she rubbed her hands over his butt, grasping the firm flesh, pulling his hips into hers. He groaned into her mouth.

In another moment he was naked. He went down on his knees, taking her with him onto the quilt. She parted her thighs, and he set himself between them as though they had done this a thousand times, as though he knew her body perfectly, as though she knew the moves he would make before he made them.

Arching over her, he bent his head and kissed her, making love to her mouth the way she knew he would make love to her body. Against her belly, she felt his erection, and it excited her to know she could make him respond to her so . . . enthusiastically.

Slipping her hands downward, she grasped him, curling her fingers around him. He choked her name, his hips rolling wildly as she stroked him.

"Have to slow down," he panted. "You make me crazy."

Pulling back, he fumbled for his jeans pocket. She heard him tear open the packet.

"Here," she said, taking it from him. "Let me."

She pushed him onto his back and moved lower until she hovered over him. With her tongue, she licked him, suckled him, nibbled along the length of him.

His hips rolled and he groaned, running his fingers through her hair, holding her head in place while her mouth and tongue drove him higher and higher.

When she couldn't wait any longer, she set the condom over him and gave a little lick under the rolled edge. Licking and rolling, she sheathed him until he gasped and begged for mercy.

Grabbing her shoulders, he gently lay her under him and thrust into her, moaning in satisfaction. His voice was rough, his movements jerky.

"I don't know how long I can hold it," he growled. "God, Evie. What you do to me."

He thrust into her again and she closed around him. Sensation rippled through her body, across her skin, stealing every thought from her head except one.

She loved him. She loved Max Galloway, loved him so much she didn't think she could form the words without weeping.

He moved inside her, and she wrapped her arms around his back, holding him close, absorbing the heat from his body, the energy expended pleasuring her. His heart beat against hers as though they were connected, made of the same ethereal stuff that had built the galaxy and all the stars and the heavens, too.

Behind her closed lids bursts of light filled the universe of her mind, the empty territory of her heart, the vast sea of her soul. She was in love and was altered forever. The joy of it, the newness, the rapture . . . she wanted to cry out of sheer delight.

So this was what it felt like to be whole, she thought. For the first time in her life, another person existed who completed her. She wanted to tell him what he'd given her, what a gift it was, what a joy.

Instead, she smiled to herself and held him tighter, letting him fill her arms and her body, and for now that would be enough.

Her pleasure mounted, the tower to heaven was built, then collapsed in a rush of release.

She sighed his name, and his mouth came down on hers to take it from her.

He stiffened, then lurched as his own climax took him over. He pounded into her, his fingers woven tightly with hers.

They lay together, bodies entangled, fingers entwined, while they floated back down to earth. Just when she was able to breathe normally again, Max suddenly wrapped his arms around her and pulled her tightly against him.

"Max?" she whispered. "What's wrong?"

His lips brushed her neck, and when he spoke, she felt his words against her skin. "Evie, I . . . I'm not much on après sex conversation. At least, I never have been."

"That's okay," she soothed, tangling her fingers in the silk of his hair. "You don't have to—"

"But I want to. I need to."

Evie stroked his hair and said nothing.

"Sometimes," he began, "well, there are times I get lonely." He spoke as though he were a sinner in a confessional, as though loneliness were a misdeed for which he must repent. "Sometimes, I'm so damned lonely, I can barely stand it. My work fills up all my days and half my nights, and I keep it that way because when I go home, nothing. I . . . Single men aren't supposed to get lonely."

"Who told you that?"

He snorted. "Take a guess. Guys like me are supposed to have a string of babes on the hook to keep
them company, and for a while I did that. Yeah, I
did that." The words came out bitterly, as though he
were deeply ashamed. "But it got old. Fast. Maybe
it was good enough for my old man, but it didn't
work for me. Since Melissa, there's been nobody
special. I think there needs to be somebody special."

She nodded. "I think so, too." Holding him in
her arms, knowing he had come to trust her enough
to share something so personal, she could almost
feel her heart burst into blossoms.

"Whatever you were," she said, "or think you
were, doesn't matter anymore."

He pulled back and looked into her eyes. "I can
be a real son of a bitch, Evie. You don't know. I
drove Melissa away, and my mother. I haven't been
able to get close to anyone. I've been afraid of
pulling the same shit, of losing—"

"Oh, Max," she whispered, the words so soft as
to be barely audible. "Don't."

Reaching past his shoulder, she fumbled for his
pants. Digging into the pocket, she found the coin
his mother had given him. It was cold, so she curled
her fingers around it, holding it tightly in her palm.

"Look," she said, and opened her hand.

By the light of the moon, she studied the image
on the metal disk. A beautiful woman in an ancient
headdress, frozen in a lovely pose for all time. Turning the coin to the other side, silvery light caught the
tips of the horse's crudely carved wings as the creature took flight.

Raising her gaze to Max, she said, "You love this

coin, carry it with you always, both for what it is and what it represents."

He nodded. His gaze darted to the object she held in her hand then lifted to her eyes.

With her free hand, she reached up and cupped his jaw in her palm. "People are like coins, Max. You . . . are like this coin. It has two distinctly different sides, and when it's tossed, it falls haphazardly to either one side or the other. But it's not like that for you. You have a choice. You can choose which side of yourself to show the world."

He took in a deep breath, let it out. She felt the rise and fall of his chest against her breast, and committed every nuance of this moment to memory. This was as close as she had ever felt to another human being. Whatever else life might throw her way, she had this moment in the arms of the man she loved, and she knew that would carry her for a long, long time.

Max's lips slowly curved into a smile. His eyes held a look in them she didn't think she'd ever seen in a man's eyes before.

"You're a pretty smart cookie," he whispered. But because of those eyes, the softness of his voice, the quirk of his mouth, Evie swore she heard, *I love you*.

"I'm a *very* smart cookie," she replied. And with her eyes, and with the whisper of her voice, and with the curve of her smile, she made sure he heard, *I love you, too*.

Chapter 23

Dear Diary:

I have been thinking about boys a lot lately. Some of the girls in my class have boyfriends, but I don't. I wish I did sometimes. Does that mean I'm a free spirit? I remember my mom, and I get worried that I'll be like her. If I got a boyfriend, would I like him so much so that when I have a daughter, I'll forget all about her? Maybe I shouldn't fall in love for a long time, just in case.

Evangeline—age 13

Sometime during the wee hours, Evie brought Max up to her room, and they actually managed to get a little shut-eye. She woke just before dawn, wrapped snugly in his arms. Contentment and satisfaction relaxing every bone in her body, she melded into him as though they had been designed to fit together.

Even though it was going to be a busy day, they took their time getting out of bed and down to breakfast. First, they had to make love just one last time, then shower together and help each other dress, which involved much kissing and many caresses. Somehow, her simple morning routine expanded, with Max's help, from thirty minutes to nearly two hours.

By the time they arrived downstairs for breakfast, the others were already assembled, chatting and munching, except for the poet, who appeared decidedly glum. As she and Max took their seats, Dabney tossed his napkin on the table, adjusted his glasses, and leaned back in his chair, a scowl on his handsome face.

Not for the first time, Evie wondered how such a hunky, athletic-looking man ended up a poet, especially a reclusive one. Immediately, she felt guilty at imposing an unfair stereotype on him, as though poets couldn't be young and studly. It was just that he seemed so utterly unpoetlike.

"We've hit a wall," he grumbled, running his fingers through his hair. "Finding our next clue has been a bust. Looks like we're out of the race."

Madame Grovda shook her head in sympathy and reached over, patting his hand. "Not to worry," she comforted. "As you Americans say, it is not over until the plus-sized lady does the singing." Her cheeks flushed as she grinned shyly at Dabney. "Politically correct, *da*?"

His shoulders relaxed a bit and he smiled at the psychic. "Thank you, madame. I'll keep that in mind."

The ten thousand gold bangles on Madame Grovda's wrist clanged together as she waved her hand at Lorna. "Besides, one treasure you have found already, yes?"

Lorna lowered her lashes and mumbled something under her breath. When she lifted her gaze, it was to look at Dabney, who looked back at her with a predatory glint in his eye.

Evie swallowed a smile, trying to ignore what was obviously going on between the secretary and the poet, since the same thing was apparently going on between the schoolteacher and the detective.

Adding cream to her coffee, she said, "So you're saying you can't find your fifth clue?"

"It's like the trail just dried up," Lorna offered. "And unless we can find it, locating six and seven, not to mention the jackpot, will be out of the question."

"There are still several days left," Evie insisted. "You never know what will happen."

Out of the corner of her eye she saw Max and Dabney exchange quick glances, but before she could say anything else, Edmunds entered the dining room with a decanter of orange juice and a tray of chilled glasses. As he began to serve each guest, Max said, "How's it going with you two, Edmunds?"

The butler set a glass in front of Evie, then tapped her on the tip of her nose with his finger.

"Good morning," she said.

He returned her smile, then said to Max, "Though we continue to study our Clue Number Five, nothing about it leads us to Clue Number Six. We are all at sea, sir. If nothing pops soon, as the saying goes, Madame and I will be out of the running as well."

Max took a gulp of his orange juice. "Lorna," he said. "You only worked for Heyworth a couple of weeks before he was killed, right?"

Raising her juice glass to her lips, she took a sip. "That's right."

"Why were you invited to the treasure hunt? Six months ago, Heyworth didn't even know you."

She took another sip of juice, then set her glass on the table. "That's simple. Six months ago, Mr. Heyworth was apparently between secretaries, I guess you'd say."

"That's a diplomatic way of putting it," Evie contributed, remembering how several of the poor souls had fled in fits of hysteria after trying to deal with their formidable employer. "Not long after I'd come to the island, one lady burst from the office, screaming she'd swim to shore and risk drowning rather than spend one more minute in Thomas's employ. I distinctly remember Thomas shrugging and chalking it up to PMS."

"How did he know she had PMS?" Max said.

"Not hers, his. 'Post Manuscript Shit.' Whenever he received a revision letter from his editor, he would rant and rave for days, drink a lot, yell at people on the phone, slam doors. It was very tense."

"Did he make the revisions?"

"Oh, heavens no. His solution was to buy the publishing company." She smiled wryly. "If Thomas didn't like the rules, he changed them."

"Well," he said with a shrug, "I guess the old guy had his moments."

"Does that mean you're coming to appreciate Thomas? See him in a whole new light?" She arched her brow, sending him an I-told-you-so smile.

"No," he growled. "Not unless today's the day hell freezes over. I'm only saying that he may not have been as bad as I'd originally thought. *May* not. The jury's still out."

He polished off his juice, then set the glass down on the table. "There's a copy of *Door-to-Door Death* in the library, right?"

She nodded. "As I recall, the story is about an encyclopedia salesman who killed the women to whom he didn't make a sale."

"What, he conked them on the head with Volume Ten, Sadism Through Sybarite?"

"Actually, I think it was Volume Seven, Mayhem Through Murder."

Max smiled. "How imaginative."

As Evie set her untouched orange juice away from her, Max teased, "You have an emotional aversion to oranges, too? Is it because they're *naval* oranges? Reminds you of those marine crabs that—"

"Dear God," she said, holding up her hands. "Will you never let me forget that dumb crab story?"

"I liked it." He grinned at her while she stood and slipped her hands into her pockets.

"Well, I need to go check on the llamas, but I won't be gone very long. You go get that book from the library. When I return, we can read through it, okay?"

Evie picked up the grooming brush and called to Fernando. She needed to do some thinking, and when she was close to Max, all she *could* think about was kissing him and touching him, and simply breathing the same air he breathed. He was so distracting, she'd never decipher their next clue if she couldn't get her brain into gear.

Though she didn't have a lot of experience, she had enough to know that Max was an attentive, inventive, caring lover. The clever things he did, the way he made her feel, the tender look in his eyes . . . when she was with him, the outside world ceased to exist. He made her feel passionate and beautiful, as though she could make love with him with abandon and never feel embarrassed or self-conscious.

But more than that, more than being in love with him, she liked him. When they were together, he let his guard down, allowed her to see a part of him that was vulnerable. Such trust attracted her like a bee to wild honeysuckle. She'd only been away from him for fifteen minutes, and already she missed him.

Smiling to herself, she knew she was probably being silly, but she didn't care. She was in love, and the world was lovely.

She swept the brush through Fernando's wool, loosening as much debris as she could. He'd picked up bits of hay and alfalfa in his fleece and it was a tangled mess.

"Been pronking again, handsome?" she said. "Now there's a suggestive word if ever I've heard one."

"Does it mean having sex?" At the sound of the woman's voice, Evie turned. It was Lorna.

Evie laughed. "No, not sex. Around dusk, sometimes, llamas get frisky and do this running, danc-ing, hopping, bounding dance. They just sort of go a little nuts. It's called pronking."

Lorna smiled, making her brown eyes sparkle. "Pronking sounds like a sex word."

Evie narrowed one eye on Fernando. "Hey, babeeee. Care for a good pronk?"

Lorna laughed. "God knows, I'm ready for one." Her cheeks flushed and she looked away.

She was dressed as she had been at breakfast, in jeans and a floral print blouse. Her brown hair hung in a thick braid down her back and she was wearing little pearl earrings. With her arms crossed on the top rail of the fence, she looked like a pretty milk-maid. Meeting Dabney James seemed to have had a magical, transforming effect on her. Apparently, the magic hadn't progressed as far as the bedroom yet, but if the look in the poet's eye was any indication, it was simply a matter of time.

Lorna moved away from the fence and walked over to where Evie was grooming the llama. Picking up a curry comb, she thrummed it with her fingers, seemingly deep in thought. Then she said, "I'm sorry I haven't had a chance to get to know you bet-ter, Evie. What with arriving only two weeks before Mr. Heyworth left on his tour, and then his murder, well, everything's been so confusing." She looked into Evie's eyes. "I'm too used to keeping to myself, I suppose. Guess that'll all change now."

"What do you mean?"

"I moved here specifically to take this job. Mr. Heyworth's agent made me an offer I couldn't re-

fuse. Now that he's gone, as soon as the estate paperwork is settled, I'll be out of work. What with
our latest clue being so difficult, I don't think I can
count on buried treasure as a solid source of in-
come." She gave a dry laugh and plucked at the
comb's teeth again.

Evie stopped what she was doing, set the brush
on the bench and turned her attention on Lorna.

"Lorna, did you like Thomas?"

"He was nice to me."

"That sounds evasive."

"I wanted to like him, but I found myself angry at
him a lot of the time."

"Did you kill him?"

If Lorna was offended by the question, she didn't
show it. "No."

"You said you came to Washington specifically to
take the job with Thomas? How did that happen?"

She pursed her lips, looked at Evie, then looked
away. "I got a letter from an agency offering me the
position. A great salary—twice what I was
making—with relocation expenses included, and
room and board at Mayhem." With a small shrug,
she said, "I grew up very poor in California. When I
was little, my mom worked two jobs to support us.
She died eight months ago, so there was nothing
keeping me there, and Mr. Heyworth's offer seemed
like a fabulous opportunity."

"What happened to your father?"

"I never knew him."

Evie ran her fingers through her hair, slipping a
stray strand behind her ear. "Seems like we have

something in common," she said sympathetically. "My mother never told me who my father was, either."

"All my life," Lorna said, "I thought my father had abandoned us, but I found out recently he'd never known I existed. She hadn't told him about me. I've never been able to figure out if she was being independent or just plain stupid."

The two women smiled weakly at each other, their common pain uniting them on some basic level.

Evie leaned back against the fence rail. "I don't know for sure who my father was, but I have my suspicions."

"Really?" Lorna said. "Are you going to contact him?"

Evie's heart sank the way it always did when she thought about Thomas and realized he was gone from her forever.

"Lorna," she said, "I—I think, well, I'm almost certain, that when my mother worked at Mayhem nearly thirty years ago, she had an affair with Thomas Heyworth. In fact, I think Thomas was my father."

Lorna's face blanched. It was as though all the blood had drained from her body, leaving just skin and muscle and bone. Her brown eyes widened and she made a soft gasping sound.

"That can't b-be," she stuttered. "That just can't be. Thomas Heyworth *can't* have been your father. . . ."

Evie blinked. "Why not?"

"Because," Lorna choked. "Well, because . . ."

"Because *why*?" Evie demanded.

Lorna shook her head, her brow furrowed, her eyes dull with confusion. Locking gazes with Evie, she whispered, "Because he was mine."

Evie stood at the library window, her arms wrapped around her waist, her eyes on the clouds moving swiftly across the sky. Another summer storm was fast approaching, and it promised to be a doozy. Violent winds were already bending the treetops. At the dock, the Hatteras and the runabout were swaying from side to side, straining their moorings.

Her gaze fell to Max, standing outside, his body braced against the wind as he talked with Dabney. They were both big men, but each struggled to maintain his balance against the violent gusts. As she looked on, the two men turned and walked around the side of the house, out of sight. Evie rubbed her sore eyes and went to one of the chairs by the fireplace.

So, the letter she'd found in Thomas's office had not been about her at all. It was Lorna who was Thomas's daughter, and he'd lured her to Mayhem with a job opportunity, but was killed before he could officially claim her.

Poor Thomas. He must have had so many regrets, having had a real daughter all those years, never aware, never able to take care of Lorna the way he'd taken care of her.

Of course, everything made sense now. She'd been in denial for so many years. Even in the face of the evidence, she had stuck to her hopes rather than her reality.

Thomas Heyworth was not her father, and that was that.

God, she could be stubborn. Why hadn't she seen the truth? Max saw it, had tried to tell her, but no, she'd been convinced she was right.

She laughed softly. Being a strong woman had its advantages. It also had a few perils. Once she got an idea into her head, it seemed it took a very hard slap of reality to knock it out again. She had been such an idiot. A blind, terrified, selfish idiot.

Pushing herself out of the chair, she strode purposefully through the house until she found him. He stood with his back to her, polishing the already sparkling silver tea service that sat in the antique cabinet in the dining room.

He must have sensed her presence because he turned to her and smiled, as he always did. She cocked her head. He was tall and handsome, and had summer blue eyes. Just like hers.

Yes, she was truly an idiot.

"Edmunds," she said, her voice suddenly gone dry.

"Hello, Evangeline," he said softly. "Is there something I can do for you?"

Without warning, her eyes grew moist. She tried to say the words, but they got stuck in her throat and wouldn't form.

"You are distressed?" he said, alarm clear to see on his face. "What's wrong, my dear?" He moved toward her and placed his hand on her arm.

She blinked away her tears, then squared her shoulders.

"Th-There's something I need to know, Edmunds," she stumbled. "And I believe you are the only one who can tell me."

He looked at her, then her meaning seemed to sink in and his eyes grew aware. Nodding once, he said slowly, "Yes. I believe you are right, my child."

She nodded slowly, letting the words seep into her soul.

My child . . .

"I should be mad as hell at you, Edmunds," she said, almost under her breath.

He set the teapot and polishing cloth on the table. "I realize that," he said quietly.

"I've had a living, breathing father all these years, but you never said a word. You let me think Thomas was my father. . . . Why?" Her mouth felt tight, but she didn't want to hate Edmunds, not now. Especially not now.

"I tried a thousand times to tell you, Evangeline," he said. "You must understand, I didn't know about you, not until your mother died. Upon her death, an item appeared in the obituaries. It stated she had left behind a daughter of eleven. At that very moment, I did wonder, but assumed Maggie would have told me."

"Why do you think she didn't?" Her eyes burned, her heart hurt, her voice trembled. But the truth . . . the truth, at last, had come out. It was as though she could take in a deep breath for the first time in her life.

Remorse shaded the blue of his eyes. "Maggie O'Dell was determined to live by her own rules. She didn't want anything slowing her down, tying her to a place she did not wish to be. Perhaps she feared I would want to be a part of her life if I knew about you."

Evie nodded. That sounded like her mother all right.

"I was thirty-six. She was twenty. Beyond beautiful. One might say ethereal. Full of life, and glorious in her youth." He shrugged. "I cannot say exactly how it happened, but one night, it simply did. I fell in love with her. I gave her my mother's necklace, the one you're wearing now."

She reached up and touched the warm gold, tears choking her, making speech impossible.

Edmunds let go a long sigh. "When I saw that she had died, I talked to Thomas, told him a former employee had passed away and left a young daughter. No other family had been found. I asked him if he didn't think it charitable to see if the child needed anything."

He smiled, his affection for his late employer obvious. "Thomas barely remembered Maggie. After all, she hadn't worked here that long." He paused, then sought her eyes. "Imagine my surprise when he returned with you and announced he had made arrangements to have you live here as his ward."

She tilted her head. "When did you know I was yours?"

"Instantly," he whispered, the word like a prayer on his lips. "Not only did you have my mother's eyes, you were wearing her necklace. And, more importantly, Maggie had named you Evangeline May Randall. That could not have been a coincidence."

"Why?"

"My mother's maiden name was Randall. May Randall. Maggie knew that. I told her when I gave her the necklace. I wanted to marry her. I believe that's why she left soon after."

Evie nodded, letting everything he said settle into her bones. She was in shock and hungry for information. But she knew that soon her shock would merge into anger, and she wanted to fight it as long as she could.

"Why didn't you ever tell me you were my father, Edmunds?"

He walked to the large window overlooking the sea. Past his shoulder, dark clouds moved toward shore, urged on by turbulent winds.

"I didn't tell you who I was because I had nothing to offer you." His shoulders lifted in a helpless way. "Thomas didn't know you were my daughter. He'd already made you his ward. He had the finances and the social status I lacked. It was obvious you adored him, right from the start. I knew I would never marry and give you a mother. I did have hopes Thomas would remarry, but he never did after Lillian died."

"Max's mother."

"Yes. She died only months before you came here. Maybe Thomas was trying to fill that void with you, I don't know. At any rate, I thought it best just to leave things as they were."

"When Thomas was killed," she said, "why didn't you tell me then?"

He doubled his fists and held his arms straight at

his sides. Turning to face her, he cried, "Because I am a coward! Because you loved *him* and I feared I could never take his place in your heart. I had let too much time slip by. I was wrong, Evangeline. I loved you so, I was terrified you would hate me. I had convinced myself you would never want to have anything to do with me once you knew the truth."

Tears filled his eyes and slid down his flushed cheeks. "I am so sorry," he choked softly. "Can you ever forgive me? Can I do anything to make it up to you, make things right again?"

Edmunds stood before her, a man tormented by guilt and remorse. What could she say to him? How could they move past such a monumental barrier between them?

Then she remembered Max's words. *If you search your heart, I think you'll realize that you've known the truth all along. You know it now, right this minute. Don't you, Scout?*

Edmunds stood, terrified, waiting, torn to pieces by what he had done, and not done. But she had been just as guilty. She'd had every clue, every opportunity, and had ignored it all.

Stubborn. Yes, she was stubborn all right.

Going to her father, she slipped her arms around his waist and lay her head on his chest. Beneath her ear his heart pounded like a fist on a wooden door. *Let me in*, it said. *Please let me in.*

Slowly, his arms came around her. He lowered his head until his cheek rested on her hair.

"I think we've both made some mistakes," she

whispered. "But I'll forgive you, if you'll forgive me. Papa."

His only answer was a tightening of his arms around her as he sobbed softly into her hair.

It was all either of them needed.

Chapter 24

Dear Diary:

I saw this movie on TV today that I figured was going to be about some car race. It didn't have any special effects, explosions, animals, children or anything! The man and the woman were perpetually arguing and seemed to hate each other. Then they had a horrible fight and he grabbed her and kissed her, and then they fell in love. It was the best movie I have ever seen.

Evangeline—age 13

Monday came and went, as did Tuesday. The storm that rolled down from Canada stalled out over the peninsula, keeping the sky in turmoil. Fists of wind punched at the house, rattling the windows. The eaves whistled from the force, like the eerie lament of a banshee.

The sea was high. Huge waves sucked away the sand on the north side of the island as massive surges thundered in, pummeling the driftwood piled against the low rock cliff. The bay was so rough, travel to and from Heyworth Island had become impossible. Inside the house, the air held a damp, salty bite.

Because the Stanleys were stranded in town, Evie and Lorna stayed busy in the kitchen preparing meals. Max, Dabney, and Edmunds helped out by doing the dishes, while Madame Grovda paced and mumbled to herself, her forehead beaded with perspiration, her eyes wide with alarm. Whenever Evie asked what was bothering her, she muttered in Russian, crossed herself, and wandered away in obvious but incomprehensible distress.

Together, Max and Evie had gone through *Door-to-Door Death* no fewer than four times, but they still couldn't figure out where Clue Number Six was hidden. The other two teams had lost their trails completely and all but given up.

By Friday morning nerves were tightly stretched. The hunt was scheduled to end the next day at midnight, and if none of the teams made it to Clue Number Seven, not only would Thomas's fortune be lost, a killer might escape.

Then, just before noon, the winds died down and blue sky emerged between the clusters of gray and black clouds. Mrs. Stanley arrived and, even though she seemed tired and distracted, immediately went to work preparing lunch.

"Earl didn't come with you today?" Evie asked as she put away the dish she was drying.

"No," the cook said, then rubbed her eyes. "Bad cold. I, uh, it's been rough. Soup and crackers."

"Is there anything I can do?"

Mrs. Stanley shook her head and silently continued on about her business, so Evie went into the library to wait for Max.

Tugging a slim volume of verse from the shelf, she collapsed into the nearest chair, letting the soft leather envelop her, making her feel like a small child snuggling into Grandma's lap.

Her vision blurred. Ironic, since she'd been blind for so long. She'd been so focused on one possibility, she hadn't seen the truth literally staring her in the face . . . or laughing at her over her tea set, or pushing her on the swing behind the house.

Edmunds was her father. She smiled a watery smile to herself. Of *course* he was.

She opened the cover of the book and tried to concentrate, but there were so many puzzles all tangled up in her brain, the words on the page became an inky haze. In frustration, she closed her eyes . . . and saw Max.

The mere thought of him sent ripples of delight through her body. Love, fresh and new and brimming with possibilities, made her heart light. A moment later that same heart sank like a rock.

Sure, she was head over heels in love and it felt beyond good. But within a few hours the hunt would end, and Max would return to Olympia. He hadn't said anything about wanting to see her again, or whether he had any feelings for her. Her heart told her he did, but it sure would be nice to hear him say it.

She sniffed away her tears, opened her eyes, and ran her finger down the crisp page. Love was wonderful, being in love sublime. It was also nerve-wracking and tense. She wanted to pluck a daisy from its stem and do a he-loves-me, he-loves-me-not petal pull. However, she knew the outcome was determined less by Cupid's will than by whether the flower contained an even or odd number of petals.

Math. Damn. Sometimes, being a schoolteacher took all the mystery out of things.

Releasing a long sigh, she forced herself to forget about Max for the moment, forget about romance and the possibility of a future together, forget about treasures and clues and her inability to analyze them, forget about her newly discovered father, about the chasm losing Thomas had created and the fact that somebody had made three attempts on her life. She pushed everything away and tried to concentrate on the most important task at hand—identifying a killer.

She hadn't killed Thomas, and neither had Max or Edmunds. That left Madame Grovda, Dabney, or Lorna. Surely, Madame Grovda could be ruled out, given her age and the complete lack of organizational skills it would take to pull off a murder.

Lorna? She was probably out, too. Since she knew she was Thomas's daughter, what possible reason would she have had to kill him? Well, there was the money. Lorna hadn't said so, but maybe she had proof Thomas was her father, and if so, the estate would go to her sooner rather than later. Yet if all that were true, what motive would Lorna have for killing Evie?

Then there was Dabney James. Evie rubbed her temples. What did she know about him, except that he and Max didn't seem to get along. Thirty-something, handsome, boyish, and totally incompetent at impromptu poetry. He must have worked like a demon for months to polish his published works enough to have them acceptable to an editor, because his spur-of-the-moment stuff sucked mightily. Even so, she didn't see him as the type—if there was a type—to plan and commit murders. And what would have been his motive?

Of course, there was Felix Barlow, though why he'd want Thomas dead was a mystery. Maybe he hated Thomas, maybe he wanted his money, too. Barlow was a relatively wealthy man, so getting his hands on the Heyworth millions seemed like an implausible motive, but stranger things had happened. But if Barlow *had* killed Thomas, then he'd also plotted to kill her. Why?

And there were the Stanleys. The cook and the gardener. Evie's understanding was that they had been handsomely provided for in Thomas's will. Were they broke? Have expensive tastes? Gambling debts? Did they need to get their hands on the money, and hadn't wanted to wait for Thomas to die?

Evie let her head fall back against the chair as a frustrated sigh escaped her. She lifted her gaze to the window.

It was growing dark, and the yacht was still gone. She wished Max were there. She wanted to talk to him about her suspicions.

As soon as the weather had cleared, Max had gone to the mainland. "Police business," was all he'd said. "Edmunds and James will keep you safe until I get back. None of the cell phones can get a signal, the land lines are down, and I need to talk to McKennitt. I'd take you with me, but I honestly feel you'll be safer here than out on the water."

His hands cupped her shoulders, but his tone had been gruff, all business. Detective Galloway, on the job.

Then he'd kissed her, and Mr. Police Officer went away, to be deliciously replaced by Mr. Sensuality Who Really Knew How to Kiss, Baby.

"Stay in the house," he'd warned, and with the weather so iffy, it hadn't been hard to comply. But after he left, the day had dragged. She'd mulled the clue over in her head, but its solution still evaded her.

As for Edmunds, he and Lorna had been busy in the office going over the estate finances, while Madame Grovda had paced the length and breadth of the mansion, her fingers rubbing her temples.

"I must go to rest," she moaned. "Not good . . . not good." Looking deeply into Evie's eyes, she said, "Be warned. With his prick in his hands, it comes. Like the Shakespeare."

Evie blinked. " 'By the pricking of my thumbs, something wicked this way comes. . . . ' "

"*Da, da,*" she'd responded, and made her exit up the stairs.

Suddenly, Evie felt like she'd swallowed a ball of snakes. Her nerves went on alert, her palms dampened. Madame Grovda was seldom right, yet the woman was obviously in distress. Perhaps she really was sensing peril. Until Max returned, she'd try to be especially aware of what was going on, just in case. She didn't have a gun, and could hardly walk around the manor with a butcher knife in her hand, but it wouldn't hurt to be on the lookout for trouble.

Thinking of the butcher knife led to thoughts of the kitchen. *Hmm. The kitchen.*

With a copy of *Door-to-Door Death* tucked under her arm, Evie left the library, went downstairs to the dining room, through the swinging doors, and into the kitchen. *Now what?*

She took the fifth clue from her jeans pocket and unfolded it. With this new perspective, several phrases jumped out at her.

> *. . . girls . . . tastes . . . packed heat . . . gal knew her place . . . good encyclopedia . . .*

It was sort of a stretch, but she was getting desperate. Thomas *could* have been referring to a kitchen. The novel hadn't taken place on an island, but in a fictional town on the Olympic Peninsula. If he'd wanted his guests back at Mayhem for the end of the treasure hunt, then it made sense the last two clues were probably hidden in the house somewhere.

She meandered around, wondering where Mrs. Stanley had gone. Such an odd woman. A terrific cook, but a very nervous person. She'd never allowed others in "her" kitchen, and shooed anybody out who came in even for a glass of water.

Evie let her gaze search the place. Large stove on the center island, pots and pans in gleaming copper hanging overhead. Cupboards and cabinets made of the finest oak and crystal, and a stainless steel refrigerator the size of a three-car garage. In the corner of

the kitchen stood a bookcase filled with cookbooks
dating back at least a thousand years. Didn't any of
the Heyworths ever get rid of anything?

She let her gaze wander over the titles, until something caught her eye. *Oh my God . . . that has to be
it. It has to be.*

There it sat, the Woman's Companion twelve-
volume encyclopedia of cookery. She picked up the
first volume. The copyright was dated 1960.

Heat began to sizzle up her spine and her mouth
went dry. She swallowed, then licked her lips. Slipping out each volume in turn, she flipped through
the pages, carefully feeling under the end papers for
an envelope-sized bulge.

And there it was. In the back of Volume 6. You
are so lame, she thought, admonishing herself for
not going straight to it. Volume 6 for the sixth clue.

Hurrying to the tile counter, Evie pulled a boning
knife from the rack and sliced open the end paper,
tugging out the envelope.

Rather than some elaborate address, this one simply said *Evie and Max.*

She returned the knife to the rack, closed the
cookbook, and replaced it on the shelf. She wanted
to read the clue right now, but Mrs. Stanley could
return at any second. Besides, it would only be fair
to wait for Max.

Eh, no it wouldn't. She'd go to her room and read
the clue. Time was of the essence, and it might take
some thought to figure out where to look for Number Seven. The *prize.* The answer to *everything, if*
Thomas had had time to change it, to name his

killer, or at least provide some kind of evidence the police could use.

Five minutes later, her bedroom door closed, she sat on her bed and opened the envelope.

Her eyes flew over the words.

He'd never believed in the institution of marriage. After all, who wanted to live in an institution? Now, here he was, sailing along through his middle years and, bam!, he meets her. Smiling eyes guaranteed to knock a man's heart from here to Kingdom Come. And he starts thinking, maybe forevermore ain't such a bad thing. . . .

T. E. Heyworth, 1991
The Changed Man Changes His Mind

Evie frowned. She remembered the book, even the passage. It had been so unlike Thomas's other novels, this one had stood out in her mind even though she'd only been a teenager when she read it.

Then her fingers relaxed and the paper fluttered to her lap.

I know where it is. I know exactly where it is. It can only be—

An angry blast of wind interrupted her thoughts, startling her. A bough near the house crashed against her window, nearly splintering the glass. Jumping up, Evie ran and looked out. The storm was raging again, worse than before. Trees bent and shivered against the roar of wind off the sea. Afternoon had been turned to night by the thick blanket of clouds tumbling low overhead. Rain splattered the window like beads thrown on a glass table.

Max. Would he get back tonight? If he'd already started for the island, he would be caught in this. Could the yacht withstand such a storm?

Her head spun. *Oh, God. First things first.* Quickly, she refolded the clue and shoved it under her pillow.

Now, the llamas. Lily was very close to birthing. It had been raining for days, and the wind's renewed force was sure to begin toppling the tall trees. She had to put the llamas inside the barn for their own safety.

As she pulled on her jacket, she heard her bedroom door open.

"Max?" She looked up, her heart fluttering and skipping and hoping.

But it was Lorna who peeked around the jamb. "I knocked, but you must not have heard," she said. "Have you seen Dabney? The last I saw of him was lunch. I was sleepy and went to take a nap. He seems to have disappeared."

Evie forced a smile even though something inside her went on alert.

"Must be the weather. Madame Grovda went to take a nap, too. Listen, I'm going to check on the llamas and put them in the barn until this storm passes. Do you want to come? We can look for Dabney on our way back."

"Sure." Relief eased the strain on Lorna's face. "It'll help me take my mind off things." With a quick glance out the window, she said, "It'll probably be pitch-dark by the time we get back. I think there are some big flashlights in the pantry off the kitchen."

Amid gusts of wind and slanting pellets of rain, the two women hurried down the path toward the barn. A sickening crack to her left caused Evie to start as a Douglas fir snapped and fell, slamming into the earth.

Fernando, Lorenzo, and Lily were huddled together next to the side of the barn. They turned their heads and blinked at her as she opened the gate and scurried toward them.

With soothing words, she took hold of Fernando's halter and began leading him toward the barn door Lorna was trying desperately to hold open.

Evie's hair blew across her face, making it hard to see, so she swiped it away and moved forward. Fernando strolled along beside her, Lorenzo and Lily following his lead.

Once inside the barn, Lorna yanked the door closed.

Evie led the trio to the far end and put them in a roomy stall where they would be out of the wind and could kush down in the soft straw to sleep. They had food and water, and they would be safe. Even if a tree fell on the barn, the structure would absorb the blow and protect the animals much better than if they were outside with no roof over their heads.

Save for the light from the flashlights, the barn lay in shadows. Outside, the wind picked up, blasting against the north wall, seeking chinks through which to enter. A shrill squeal high overhead told her it had found a spot.

The gust passed, and in a moment of calm Evie heard a different noise. It seemed Lorna heard it, too.

"What's that banging?" she said. Her brow furrowed. "Is it the wind?"

Evie stood very still. A thumping, rhythmic and steady, echoed up from beneath them.

"I don't think so," she said. "I—I think somebody's down in the *cavern*."

As they stared at each other, they heard the sound again.

Evie looked at the floor beneath her feet—the floor that had opened up one day and swallowed her whole. Falling to her knees, she shone her flashlight on the newly replaced boards.

"We'll have to pry it up."

Chapter 25

Dear Diary:

For my birthday, Thomas gave me a book of fairy tales with gorgeous illustrations by a man named Rackham. They are mostly stories about princesses who are rescued by handsome princes. I adore the book, and the princes are certainly handsome, but the stories aren't realistic in any way! I mean, I'm not exactly brave and I'm definitely not as strong as a prince, but if I were one of those princesses, I think I'd find some way to rescue myself instead of just sitting in the face of danger and waiting for the love of my life to come. I mean, hello!

Evangeline—age 13

The wind beat against the sides of the barn like angry marauders as Evie watched Lorna raise her flashlight.

Over the din, Evie yelled, "Lorna? What are you doing?"

"There's a crowbar hanging up there," Lorna shouted. "On that hook. Do you see it?"

Evie got to her feet, stretched up and grasped the crowbar.

The sounds of intermittent thudding still echoed from beneath the floor, and both women dropped to their knees and began prying up the boards.

When the last section of wood came loose in Evie's fingers, she shone her flashlight into the yawning cavity and felt her blood turn to ice.

"Been there," she whispered to herself as a shiver of fear assaulted her. "Done that."

"I can go," offered Lorna.

"No." Lifting her gaze to the other woman, she smiled weakly. "I know the way."

Evie flicked the light down the slope of rocks that had nearly cost her life just two weeks ago. With a shake of her head, she rose to her feet and went to the storage bin. Rummaging through it, she found a coil of rope.

Her fingers shook as she twisted one end into a bowline and wrapped it around one of the stall posts, shoving the end of the rope through the loop. As quickly as she could, she tied knots in the length of rope at three-foot intervals, then tossed the line through the chasm. Grabbing her flashlight, she shoved it into the waistband of her jeans.

"Shine your light down there so I can see where I'm landing," she said, gesturing to the floor.

Lorna directed the beam, and Evie took hold of the knotted line. "No matter what," she warned, raising her voice above the screaming wind, "don't come down after me. If something happens, go to the house and get help. Promise?"

"Evie, I—"

"*Promise* me!"

"All right!" she yelled. "I promise!"

With that, Evie began letting herself down into the darkness, with Lorna's light on the rocks the only guide she had.

In her hands, the rope felt cold and slippery. Nausea tightened her stomach as she relived her fall into the cavern, the pain it caused, how it had nearly taken her life. She remembered the feel of Max's strong arms around her, and she wished he were there now.

The toe of her boot, then her heel, touched the rock. Panting, sweating, fearing she might vomit, she paused for a moment.

Beneath her, the pounding noise had slowed, but was still steady.

"You okay?" Lorna shouted from above.

"So far so good."

Evie pulled the flashlight from her waistband, flicked it on, and shone the beam at the rocks at her feet. Tucking herself down as low as she could, she began the slippery descent. The circle of light illumined the cavern, showing the rock walls, which were damp and covered with lichen. The floor beneath her seemed to be moving.

When she stepped down, cold seawater covered her boots to her ankles.

"Hello!" she shouted. "Hello? Who's there?"

The thumping grew louder, more insistent.

She swished through the cold surge until she came to two rocks butting up against each other. Down near her knees, a gap between the rocks allowed seawater to rush in at an alarming rate. Shining the light on the opening, she could see that there was enough room for a person to crawl through—if they truly, with all their heart, wanted to go there.

Beyond the rocks, the thumping continued.

Taking a deep breath, Evie forced herself onto her knees and into the inches-deep surge. Squirming through the hole, she came through on the other side just as a slap of saltwater hit her face, filling her mouth.

Spitting and cursing, she pushed herself to her feet. With her wet jeans and sweater clinging to her body, chilling her, making her feel a hundred pounds heavier, she ran the beam of light along the walls, over her head, and down the passage in front of her. It was some kind of tunnel. Dark water rushed toward her, obviously pouring in from the sea. If it continued rising at that rate, she thought, the passage behind her would be underwater in minutes and she'd be trapped.

She considered going back, then heard it again—the thumping.

Cold water swirled around her calves now. Each passing minute brought the level up a few more inches.

"Damn it," she swore out loud. "Somebody had better be in *really* deep doo-doo over there, or I am going to be really, really pissed." She wanted to pinch her nose closed as a god-awful smell assaulted her.

To her left, a huge boulder blocked her view of the tunnel. Moving toward it, toward the sound, she turned the corner and the tip of her light touched something lying under the fast rising water.

A dead body? No, a man, alive, kicking frantically against a wooden support. His hands and feet were bound and a piece of silver duct tape had been pressed over his mouth.

Shoving her flashlight under her arm, Evie splashed forward, reached down and grasped his shoulders. With all the strength she possessed, she lifted him, bringing his head and upper body above the swirling foam.

She yanked off the tape, and he began to cough and choke, gasping for air. He pushed with his bound legs until he scooted to a rock, which he leaned against for support.

Evie shined her light on his face. It was Dabney James.

"Thank you," he rasped between coughs. "There's a knife in my right boot, but I couldn't reach it."

She shined the light down his legs and reached into the water-soaked leather to retrieve a Swiss Army knife. Her hands trembled from cold and sheer terror as she yanked open the biggest blade and began sawing at the ropes that bound his hands. When they came lose, he took the knife from her and quickly cut through the ropes binding his feet.

"Who did this to you?" she asked.

"Later," he said. "We have to get out of here."

"What's that horrible smell?" she yelled.

He gestured to a pile of rocks near the opening to

the sea. "Earl Stanley. He's been dead for days. Just like I would have been if you hadn't showed up."

Evie tried to process this shocking information, but they had a more pressing problem to deal with—the water had risen to her waist.

"Can you stand?" she asked.

Dabney snapped the knife closed and shoved it into his pocket. With her help, he was able to grab a hold on the rock and pull himself to his feet.

"Go ahead," he said to her. "I'm right behind you."

Flashlight in hand, Evie splashed around the rock, to where she had entered the tunnel, but every step seemed to take forever. By the time she reached the gap, it was submerged under several feet of churning seawater as more continued to pour in. If they tried to go underneath it, the storm surge would either shove them into the rocks or suck them back out to sea. Either way, they'd probably drown.

Their only escape route had been cut off.

It was dark as pitch now, a windy, storm-ravaged, moonless night as Max stalked from the dock to the house.

He'd been anxious about Evie all day, but he'd had to get to the mainland and see McKennitt. Besides, anybody set on hurting her would have to be a complete idiot to try to navigate out to the island in weather like this. And with both Edmunds and Nate watching out for her, he told himself, she would be fine.

Just as he got to the back door, the lights in the house flickered. Around him, the wind screeched like a demon, bending the trees, creating a wall of noise he could barely think through. The lights flickered again, then went out.

Great. Just frigging great.

The kitchen was empty. Unable to see anything in the dark, he headed for what he remembered was the storeroom where the flashlights were kept. Finally finding the knob, he turned it, then felt around until his fingers curled around a likely handle.

One flick, and the flashlight's bright beam lit up the small room.

Moving quickly through the house, he took the stairs two at a time until he reached Evie's bedroom door. Without knocking, he flung it open, calling her name. Empty.

He searched from room to room until he heard voices in the library. As he approached the wide double doors, he stopped and flicked off his flashlight, peering inside.

"My dear madame," Edmunds was saying to the frantic-looking psychic. "I assure you, we possess enough hurricane lamps to light a Broadway stage. We often lose power at Mayhem Manor, and have come to take it in stride."

She responded in near hysterical Russian, and the butler continued, "I have some matches just here. I don't mind losing power, actually, save for when I'm in the middle of a good book, or watching *The Daily Show*."

"Edmunds," Max said as he entered the library, flicking on his flashlight. "Where's Evie?"

The butler lit a lamp, then turned to face him.

"Detective Galloway," he said with a smile. "Just

before the lights went out, I saw her and Miss Whitney go down to the kitchen. I'm sure if you—"

"I just came in through the kitchen. Nobody's there."

Edmunds lit another lamp. "Oh. Well, then. Perhaps her room—"

"Max!"

He turned to see Lorna rush through the doors behind him, a flashlight in her hand, a look of panic on her face.

"What happened?" He grabbed her by the shoulders, alarm chilling his blood. Through clenched teeth, he growled, "Where is Evie?"

"I'm sorry!" she cried. "She . . . she . . . we heard a noise under the floor of the barn. So we pried up the boards, and she went down there. The cavern is flooded with seawater. Oh, Max," she sobbed, "I think she may have drowned!"

In the total darkness outside the library doors, Felix Barlow clutched the piece of paper in his hands, the paper he'd retrieved from the Randall woman's room, the paper that would bring it all to an end. It hadn't taken him long to find it under her pillow.

Clue Number Six. He didn't know what it meant, but he'd wager everything that *she* did.

For days, the weather had prevented him from getting to the island to finish his work, but the break today had been all he'd needed—until the storm had picked up again. He hoped his boat was where he'd left it, otherwise he'd be in really deep shit.

Time was running out. His plans were going to hell, and he'd decided the best he could do now was leave the country. He had to get back to Port Henry, retrieve his laptop and papers, then get to Canada and from there hop a flight to parts unknown.

But he still had time. He'd retrieved her clue, and if he could just decipher the fucking thing, he could steal Number Seven, and maybe prevent his having to flee to Canada.

The truth was, he didn't want to leave Port Henry or the life he'd established for himself there, but he didn't want to end up in prison, either. He could barely imagine sharing breathing space with the low-life scum who inhabited penitentiaries. The prospect was unthinkable.

Curling his fingers into fists, he stood absolutely still. While they all went looking for that Randall bitch, he could get the last clue and slip away.

These people were such fools.

Hope lightened his heart. He could still pull it off. Once he destroyed the last clue, they'd have nothing with which to pin Tommy's murder—or anybody else's—on him, and they never would. He'd been too careful, too patient, too clever. There were no loose ends to tie him to anything. *None.*

He pressed himself against the wall, deep in the shadows, and waited.

Go away now, he thought. All of you. Go and run and look for Little Miss Pain in the Ass. She'd be dead by now, which was as it should be for all the trouble she'd caused him.

You people are such fools.

Chapter 26

Dear Diary:

Thomas is very famous and writes books. I asked him if I could read one, and he said that it would be all right. It was a murder mystery, and you aren't supposed to guess who did it until the very last second. But I knew who it was all along.

Evangeline—age 13

Max refused to believe what he was hearing. His brain felt sharp and dull at the same time. Evie, in that cavern? Drowned? No. *No!*

A glass funnel from one of the hurricane lamps slipped from Edmunds's hands and crashed to the floor. He looked up, stricken, and moved toward Lorna, trying to form words, but none came.

Grasping Lorna by the elbow, Max began dragging her toward the doors. "Show me!"

"Nyet!"

He stopped in his tracks and turned to face the distraught psychic. Her eyes were huge, her mouth gaping. Her hands reached for him, fingers splayed, clawing the air like a cat kneading a blanket.

"Not to go," she begged. "Not to go. Here. Stay *here!*"

"We cannot wait," Edmunds choked. "There is no time—"

"Nyet!" she shrieked, a shocked expression on her face, as though she couldn't believe the words were coming from her own mouth. Shaking her head frantically, she choked, "Evie. She ... she is good. She is fine. She comes. Much danger!" Closing her eyes, she placed her fingers to her temples. "I see ... ehm, the dark place ... cold ... she is near ... she comes to you ... I don't ..."

Against the far wall, a noise drew everyone's attention. A thump, a squeal, and the middle section of the large bookcase creaked open to reveal a narrow gap in the library wall, not ten feet from where Thomas Heyworth had been slain.

The beam of a flashlight bounced off the darkness, and a figure moved toward the opening.

Evie? Max released Lorna and took a step forward.

Then she emerged, and through the dusky light of the vast room, their gazes locked. In that instant, he saw everything. In that unguarded, vulnerable, open moment, he saw in her eyes what she felt for him, and his heart wanted to burst.

She loved him.

"M-Max ..."

In four strides he reached her. "Evie," he murmured as he wrapped his arms around her in a rocking embrace. Holding her close, seeing her safe, brought breath to his lungs, color to his shadows, dimension to his dreams.

She was drenched and cold as ice, but he didn't care. It had become a sort of tradition with them.

Raising her face to his, she smiled, and it soothed and healed him, and made him whole.

"I'm sorry, Scout," he whispered. "I tried to get back sooner but the storm got so bad. I never should have left you." He bent his head and kissed her.

Her lips were cold, but her kiss the sweetest thing he had ever tasted.

Behind Evie, a deep male voice said, "Gosh. Don't I get a hug and kiss too?"

Max's head came up. "Nate?"

With no small amount of fanfare, Nate stepped through the secret door and into the library. He was soaking wet, had ropes dangling from his wrists, a bruise on his jaw, a pissed off look on his face, and no glasses.

"What in the hell happened to you?"

Nate shrugged and squinted at Max. "Nothing that my hands around a certain son of a bitch's neck won't cure."

"Dabney? What on earth . . ." Lorna's eyes filled with concern as she rushed forward and placed her fingers on his bruised jaw. He covered her hand with his own. "Max called you Nate? I don't understand."

He shot a quick glance to Max, then said softly, "Detective Nate Darling, ma'am. The real Dabney

James was incapacitated, thanks to a serious case of murder, so, when we discovered he'd been invited to Heyworth's treasure hunt, we thought there might be a connection. I took his place. I'm sorry to have to fool you, but we needed—"

Lorna interrupted Nate's confession by flinging herself into his arms. He grinned and pulled her close. Against his soggy shirt she whispered, "Thank God. I couldn't believe I'd fallen in love with a man whose poetry gave me stomach cramps."

"You didn't like my poetry?" With his cheek resting on her hair, he said quietly, " 'Live with me, and be my love / And we will all the pleasures prove / that hills and valleys, dales and fields / And all the craggy mountains yields.' "

Lorna closed her eyes, curling her fingers into Nate's battered shirt. "Much better. Courtesy of Christopher Marlowe, of course, but much, much better."

"You okay, Darling?" Max said. "You look like shit."

Nate ran his fingers through his hair and nodded.

"After lunch," he said, "I couldn't keep my eyes open. I think the food or juice was drugged. Anyway, I went to lie down, and when I woke up, I was bound and gagged and being dragged through a dark tunnel so I could become fish food."

"Did you see his face?"

"No, dammit," he growled. "It was too frigging dark, I'd lost my glasses, and I was still woozy from the drug." He nodded toward the bookcase opening. "What I did see was that the tunnel leads all the way down to the cavern and then out to the beach. It must be how Heyworth's killer came and went without being seen."

Edmunds, meanwhile, had stepped forward to embrace Evie, his face pale, his eyes filled with relief.

"Thank God you are safe," he murmured. "To lose you now . . ."

She looked up at her father and smiled. "I know."

Edmunds looked at Max. "It's Felix Barlow, isn't it?" he said.

"Yes."

Evie made a choking sound. "Barlow?" she said, looked thoughtful for a moment, and nodded. "Yes, I can see that."

"Edmunds," Max said, "did you know about this passageway?"

Stepping away from Evie, the butler shook his head. "No, sir. I had no idea this particular tunnel existed." He gazed at the gigantic bookcase. "Imagine," he said softly. "All these years. Astonishing." Clearing his throat, he said, "I am aware of several shorter secret tunnels, most of which simply lead from one bedroom to the next. They were designed for, eh . . ."

"I know what they were designed for," Max said, sliding a wry smile to Evie, who pressed her lips together and averted her eyes.

Returning his flashlight beam to the gaping hole in the wall, Max said, "If this goes all the way down to the cavern under the barn and then out to the beach, it must have been the one they used way back when, to bring in bootleg booze from Canada—"

"Oh, Max," Evie interrupted. "Earl. It's *horrible*. He's dead."

"Pretty nifty setup," Nate chimed in. "Tie somebody up, leave them down there to drown. Their body is never found."

Lorna laid her head against Nate's shoulder. "Thank God Evie and I heard you."

"The sixth clue, Max," Evie said anxiously. "I found it in a cookbook in the kitchen. It's up in my room, and I think I know where—"

A shot exploded from the doorway of the library. A window on the far side of the room shattered, and wind screamed through the opening, knocking the hurricane lamp to the floor, dousing the flame.

In the dark, Madame Grovda screamed and began yelling in Russian. Nate shouted something, and Edmunds made a choking sound. In the noise and confusion, Max heard footsteps, running, and behind him a woman's muffled cry.

He swung his arm wide, making a grab for Evie, but she wasn't there.

"Evie!" he yelled, spinning around, trying to find her with the beam of his flashlight.

The light skimmed Edmunds, sprawled awkwardly on the floor, holding his head with both hands. Max ran the light around the room in a frantic attempt to find her. But wherever the beam touched, there was only emptiness. She was gone.

Fingers held her hair in a cruel grip. He yanked her against him with one hand as he used the open palm of the other to slam the wall. She heard the panel slide closed between them and the library, and the man she loved.

He began dragging her along the tunnel, back the way she and Nate had come just minutes before. The walls shuddered and echoed a dull thudding sound, and she knew Max must be tearing the bookcase apart, trying to find the latch that would reopen the secret panel.

"They won't find it," he growled into her ear.

Felix Barlow.

Still holding her by the hair with one hand, he moved the other. She heard a click, and light illuminated the tunnel around them.

Evie doubled her fists and slammed them against whatever parts of her abductor she could reach. She squirmed and kicked at him and tried to turn in his grasp so one of her flailing fists would connect, but he moved too swiftly. He released her hair, and for a moment she thought he'd let her go, but it was only to slap her across the side of the face.

"Don't give me any trouble," he spat, "or after you're dead, I'll come back and kill your boyfriend."

Her head hurt like hell where his fingers dug into her scalp. Tears formed in her eyes, but she was too busy stumbling along the corridor after him to worry about it.

The main tunnel came to an end and divided into two. She knew the one on the right led back down to the cavern, but Barlow yanked her through the one on the left.

Far behind them the pounding ceased.

Barlow halted, shining the flashlight into her eyes. "Where's the last clue?" he bit out, his face only inches from hers. She could smell his breath, feel the warmth from his overheated body. She wanted to gag.

"I don't know," she choked.

He yanked on her hair so hard, she thought he must have pulled clumps of it out by the roots.

"Liar! I heard you telling Galloway. You know where it is, don't you?"

"Y-Yes," she stumbled. Her heart pounded in her ears. Terror kept her voice low, soft, almost intimate. "What's it w-worth to you?"

He moved closer, pressing her body against the rough wall. Sweat from his brow dripped onto her cheek. "I destroyed the sixth clue," he whispered roughly. "Stalling won't help you. Galloway has no idea where to look, so he can't show up to save your ass. *Where's the last fucking clue?*"

"Why?" she said. "It's p-pretty obvious you killed Thomas, or had him killed. What good will finding the last clue do? They know it's you."

He shoved her so hard, the back of her head hit the wall, and a burst of stars glistened behind her lids.

"They have nothing," he bit out. "*Nothing.* Nothing ties me to anything. James, or whatever the hell his name is, never saw me. I want whatever Tommy had on me. The police can't do a thing to me without evidence, and they don't have *anything*."

"What about me? Kidnapping me should tell them something."

"Nobody saw me, princess," he said, with a sneer in his voice. "It was too dark. And after you're dead, there won't be anybody left to tell."

She was having trouble breathing. He was too

close. There was no air in the tunnel. The bruises on her back ached where he had her shoved against the wall.

"How do you know about the tunnels? N-Not even Edmunds—"

"I played here when I was a boy," he panted. "My brother and Heyworth were friends. They were older, went off fishing and the like, and while they were gone, I explored. I think I know this place better than Tommy ever did."

"If you were friends, why did you k-kill Thomas? Was it for the money?"

"Hell no!" he shouted, his voice ricocheting through the narrow corridor, echoing down and back, assaulting her ears. "I *hated* him. He took everything from me, and I wanted to take everything from *him*."

Barlow was on the move again, dragging her behind him as he stumbled through the passageway, his flashlight a meager force against such total darkness. They turned a corner and he stopped, slamming her against the wall. "I can hit you again, I can hurt you—hell, I can rape you—and there's nobody who can stop me. Tell me where the clue is!"

Evie's brain was fuzzy. Her mouth hurt where he'd hit her. She took a deep breath, trying to pull in more oxygen, trying to hang on until Max could find a way to help her.

"Why did you hate Thomas?"

"He killed my brother!"

An animal sound, a choking sob, primal, crazed, escaped him, and she raised her gaze to look at his distorted face.

"Tommy was rich," he spat out. "We were poor. Hell, the war to end all wars was over. There would never be another one. Everybody knew it! My brother couldn't find work. Our parents were sick. I was just a kid. He joined the Army reserves, for a little extra cash, make ends meet. Tommy encouraged him to! There weren't going to be any more goddamn *wars*! But then, Korea . . ."

Evie swallowed. "That's not Thomas's fault. He couldn't have anticipated—"

"He could have given us money! He was loaded, dripping with wealth. He *could* have helped us out, but he was stingy, cheap, never thought of anybody but himself. The war started, my brother was called up, and—"

Another sob escaped him, and his grip on her relaxed a little. "He was everything to me," he whispered. "The world is an evil place, and my brother was good. He was good and he was fine, and that son of a bitch let him die!"

With renewed energy, Barlow raised his hand to slap Evie again, but she lifted her arms, blocking the blow.

"Stop!" she shouted. "I'll tell you!"

Slowly, he let his arm drop. Shining the light into her face, he said, *"Where?"*

Blinking against the bright light, she whispered, "I'll have to show you. I won't know if I'm right until I can see for myself. Where does this tunnel lead?"

A second passed, and another, then he turned the light away and shined it down the passage. "It splits again, around that corner. One tunnel leads to a cave that opens onto the beach, the other to Tommy's bedroom."

She licked her dry lips. "That's where the last clue is hidden. Thomas's room."

They moved along at a brisk pace. Considering that Barlow was yanking her by the hair, she tried to do whatever she could think of to slow him down.

Her mind raced along ahead of them. The tunnel was fairly wide. If she could just get free of Barlow, maybe she could make a run for the beach.

Rounding another corner, he halted, shoved her against the wall and clamped his hand over her mouth.

"If you make *one sound*," he threatened, "the tiniest squeak, I'll shoot you in the gut so you'll slowly bleed to death. And when your boyfriend shows up, I'll do the same to him and you can watch each other die. So keep your fucking mouth *shut*. Are we clear on that?"

She nodded.

With his free hand, he pressed the wall, and a panel opened. The lights were still out, the room dark. Nothing stirred.

He turned the flashlight into Thomas's room. With his fingers still wound tightly in her hair, he thrust her in front of him, then shoved her through the open panel. Against the small of her back, she felt the hard angles of the gun in his waistband.

They stood alone in the enormous room. No one came here anymore, not since Thomas died. Outside the uncovered windows, rain smashed against the glass, driven hard by the howling wind.

Evie's heart sank. She'd hoped Max had some-how figured out where they were going and been waiting. But how could he? Barlow had destroyed the sixth clue. It would take Max and the others hours to search the place, room by room. By then it would be too late.

And if Max did miraculously show up? Barlow would kill him. Maybe it would be better just to give the bastard the clue he wanted and make a run for it in the dark.

The beam of Barlow's flashlight moved about the room, touching on the large bed, the cherry desk in the corner, and various oils, watercolors, and photo-graphs that adorned the walls. Above the massive stone fireplace hung a portrait of Lillian Galloway Heyworth, Max's mother. Evie had always loved that portrait, even though she'd known so little of the woman. She raised her gaze, looked into Lillian's eyes and saw the woman's son there . . . Lillian's son, the man she loved.

"Where is it?" Barlow hissed, releasing her with a shove to the head.

The moment she was free of him, a shadow sepa-rated itself from the wall and slammed into Barlow, knocking him to the floor. He dropped the flash-light, its beam making crazy patterns on the walls as it rolled away.

Evie reached along the floor until she felt the rounded handle. Picking it up, she shone it on the two men.

Max rose up, his fist slamming hard against Bar-low's jaw and then into his body. Blood trickled from the lawyer's mouth and his eyes glazed over.

His jaw dropped, his body crumpled, and he slumped to the floor in a heap. Reaching down, Max pulled the revolver from his limp grip.

Out of breath, Max turned to her, grabbing her, enveloping her in his arms. "Tell me you're okay," he choked. "Tell me he didn't hurt you."

Her arms wound around his neck and she let herself sink against his strong body. "I'm all right. He admitted killing Thomas."

"We know," Max panted. "He systematically robbed him blind, then killed him."

"How did you find me? How did you know where to come?"

Max wiped a smear of blood off his mouth. "We found Mrs. Stanley wandering around in the dark. She knew about the tunnels. Nate and Lorna went out to the beach to see if he'd bring you out that way. I came here."

"You were so quick. I didn't expect—"

"I told you I could run fast." Though she couldn't see him well, his voice was rich and gentle, and when he touched her cheek, she turned her face into his warm palm.

On the floor at their feet, Barlow groaned, then sat up. Staggering to his feet, he sneered, "You can't prove any of it, Galloway. Maybe you can get me on embezzlement, but there's nothing, not a goddamn shred of evidence, that will tie me to any murder."

As Max turned to face Barlow, the lawyer raised his arm, a heavy bookend clutched in his fist. He swung at Max's head, but Max ducked, shoving Evie away to safety.

Barlow raised his arm again, to land a massive

blow, when the blast of a gun rang through the room, stopping his movement.

Evie scrambled to cover Max's body with her own just as Barlow yelled. A second shot echoed through the room.

Barlow clutched his chest, a look of shock distorting his features. The bookend fell from his hand to thud softly onto the thick carpet. Lowering his head, he seemed mystified by the bloom of red blossoming on his shirt. Then, with an amazed little laugh, he dropped to the floor.

With a quick twist, Max rolled Evie under him. The lights flickered, then came back on, illuminating a person standing in the bedroom doorway, a .357 Smith & Wesson revolver held tightly in both her hands.

"Mrs. Stanley?" Evie whispered.

For a moment the woman said nothing. Then, "I helped him." Her voice was quiet, calm, as though she was telling a story to a group of small children. "Did all his dirty work for him. Put the sleeping stuff in the orange juice and the food so's he could creep around the house with nobody the wiser. His mole, he called me. Gonna be filthy rich, he said. Promised. After all I done . . . he killed my Earl. Tried to kill me, too. Left me in the tunnel . . . to die. But I got a few tricks of my own."

"Where'd you get the gun?" Max said as he got to his feet, bringing Evie with him. In the shadows behind Mrs. Stanley, something moved.

The woman let her arms go limp as Nate approached her and carefully removed the weapon from her hand. She didn't even acknowledge his presence.

"Gun belonged to Thomas," she murmured. "I stole it and gave it to Felix. He gave it back to me to hide from the cops." Her eyes were glazed over and her mouth was slack. She looked like a woman who had absolutely nothing to live for.

Max went to Barlow, knelt, and felt for a pulse. He looked up at Nate and shook his head.

"What about the attempts on Evie's life?" he said to the cook.

"I found part of a letter, about an heir," she whimpered. "Told Felix. He was furious. Didn't want nothing standing in his way, he said. But it had to look like it was an accident. Put him in touch with my nephew, Sam. My sister's boy, see? I raised him. He's an expert marksman, so I knew he'd be good at the work."

Max said, "Sam Ziwicki's dead, Mrs. Stanley. Felix Barlow killed him."

Her blank gaze drifted toward the body on the bedroom floor.

"That so?" she mused softly. "Well, that boy never was no good, anyhow. Pork rinds and beer, that one. Just pork rinds and beer."

Epilogue

My dear Evie:

So, you found it, the last clue. I knew you'd be the one to think of looking behind Lillian's portrait. You always were smart as a whip.

Take the key enclosed in this envelope and go into my office. Behind the autographed photo of Rod McKuen, Barry Manilow, and me, there's a hidden safe which contains enough evidence to hang that goddamned Felix Barlow by his balls (if he has any, which I doubt). Not for killing me, God knows, but for the murder four years ago of my friend, Charles Steele. That's right. Barlow killed his own partner. You give whatever's in there to Galloway. That cocky son of a bitch will know what to do with it.

Yeah, Galloway. I know, I know. I've got no love for that little prick, but Lillian spoke highly of him, and her opinion meant a lot to me. Lovely woman. A truly lovely woman. Loving her, and losing her, led me to you, my darlin'. She made me see how lonely I was and how I'd wasted most of my life shutting people out. When I learned about you, that you were alone, I thought it would be a fitting tribute to her to give you a home, in her honor. I'll rest in peace if I know I did her proud.

As for Galloway, if you could see your way clear to falling in love with the bastard and marrying him, that would likely make his mother very happy. I think you're just the woman for that arrogant son of a bitch. Maybe bring him down a notch or two. Even though you're far and away too good for him.

As for you, Galloway (yeah, I know you're there), Evie's too good for you (that was definitely worth repeating), but your mother said you'd turn out to be a fine man someday, so I've followed your career and discovered she was right. If you have half the brains you're supposed to have, you'll know a good thing when you see it and marry Evie, get her off this island, give her some kids, make her happy. Something I've learned along the way is that nobody likes to end up alone. Nobody should, either.

Evie, honey, though you've been like a daughter to me, the truth is, I'm not your father. I hope the man who is has finally figured out how to tell you. Don't be too hard on him, honey. He adores you. Just sort of go with that.

As for my estate, I could have left it all to you, but what would you have done with it? You'd have spent the rest of your life on the island avoiding love—much as I have done—hiding away with your shy heart and your sweetness and never knowing the kind of joy I found with Lillian. I'd like to spare you that, if I can. Maybe I'm old fashioned, but you don't need money, honey; you need a good man.

I'd be doing you no favor by making you a rich recluse. I was hoping that, if you won the hunt, you'd already be in love with Galloway and would no longer want to hide away. Besides, I've recently discovered I may actually have a daughter, and she, as rightful heir, would be entitled to everything. My dearest wish is that I have a chance to talk to her before something happens to me. If I don't, it'll be up to the frigging lawyers to figure it all out. Damn. Even in death, the bastards win.

So, you've solved the riddle and conquered the day. Now, my sweet, go conquer life. . . .

Yours,
Thomas

Two weeks later, lying in bed in her sunny cottage in Port Henry, Fernando tied in the yard after another trip to the Rhododendron Senior Center, Evie moved her hands over Max's naked back. She loved touching his strong, smooth muscles, feeling the warmth of him, luxuriating in the essence of who he was by himself, and who they were together.

Being with him, making love with him, was nothing short of miraculous.

"I love you," she whispered, then bit her lip and waited. She'd said it before, but he'd never said it back. It wasn't as though she was expecting him to, except that . . . well, she'd pretty much begun counting on him saying it any second now. Any second.

With his upper torso resting on his elbows, he smiled down at her. His hair was tousled, his cheeks flushed, his eyes gleaming. God, he was beautiful.

Cocking his head to one side, he said, "Do you think the probate court will find in Lorna's favor and award her the estate?"

Any second . . .

Evie's heart fell a bit, but she said, "I don't know. If she can prove she was Thomas's daughter, I guess I don't see a problem. At any rate, Edmunds—I mean, my father . . . I just love saying that—my *father* has decided to retire so he and I can spend some time together, and Madame Grovda is going to stick around, too. She said she, uh, she wants to play with my babies."

Max raised a brow, but didn't comment on that.

Evie squirmed a little. "What about Nate?"

"Oh, he probably doesn't want to play with any babies."

She chuckled. "You know what I mean. Are Lorna and Nate an item?"

"I guess time will tell. He's back at work, though, and not composing sucky poetry anymore."

She ran the tip of her finger over Max's ear. "I've been wondering. Why did Barlow have the real Dabney James killed?"

Max settled himself more comfortably between her thighs. "It's difficult to know, what with all the major players dead, but according to Mrs. Stanley, when Barlow found out about the treasure hunt, he went absolutely nuts. Maybe he thought by killing off some of the guests, he could throw the game or maybe get it nullified. Nate was working the James case and decided not to let it out that he was dead, but to take his place instead. The fact that the real Dabney James hadn't been seen in public for years helped a lot."

"Then how did Sam Ziwicki know who to kill?"

"He probably didn't," Max said. "He just went to the address Barlow gave him and shot whoever opened the door."

Evie kissed Max's chin. "What's going to happen to Mrs. Stanley?"

Max lowered his head and kissed her, sending her heart rate up another twenty beats per second. When he was through thoroughly arousing her, he said, "It's funny about some people. Once they're caught, they start talking and you can't shut 'em up. She confessed to helping Barlow for years. He'd promised her a huge cut of the inheritance if she'd spy on Heyworth and report back if anything suspicious turned up, like a possible heir. But in the end, he betrayed her. Killed her husband, then left her for dead, too."

He quirked his lips. "Okay, now. On to the really important stuff. Do you think a month is too short a time to know somebody before you ask her to marry you?"

A month? "Are . . . are you talking about us?"

"Of course." He shrugged. "I wanted to ask you to marry me now, but I thought maybe you'd like it better if I waited a more reasonable period of time."

While she tried to form some kind of answer, he reached for his jeans, crumpled on the floor next to the bed, and pulled something from his pocket. Holding it to his chest, he waited a few moments, then said, "I'm warming it up for you."

"What are you—"

"Here," he said. "Lift your head a little."

Evie did as he asked. He slipped a slender chain around her neck so the metallic disk rested between her breasts. She curled her fingers around it.

His mother's coin.

"Max!" she cried. "You put it on a chain? For me? But you can't give this to me. It was your mother's and she—"

"Gave it to me," he finished for her. "I know. But I think she and Thomas would want me to give it to you. After all, it represents something much more precious to me than a mere memento. It's a part of my heart," he said shyly. "You can, um, pass it along to our firstborn someday, if you like."

"Max—"

"About the month thing," he interrupted softly. "If I confessed my undying love for you now, and asked you to marry me and spend the rest of your life with me, won't you think that maybe I am the kind of man who leaps before he looks? That maybe

I'm the kind of man who doesn't think things through before making life-altering decisions?"

She clutched the warm coin in her fingers. "No," she said tightly. "I'd think you are a man who is absolutely crazy about me and can't stand to live without me for one second longer."

"Good enough," he said, and smiled. "So, we're going live in three, two, one . . ."

He took a deep breath.

"Evangeline May Randall," he said gently, tenderly. "I absolutely adore you. Will you do me the honor of becoming my wife?"

Her heart pounded and her vision blurred. "You mean it?" she squeaked.

"Of course I mean it." His eyes grew serious. "I'm your crab, Evie. I love you. And I'll never leave you, not even after your shell hardens and you give birth to two million of my children."

"Oh, Max," she sobbed, wrapping him in her arms. "You have no idea how I've longed to hear you say those words."

"Well," Max whispered as he crushed her lips beneath his own, "ooo-*rah* . . ."

*It's time to crank up the Summer heat
with these releases coming in June
from Avon Romance!*

Marry the Man Today by Linda Needham

An Avon Romantic Treasure

The very last thing lovely Elizabeth Dunaway plans to do is marry! Determined to liberate the women of Britain, Elizabeth opens a private Ladies Club, scandalizing every male in Victorian London. Of course, Ross Carrington, the Earl of Blakestone isn't like most other men. Ross sets out to tame her rebellious spirit, but soon finds that he's met his match!

Running on Empty by Lynn Montana

An Avon Contemporary Romance

Josie Mayne is on the verge of accepting a bad marriage proposal when her ex Pardee reappears. He needs Josie in an incarnation she's left behind, as his former partner in a bounty hunting business, to help him rescue his kidnapped son. Torn between her crazy old life and a promising new one, Josie takes one last plunge—headfirst into passion with her old flame . . .

Beyond Temptation by Mary Reed McCall

An Avon Romance

Lady Margaret Newcomb is a disgraced daughter of a powerful English earl. Sir Richard de Cantor is a highly skilled warrior of the Templar Brotherhood. Though of different backgrounds, in truth they have both been battered by the world, and only the acceptance—and love—of each other can save them from dangers afoot in this time of battle . . .

The Runaway Heiress by Brenda Hiatt

An Avon Romance

Dina Moore lives under the watchful eye of her bullying brother, Silas, until she learns he has a financial interest in seeing her remain unwed. Never a passive victim, she runs away in the hopes of marrying a kind stranger. Instead, she finds roguish Grant Turpin, and their marriage of convenience turns quickly into a marriage of passion . . .

REL 0505